As Sounding Brass

As Sounding Brass

Alan T. Nolan

HOUGHTON MIFFLIN COMPANY BOSTON
THE RIVERSIDE PRESS CAMBRIDGE

For

BETTY

and

for

JOHN VAL NOLAN

As Sounding Brass

I

AT 11:32 ON THE NIGHT OF THURSDAY, May 19, 1960, a middle-aged woman parked her car in front of her house, just north of the northwest corner of Park Avenue and Twelfth Street. The neighborhood, near the center of the large city, was old and declining, a mixture of storefronts and aged houses, many of which had been cut up into cheap apartments. In the indistinct light of a lamppost, the woman turned toward the car, a 1958 Ford sedan, to lock it. As she turned, someone grabbed her from behind. He put one hand over her mouth, jerked her pocketbook from her left hand, and pushed her hard in the back. The woman fell to the ground on her hands and knees.

As she fell, she caught sight of the feet and legs of her assailant. Then she heard the footfalls of someone running up Park Avenue.

Huddled on the ground on the curb beside her car, for a few moments the woman was breathless and too frightened to scream. Then she began to scream at the top of her voice.

The corner was a busy one at night and people came running to help the woman up. Between her gasps and exclamations, she told what had happened. A man ran into the corner house to phone the police, but before the call was placed a squad car arrived with two policemen. One of them was John Sullivan, twenty-one years old, in his first year on the force. The other was John Mueller, a middle-aged veteran only recently transferred from the traffic division.

The police jumped out of the car and the woman repeated her story. Then the officers quickly re-entered the car and drove rapidly up the street. As the car approached the middle of the block, they saw a man ahead, standing back in the shadows on the sidewalk on the left side of the street. The car swerved to the left toward where the man was standing.

The man started to run. He disappeared into a yard. The police stopped and leaped from the car, shouting for him to halt. Then they plunged into the yard after him.

At the rear of the yard was a low board fence. One of the officers ran through a gate and the other vaulted the fence. Each switched on a powerful flashlight that swept up and down the alley. Each also drew his gun. To the north a shadow appeared and then the figure of a man was visible, running, darting in and out of the caverns beyond the searching beam of the flashlights. The policemen shouted again for the man to stop. Then they opened fire, the loud and hideous reports echoing back and forth across the alley.

Perhaps ten shots were fired in as many seconds and suddenly the man went down and lay still. The officers raced to him. He was perfectly still, face down. His head was turned to one side and his eyes were closed. He was young, with close-cropped sandy hair, a fair complexion and a plain, almost handsome face. Lying there, he appeared to be of medium height and his arms and shoulders looked well developed and strong. On his white shirt, just above his belt, was a red stain. In the few moments of silence as the officers stood there, the stain grew larger, gradually also marking his brown pants.

Nobody quite remembered what else had happened at first. John Sullivan said, "Jesus," and a conviction came over him that his shots had missed. But Sullivan's thoughts were interrupted by Mueller's voice.

In a flat tone Mueller said, "Son, please go to the car and call in. Tell them to send an ambulance." Sullivan started back down the alley, and Mueller called after him, "Hurry! And bring the woman!"

Sullivan began to run, and as he did he tried to remember what had been said in police school about shooting a fugitive. He couldn't remember exactly, but a picture flashed through his mind of policemen exchanging shots with heavily armed and desperate men. At the car, Sullivan made the report. Then he walked briskly to the corner. Ignoring the questions, he pushed through the crowd to find the woman.

She was sitting on the curb, surrounded by the neighbors who had come out to talk to her. She said that her knees were skinned a bit, but she seemed composed.

"What's your name, ma'am?" Sullivan asked.

"Wallace," she said, "Josephine Wallace." More words tumbled out. "This is my house. I live here with my mother . . . I've been to my club meeting." She shuddered. "I was just coming home and that man jumped out at me."

Sullivan felt sorry for the woman. She reminded him of his Aunt Mary, who was just about the same age. "Mrs. Wallace . . ."

"*Miss* Wallace," she corrected.

"O.K.," he said, "Miss Wallace, I guess you better come with me. Can you walk all right?"

"Yes, I can walk." She got up gamely, holding on to Sullivan's arm.

"Let's go now, please," Sullivan said, and they started to walk up the sidewalk, trailed by the interested neighbors.

Halfway up the block, the group cut through a yard to the alley. Mueller was ahead, standing over the man on the ground and now joined by three or four other men. The assembly presented a strange tableau in the light from the flashlights.

As Sullivan and Miss Wallace advanced, the policeman said, "We're sure he's the one, ma'am. Can you identify him?"

"I didn't see anything but his pants and shoes."

"Well, we're sure," Sullivan said.

By this time, they had reached the place where the man was. As soon as Miss Wallace saw the body and the blood, she shuddered again and leaned heavily against Sullivan. He steadied her and then Mueller took over.

"I know this isn't fun, ma'am, but you've got to identify him for us," Mueller said. "Is this him?"

The woman hesitated as the flashlights played up and down the still form. The lights paused at the pale, plain face but Miss Wallace said, "I didn't see his face."

"She saw his feet and legs," Sullivan said.

At once the flashlights were concentrated there. The brown pants were some kind of plain cotton material, like an army summer uniform but slightly darker. The shoes were brown, too, oxfords, inexpensively made and with a plain toe. Miss Wallace could see the toe because one foot was turned in an odd way. As she realized this, she began to get sick again.

"Well?" asked Mueller.

"Yes, that's him," Miss Wallace said. "Is he dead? He's so young . . . I hope he isn't dead."

"He's not dead," Mueller said. Then he knelt and began to search the man. No weapons were found. The purse wasn't there either, and Mueller told Sullivan that he'd been unable to find it anywhere nearby.

In the man's left hip pocket was a cheap leatherette wallet containing three dollars and an identification card. The identification card said that he worked at Faultless Pump Company and lived at a nearby rooming house. In his right hip pocket was a handkerchief with lipstick on it. His other pockets contained some change and a brass key, a little sticky with blood which had run across his back and dripped down his sides.

Mueller placed the articles on the man's back, arranging them into a neat exhibit. He looked up at Miss Wallace and asked, "Is any of this stuff yours, ma'am?"

"I don't think so, unless that's my change. I had some change, in a little red coin purse. I don't know whether that's it or not."

"Did you have any other money in your pocketbook?"

Miss Wallace blushed. "No. Pay day's not till Wednesday. I work at Hal Tobin Cleaners. My wallet was empty."

Mueller said, "What else besides the coin purse and the wallet was in your pocketbook?"

"Oh, a compact, and a few other things," she said vaguely. "Just the usual things you carry in a pocketbook."

Mueller stood up and looked at Sullivan. "Well, John, it looks like we've got our man. His identification card says his name is Adam Johnson."

"Will I get my pocketbook back, and my things?" Miss Wallace asked.

"We'll do the best we can, ma'am," Mueller said.

2

Just after midnight, in the early hours of May 20, an orthopedic surgeon, a neurologist and a radiologist were summoned to City Hospital. Before they had completed their medical findings—the man's spinal cord was severed—the police work in the Johnson case was resumed.

At 8 A.M. on the 20th, Officer Mueller and Detective Terry O'Neal arrived at the corner of Twelfth and Park. John Sullivan was not with them. He had been scheduled to go, but his wife had called in to report that he had the stomach flu and was in bed for the day. Having read Miss Wallace's 2:30 A.M. statement, Detective O'Neal was to be introduced to the case by Mueller alone.

The officers had a particular interest in the scene of the

crime, or rather the scene of the prisoner's flight. They left their unmarked car at the curb on the east side of the street, opposite the place where Miss Wallace had parked on the night before. They crossed and, after a momentary stop at the site where the woman had been attacked, they began walking slowly up the sidewalk.

Fortunately for their tasks, it was still too early for the school crowd, and the policemen were unmolested by the usual stream of children. A few pedestrians were about and cars passed up and down the street, but police officers were nothing new in the neighborhood and no particular notice was taken of them now.

Mueller stayed along the right side of the sidewalk, scanning it and the curb and gutter to his right. O'Neal was to Mueller's left, next to the yards. Although each man paused more than once or halted occasionally to kick at something, and O'Neal crouched down once beside a bush, they were empty-handed when they reached the yard that Adam Johnson and the police had cut through. Together they entered this yard, moving west toward the alley.

The officers' journey was now quite slow. Each bush and irregularity in the ground was a possible hiding place and the yard was untidy and unkempt, littered with bits of paper and trash. On the north side of the house, the side on which the chase had taken place, was a cement stairwell leading to a basement entrance. Both men checked this place, picking about in the leaves and waste that had blown into it. Then they reappeared on the surface of the ground and worked their way through the backyard to the alley.

"I went through here," Mueller said, pointing to a weathered wooden gate. "Sullivan took the fence. He was a little ahead of me the whole time, and he didn't see him right away in the alley. But he says the guy didn't leave the alley once he got into it except to jump in and out a little bit."

O'Neal said, "If that's what happened, we can follow the

alley first, before covering the backyards. I'll take the right side. You take the left."

They went into the alley and turned north, moving slowly, poking into the corners, boxes and barrels along the way. After a search of perhaps half an hour, they reached the place where Adam Johnson had fallen. At O'Neal's suggestion, they split up at this point. The detective took the west half of a theoretical circle and Mueller was assigned to the other half.

The detective had the first break. He had moved into the backyards and was several feet north of the site where Adam had lain. Suddenly stepping quickly, he leaned over and called out, "Here's the purse!"

Mueller hurried to him. The pocketbook was empty, but it fitted Miss Wallace's description perfectly.

O'Neal now reorganized the search. Pointing to the spot where the pocketbook had been, he said, "Let's concentrate in this area. The other stuff should be right around here."

An hour's further effort yielded nothing and the men gave up on the west side of the alley and decided to check the backyards on the east side. There, considerably south of the point at which Adam's flight had ended, Mueller turned up a compact and lipstick. Nearby was a handkerchief and an unopened coin purse containing a door key and ninety-two cents in change. Three letters were also found, each addressed to Miss Wallace. Finally, O'Neal discovered the wallet, engraved with Miss Wallace's initials and enclosing a card with her name and address, a laundry receipt and two raffle tickets.

"This is about it," O'Neal said, and by tacit consent the men turned back to the alley and walked silently to the car, carrying the results of the search. They climbed into the car and, without comment, O'Neal handed Mueller a plain sheet of white paper. Across the top, Mueller wrote, "Found near prisoner's course of flight." Then he listed the articles and at the bottom set forth the date and the time and signed his name. O'Neal wrote his name under Mueller's and produced a large manila envelope. The articles and the piece of paper were put into the envelope and O'Neal placed it beneath the seat.

Before going to Adam's rooming house, Mueller and O'Neal drove to the Hal Tobin Cleaners. Miss Wallace was shown what they had found and she identified all of the objects. The only thing missing, she said, was an inexpensive plastic comb. Mueller wrote "Identified" on the back of the piece of paper listing the articles and Miss Wallace wrote down her name, the date and the time. Then Mueller gave her a receipt and he and O'Neal left, taking the articles and the piece of paper along. Returning to the car, they headed for the rooming house.

The rooming house was near the corner of Tenth and Central, about two blocks south and two west of the scene of the crime. It was a large brown frame building that badly needed paint. The officers parked in front and took the walk that crossed the narrow front yard between two old automobile tires covered with luminous silver paint and enclosing flower beds.

In the middle of the porch was the front door. It was glass and was covered by a net curtain. O'Neal knocked, and knocked again, but there was no sound from within. After a few minutes, Mueller tried the door and it opened, admitting the men to a large entry hall with wallpaper hanging loose from the ceiling. Three doors were visible, each with a name card attached. There was also a stairway extending upward to the right of the front door. The officers knocked on each of the doors but there was no answer.

"Before we go up, let's try the back," O'Neal said.

Mueller nodded and they left the house and followed a

narrow cement walk around to the back door. There, secured by a thumbtack, was a small card with the inscription, "Mrs. Emile Davis, Proprietor."

O'Neal knocked. After a few minutes the door opened about three inches and part of an old woman's face appeared.

O'Neal said, "Good morning, ma'am, are you Mrs. Davis?"

"Yes," the woman answered.

"Well, we're police officers and we'd like to talk to you." O'Neal flipped open his wallet and showed his badge and credentials.

After a pause, the woman said, "What do you want to talk about? I'm not even dressed yet."

"We want to ask you about a man who's committed a crime who lives here. We don't want to trouble you, but we're kind of in a hurry. Maybe you could just put on a robe or something."

"Well, I've got my robe on anyway," she said, but she did not open the door. Then she added, "I don't know nothing about any crimes, but I guess it's all right." Releasing the door, she stood aside and the officers entered.

The room was the kitchen and the officers were assailed at once by a variety of heavy cooking smells. A rumpled bed was in one corner with a washbasin on a chair beside it. On the other side of the room was a sink with a wooden drainboard and an antique gas stove. The floor, a cracked linoleum, was covered with frayed cotton rugs. One overstuffed chair and a lamp were at the foot of the bed.

Mrs. Davis sat down on the bed. Her face was heavy and wrinkled and her gray hair hung to her shoulders. A dirty blue man's bathrobe covered everything but her feet and they were partially hidden in worn felt carpet slippers. She lighted a cigarette and turned toward O'Neal who had sat down in the overstuffed chair, leaving Mueller standing against the sink.

O'Neal produced a notebook and a pencil. "Does a man named Adam Johnson room here, ma'am?"

The old woman exhaled a large cloud of smoke. "I don't pay much attention to my roomers' business."

Accepting this as an affirmative answer, O'Neal said, "Well, a woman was hit and had her purse snatched last night over at Twelfth and Park. This man Johnson did it."

Without changing her expression, Mrs. Davis said, "I doubt it. He don't seem the type."

Mueller, who had said nothing until now, spoke up. "The woman identified him."

Mrs. Davis did not look toward Mueller, but she said, "She probably didn't even see him." Then, looking down at her feet, she added, "My husband was a railroader. He was mixed up with the union once and the railroad cops. He used to say that policemen were dumb . . . and mean to boot."

To O'Neal's annoyance, Mueller rose to this too. "Did your husband have a record?"

Still looking at O'Neal, she answered, "My old man's gone, you can't hurt him. Nobody can hurt him." The woman swung her head toward Mueller and looked closely at him. "He was just about twice as big as you, and he had hands like a bushel basket."

Mueller continued the contest. "How about you? Have you been in trouble with the police?"

"No," the woman said, "unless, of course, I might be John Dillinger in disguise." Without the trace of a smile or emotion, she added, "Of course, I do quite a bit of purse snatching nowadays. I'm real good at it, because I'm so fast on my feet. I just run up so quick nobody sees me. Then I run away. I always wear gloves and sometimes they don't even know I got the purse. I don't leave no fingerprints 'cause of the gloves, you know."

Taking advantage of Mueller's effort to recover, O'Neal

said, "We'd like to look at Johnson's room, Mrs. Davis. We've a warrant, of course, and we'll be grateful for your cooperation." The woman sat smoking for a few minutes. O'Neal said, "Let's go up, shall we?" and he rose from his chair.

Mrs. Davis got up reluctantly and opened a small drawer in the table by the bed. She took out a ring of keys and crossed to the back door and opened it. The officers followed her, into the yard and around the walk to the front of the house. They went in the front door and were in the hall in which they had been before.

With considerable effort, Mrs. Davis began to climb the stairs, the officers behind her. At the top of the stairs, she paused, breathing heavily. She lighted another cigarette and drew deeply on it, as if to clear her lungs. The officers stood together on the steps waiting for her to move, and then went down the hall behind her.

The last room was Adam Johnson's. Mrs. Davis unlocked it and drew back, letting the men enter. But she did not leave. Instead, her face as immobile as ever, she stood in the doorway to oversee the violation of her roomer's property.

The room was painfully plain. There was a bed, a chair and an unpainted dresser. The closet was in the corner, covered by a plastic curtain. The remaining furnishings consisted of a metal ashtray, a wooden floor lamp, a wooden bed table and a small rag rug on the floor beside the bed. There was little evidence of an occupant. Two paperback books were stacked on the bed table. On the dresser was a razor, a shaving brush, a tube of shaving soap and a comb. A toothbrush, toothpaste, and a bar of soap lay on a shelf above the dresser.

O'Neal moved to the dresser and opened the drawers. In the top drawer was nine dollars, neatly piled in the corner and covered by a pair of white socks. Three more pairs of socks, six heavy work shirts, two white shirts, four pairs of cotton shorts and three pairs of brown cotton pants were also taken from the dresser and placed on the bed. This was all. The pants were exactly like those that Adam Johnson had worn the night before.

The closet yielded a pair of dirty pants, just like the others, two dirty work shirts, and a pair of cotton pajamas. A pair of heavy work shoes was on the floor. Hanging on a wire hanger was a dark blue wool suit with two pairs of pants, neatly pressed and new looking. A dark blue necktie was draped around the shoulders of the suit.

The officers placed everything on the dresser. Stripping the bed, they prodded the mattress and turned it upside down. Nothing appeared but a large suitcase under the bed with Adam's name on it. It was made of black cardboard. coated with shellac, and it was empty.

After more poking about, O'Neal said, "Well, John, it looks like that's it."

Mrs. Davis, silent until now, said, "Looks like you've really caught a big bug, don't it? He's been hiding the loot up here, waiting to fence it all at once."

Mueller swung around to argue with the woman, but O'Neal touched his arm. "When did he rent this room?" O'Neal asked.

"Early last month, April, maybe about the first week."

"What's the rent, if you please?"

"Eight dollars a week, in advance. He always paid on time. He paid me yesterday for next week, starting Monday, so he's paid up in advance." As if to herself but loud enough for all to hear, she added, "He probably stuck up a bank to get the money."

"Where was he from, do you know?" O'Neal said.

"Tennessee. He just got in town and saw my sign and

come in. He was a nice boy. Regular hours, no women, at least not here, and no whiskey either." Again she digressed. "Of course, I didn't know he was a big-shot criminal or I wouldn't have rented it out to him. With the cops as mean *and* dumb as they are, a woman had ought to be careful as she can."

O'Neal said, "Well, thanks a lot. We'll take this stuff along." He opened the suitcase and began to fill it.

"Who gets the money, the chief or you two?" she asked.

"Mr. Johnson will get it, we'll deliver it to him," Mueller said heatedly.

"Fat chance," said Mrs. Davis.

Having packed the suitcase, O'Neal put the nine dollars in an envelope and marked it. Then he picked up the suitcase and he and Mueller left the room. Mrs. Davis followed them down the hall and the steps and out the door. They walked to the car and got in. She stood on the porch as the car pulled away.

Mueller let out a loud breath of air. "Jesus, poor old Emile Davis. I'll bet she killed him with a knife."

O'Neal smiled. "Oh, I don't know, John. She spoke real respectful about him. My guess is that he could handle her all right."

Mueller said, "Oh, well, to hell with it. It's time for lunch. Let's eat."

After lunch at a drugstore, the officers proceeded to the Faultless Pump Company. It was one of the larger plants, employing almost nine thousand people. Both men had been there before, so they had no trouble in locating the employment office. They asked for the personnel director, Fred Wampler, and were almost immediately shown in to his handsomely paneled office.

In his mid-thirties, blond and immaculately groomed,

Wampler shook hands with the officers and waved them into modern and comfortable chairs. He moved gracefully around his desk and sat down. At the front of the desk were several colored photographs of his wife and children, turned conveniently toward the visitors. Between bookends, miniatures of a Lincoln statue, were several books. The officers caught sight of a few titles, including *Getting People to Work For You* and *Employment and Self-Respect.* Also on the desk was the emblem of an organization, surmounted by the motto, "Others, Not Self."

But all of these ornaments were overshadowed by a large photograph hanging behind Wampler's head. The policemen recognized the picture, a Karsh of Dr. Raymond Pate Moore, the clergyman. Wampler had been in charge of a seminar on salesmanship which the minister had conducted in the city the year before. He had been rewarded with this picture, inscribed to Wampler, "A young man who is going places." Below this, in slightly smaller script, were the words, "Believe in *yourself!*" Then came "In Christ's Name," followed by the flourishing autograph.

The visitors scarcely had the chance to appreciate these things when Wampler cordially opened the interview. Fingering the miniature Boy Scout pin in the lapel of his sports jacket, he said, "Well, gentlemen, what can I do for you?"

O'Neal answered, "We've got an employee of yours in custody, Mr. Wampler, a man named Adam Johnson, held for robbery." He glanced at his notebook. "According to his Faultless ID, his clock number is 16172."

"I'm reassured to find that it's an hourly man," Wampler said. "Of course, I'm always sorry if any of our people are in trouble. The clock number would indicate that he's a new man. Just a moment."

Wampler pressed a buzzer and a young girl opened the door. She was quite pretty, with an excellent figure and beautiful legs, and she wore a clinging black wool dress, dark stockings and high-heeled shoes. Poised attractively on one foot with her arms extended backward, she said, "Yes, Fred?"

Wampler said, "Judy, honey, please tell Ed to bring in the file on Adam Johnson, Number 16172. I'll also need an IBM check to identify his present department."

"O.K.," the girl said. She looked at the police, returning their stares, and left the room.

In a few moments a man entered, carrying a file jacket.

"This is Ed Volger, my employment manager, gentlemen," Wampler said. "These men are police officers, Ed, they need some information."

Volger nodded, sat down beside Wampler and opened the file. After briefly shuffling the papers, he said, "Adam Johnson was hired here on April 23, this year. Classification: Common labor. Rate: $1.8755. He was assigned to Department L, that's our cost code for warehousing indirect. He hasn't completed his probationary period under the collective bargaining agreement. It's up next Tuesday. No reprimands. No absences." Volger looked up. "That's what the file shows as of the 5 P.M. register yesterday."

O'Neal wrote in his book and said, "What kind of pre-employment history have you got on him?"

Volger took an application from the file. "Well, he was born in Kingsway, Tennessee, January 19, 1941. He's nineteen years old. He's had eight years of common school and four years of high school. He graduated at both places." Volger again looked up, as if this fact were impressive. Then he read on. "Lived his whole life in Kingsway, apparently, until April of this year. Came directly here from Kingsway. Previous employment—odd jobs during school and summer vacation and worked at a grain elevator from high school graduation in 1959 until April this year." Again Volger looked at the policemen. "He quit that job voluntarily."

Returning to the file, he droned on. "No criminal record. No church affiliation."

"Do you pick up family stuff on your applications?" O'Neal asked.

"Yes, we do, but this guy's family data is sketchy. Father, presumed dead. Mother, died 1950. No brothers or sisters. Next of kin, none. 'Mr. and Mrs. Abernathy, Rural Route 3, Kingsway' is written below the word 'None' in the next-of-kin box. Here's his picture. We took it here . . . looks all right. Incidentally, the Testing Division ranks him pretty high in terms of aptitudes, motivation and adjustment. That's about it on Johnson."

O'Neal glanced at the photograph. "Does anyone in this office know him?"

Wampler answered, "No. We can't know all of them, although our communications program is the best there is. There are just too many. His foreman would know him, of course." Glancing at Volger, he said, "By the way, that would be Fitz Hogan, wouldn't it?"

"Yes. Hogan's his boss."

"We'd like to see Hogan if we could. Could you get him over?" ONeal said.

"Sure, we'll just put him on the auto-call. His department's at the far end of the plant, but it'll only take five minutes on the monorail." Wampler picked up the phone and issued the order for Hogan. Then he asked, "How about some coffee?" The officers accepted and Wampler again pushed a button and the very pretty girl reappeared. "Four coffees, Judy, please—no, you'd better make it five, one for Hogan, too."

In a few minutes, the girl was back. With all eyes upon her, she wriggled to Wampler's desk and put down a tray with five cups of coffee and plastic packages of sugar and cream.

As the girl left the room, Hogan arrived. He was a big, rough-hewn man, middle-aged and with large, dirty hands. On the back of one of them was a tattooed cross, with the words "My Lord and My God" above it.

Wampler introduced the officers.

"What's it about," Hogan said, "the Johnson boy?"

"Yes," said Wampler, "how'd you know?"

"One of the boys seen it in the paper." Hogan reached into his shirt pocket, pulled out a slightly smudged clipping, and handed it to Wampler. The officers rose and read over his shoulder:

ALLEGED PURSE SNATCHER SHOT BY POLICEMAN

Shot by police while fleeing with a purse he allegedly grabbed from a woman late yesterday, a man slated as Adam Johnson, 19 years old, 1041 Central, was taken to City Hospital last night. He was wounded in the back.

Bullets from the revolvers of Patrolmen John Mueller and John Sullivan downed Johnson in the 1200 block of Park Avenue after a foot chase through alleys and yards.

Miss Josephine Wallace, 46, 1212 North Park, identified Johnson as the youth who snatched her purse and struck her as she alighted from an automobile in front of her house.

"I didn't know he'd been shot," said Wampler. "Is he hurt bad?"

"He might be," O'Neal answered.

Hogan, who had sprawled on the corner of Wampler's desk, suddenly said, "Well, I'm pretty sure they got the wrong man. That boy was all right." When this gratuitous opinion was not challenged, Hogan became combative. "*Jesus Christ,* I usually get these hot rodders, young punks with nothing but tail on their minds, and dirty tail at that. This kid is different. He ain't no sissy, by God, I don't mean nothing like that, but he was smart and a hard worker. Most generally these guys loll around in the can so's you've got to lock the coke machine to keep 'em on the job. But this boy was a worker. And he was grown up, too. None of this crap like putting an air hose in your behind. He was a good guy just doing his job." Turning to the officers, Hogan stuck out his considerable jaw. "I say you got the wrong man. Kids like that ain't robbers."

Sensing the embarrassing situation the foreman had created, Wampler said, "Well, Fitz, we're all sorry about this, but unfortunately criminal tendencies may be latent in a personality. You can't always predict a man's future from his . . ."

Hogan stopped him. "Now don't give me all them college words, Fred, by God. I used to do my own hiring out there, back before you was born, and I've been supervising these men for a long time, before you got your God damn school degrees and all the fancy tests you give these guys. I *know* people and I know this boy, by God. He's a good one, and that's that." Hogan folded his arms across his chest. There was a sticky silence as he glowered around the room, as if to dare anyone, or all, to settle the question manfully.

At last O'Neal said, "Mr. Hogan, you may be perfectly right. You're certainly entitled to your opinion. The boy will get a fair trial and if he's innocent he'll go free. We're trying now to get some facts about him. You've already told us something . . . he was a good employee. What about his family?"

"He don't have one," Hogan answered, mollified. "His old man, I guess, deserted them, him and his mom, when he was a kid. Then his mother got married again, and then her and the stepfather was killed." Hogan struck his palm with his fist. "It's a lousy story, and the most funny thing is for him to turn out such a good boy." Glancing from one to another of his listeners, he continued. "Then he lived with some people named Abernathy. He called 'em 'aunt and uncle,' but they was friends only, but, *by God,* they was good people else they wouldn't have took him in. The kid even went to high school down south. He come up here on his own, he says, so's he could get himself a good job." With becoming modesty, Hogan said, "Of course, working for me ain't exactly like being President of the U.S.A., but the boy's a comer in my opinion. No behind-kissing, I don't mean that, just an honest hard-working kid. The kind that had ought to have a chance at Wampler's job, but they don't have the schooling, or the manners and fancy clothes either, by God." Hogan suddenly brightened up and, to show that this was all in fun, he doubled up his fist and hit Wampler hard on the chest.

O'Neal wrote further in his notebook. "Who were his friends, Mr. Hogan, besides you? Who'd he run with?"

"Well, nobody particular. He didn't have no special friends as far as I know, 'cept this girl . . ."

O'Neal looked up sharply. "What girl?"

"Well, maybe two weeks ago he ate lunch with this girl, Annie's her name, that works in the office over at the warehouse. A nice girl, a young one, just out of high school. Her old man used to be in the machine shop here years ago. Now he's with this die shop here in town."

"Is that all he did, eat lunch with her, once?" asked O'Neal.

"Hell, no, it ain't all," Hogan said scornfully. "He ate lunch with her regular since then and I think he's took her out a few times, by God."

O'Neal turned to Wampler. "What's this girl's name and address?"

Ed Volger said, "Her name is Anne Webster. She's an inventory clerk 1–c. Fitz is right about her dad . . . Joe

Webster. He works for the Keene Engineering Company."

O'Neal made some final notes, and he and Mueller stood up. It was almost three-thirty, and they had finished with the Faultless people. "We thank you all, gentlemen, for your help. You may hear from us again if we've got any more questions."

"You're surely welcome," said Wampler. "If we can help at all, just call."

The officers shook hands all around and left the office. As they took their last lingering look at the girl in black, Hogan called after them, "I still say you got the wrong man."

"We'll see," Mueller answered.

"Anything else, Fred?" Volger asked after the police had gone.

"No, that's all, thanks, but keep Johnson's folder handy. They may want it again."

Volger left the room and Wampler and Hogan were alone. The foreman sat down at Wampler's desk and then got up and walked to the window to watch the police get into their car. Picking up a form from his desk, Wampler said, "Here's the ERF, Fitz, you'll need a new man."

The foreman swung around belligerently. "I ain't requisitioning anybody yet. The boy's only been absent for today."

"That's true, but it's obvious that he's going to be absent for a while, at least, and in view of the reason, he'll be terminated right now, anyway."

"Why in the hell should he be terminated, he ain't even been tried yet," Hogan said angrily. "He's innocent till they prove him guilty, by God."

Checking an urge to tell Hogan that *he*, not Hogan, was the personnel manager, Wampler collected himself to end the debate. "Look, Fitz, I don't have to remind you that

this guy is a probationary employee. Under the union agree-
ment, we can terminate a probationer for *no* reason. This
guy's been arrested for robbery and socking some woman.
He's also been shot and is probably hurt pretty bad. As a
matter of company policy, we don't carry probationers over
in any extended-absence situation. We certainly can't carry
this guy over."

Hogan was silent, but Wampler continued. "In a few
days his probationary period will be over. If we don't sever
him now we'll be stuck with him, in jail and hurt at that,
and he'll start on group insurance, weekly indemnity, and
everything else. Don't you see? I'm as humane as anybody,
Fitz, but I work for this company and so do you. It's a matter
of *policy*. I can't change the policies of this company and
this man will have to be severed, that's all there is to it."

The foreman, his hands in his pockets, stood looking down
at Wampler. He had heard him and he knew that he had
no answer. The "company policy" expression was Wampler's frequent method of closing off discussions. In this
situation, it was also an honest statement of the facts. A probationary employee was out of luck in any kind of scrape,
and Adam Johnson was surely in a first class scrape. Resignedly, Hogan said, "O.K., Fred, you win. Give me the God
damn requisition form and you go ahead and terminate
him."

Wampler handed over the form and Hogan filled it in.
Wampler picked up the telephone and called the employ-
ment manager. "Terminate the Johnson boy as of today."
Glancing up at Hogan, he added, "Mark it 'absenteeism.'
Make no reference to this police business, but get him ter-
minated."

Fred Wampler hung up and turned again to Hogan. Perhaps a minute passed before the big man said, "He ain't
even eligible for health and welfare is he, Fred?"

"No. That's got a seniority requirement, too. He's s.o.l.
on all the fringe benefits."

"Well, if it's O.K. with you, I think I'll ask the union about
him. Isn't that O.K.?"

Wampler stiffened at the mention of the union. "What
the hell for?"

"Well, they've got this Flower Fund they call it, from
the vending machines. It's not only for flowers. It's for all
kinds of things, pretty loose, and maybe they'll give something here."

Wampler said, "If I were you, I'd stay away from the
union. You're on the other side of the street, and my experience is that those guys will compromise you every time you
get cozy with them."

Hogan exploded. "And who in the hell said anything
about getting cozy? This boy's an employee, the union rep-
resents the employees, the union's got a sock full of money
for guys when they're in a crack. So I ask them to help a
guy who's in a crack. What's wrong with that?" He had
again assumed his naturally aggressive aspect, and Wampler
began to backwater.

"Well, O.K., I guess you're right," Wampler said, adding,
"It's probably a good idea. Maybe the union *will* do something. After all, purse snatchers ought to stick together."

Before Wampler could get much pleasure from his little
joke, Hogan, who hadn't thought it was funny, was at the
door. "See you later," he called, and walked out.

The foreman left the office grounds, walked to the corner
and turned down a street bordering the plant. At the end
of the block across from the plant was an unpainted cement
block building with a large sign, LOCAL 980, above the door.
As Hogan approached the building, he saw the business
agent's car, a shiny Oldsmobile 98, parked at the curb. At
the building, he pushed open the door and went in.

There was one large room, a cashier's cage and a small

office. On the wall of the large room was a tinted picture of Franklin Roosevelt, flanked by smaller pictures of George Meany and General MacArthur. Next to these was a calendar, surmounted by a color photograph of a buxom girl leaning over a fence and wearing only a hat and a pair of shoes. A few small tables and some metal chairs were placed about the plastic tile floor.

No one was in the large room or in the cashier's window, but Lou Rosa, the business agent, was talking on the telephone in the small office. He was a short, muscular man. He wore a black business suit and a maroon sport shirt and his left sleeve was pinned up where his arm had been cut off at the elbow.

Hogan looked in and Rosa waved to him and continued to talk over the telephone. Hogan sat down and waited, overhearing the conversation and watching as Rosa, writing with his right hand and cradling the telephone on his shoulder, skillfully maneuvered papers around on the desk with the stump of his left arm.

To Fitz Hogan it was at once obvious that Rosa's telephone call concerned a grievance. From the end of the conversation he could hear, Hogan guessed that the business agent was talking to the assembly foreman. Rosa was in good form, wheedling and threatening alternately, interspersing his arguments with profane outbursts.

Hogan caught snatches of the conversation. "We cooperate with this company and it don't cooperate with us . . . Of course you got to be efficient, but you got to be fair, too . . . I ain't only concerned about the language of the contract, I'm concerned about the spirit, and you violated both . . . This is getting to be an old-fashioned sweat shop, by God, you foremen think you got some kind of rights from the Pope . . ."

It was the usual Rosa treatment. Hogan had experienced

it himself a couple of times, and Rosa had been at it since 1941 when he had lost his arm in a press and was elected business agent. To Hogan it was pretty boring, but, unlike many of the younger foremen, he didn't dislike Rosa. He had known him "when," when the plant had reopened in 1935 and they had been among the first to go to work.

Finally the conversation ended and, red-faced and sweating, Rosa came out of his office. "Hi, Fitz, Jesus, it's nice to see a foreman who's got a head on him. Honest to God, the things those guys do sometimes you wouldn't believe. This company must give some kind of awards for stupid foremen. It really stinks." Switching off abruptly, he said, "Well, how the hell are you?"

"I'm O.K., Lou," said Hogan and, suddenly reticent about his errand, he asked the business agent what the grievance was about.

"It's a layoff question, on the third trick last night. Under the contract, there's only one department in assembly. It covers bench, automatic, and subassembly, all of them together. After six hours last night, the subassembly people run out of parts. So that son-of-a-bitch foreman sends *them* home for the two hours instead of sending out the junior guys from the whole department." Rosa's voice rose. "Six senior men end up with six hours pay. It's lousy, and the son-of-a-bitch knows better. He just done it and figured we'd either let it pass or wouldn't go all the way on it. Well, he's wrong." Assuming the tone and mien of a hundred union meetings, Rosa said, "On a matter of principle, we'll go to arbitration if it costs even a thousand dollars." He pointed his finger at the foreman. "I don't like to get snookered, Fitz, and that's all there is to it. God knows, I'm reasonable, but I won't let this company negotiate a contract and then welsh on it. A contract's a contract. Ain't that the way it has to be?"

Although Rosa's question was surely rhetorical, Hogan diplomatically acknowledged that a contract was, indeed, a contract. But he avoided any opinion of the grievance.

Anxious to close up the office and go home, Rosa brought Hogan to the point after a few more comments about the grievance. "What's on your mind, Fitz? What can I do for you?"

"Well, it's about a boy who works for me who needs help."

"Who is it?" asked Rosa.

"His name's Adam Johnson."

"I never heard of him," said Rosa. "What about him?"

Defensively Hogan started in. "Well, you may not know him yet because he only started a while ago, but he's a very good boy and he's been accused by the police of grabbing some woman's purse. . . . I'm sure he didn't do it, but the cops shot him anyway. And he's broke, and hasn't got no family, and now the company's fired him."

Rosa had sat down, but he was out of his chair at once. "They got no right to fire him until he's put away," he shouted. "Hell's fire, we settled that two years ago in that Dolton case. Just a minute, let me get his check-off card."

As he turned to go to his files, Hogan sheepishly said, "You ain't got anything from him. He ain't finished his probationary period, so he ain't joined the union yet."

Rosa froze in his tracks and turned around, staring at Hogan in disbelief. "You mean he *ain't even a member?*"

"That's rght."

The business agent's voice was shrill. "Well, what in the hell are you talking to me about? I don't have no right to represent probationers on discharge, you know that, Hogan . . . and I don't break my ass for nonmembers anyway."

"I ain't asking you to represent him in the discharge. That's over with. I was wondering about the Flower Fund. The boy is hurt, he's broke, and he ain't got no family. He needs help. I thought you might maybe want to help out some, seeing as how he needs it so bad."

It was hardly perceptible, but at the mention of the Flower Fund, Lou Rosa's expression changed. He was suddenly a banker or a trustee, confronting some outrageous call on his wherewithal. Sincerely perplexed, he said quietly, "But, Fitz, if he ain't a *member*, what business is it of mine? You ain't makin' sense."

Hogan at last felt equal to the debate. He struck the table and said, "Now wait just a minute, Lou, by God. *I* know about that fund. *I* know the guys on the committee, and I know you can spend it for any *God damn thing* you want to and the committee will go along with anything you say about it. There isn't no requirement about being a member. What about them kids in the Little League you bought baseball suits for? They ain't members of the union." Hogan paused and lowered his voice. "I'm telling you . . . I'm not telling you anything . . . I'm *asking* you to please help out a man who works here who's a good boy and who's in a helluva shape. If you won't help him, O.K., but don't for Christ's sake give me any crap about having to spend the money only for members."

Hogan, in anger, was imposing and the smaller man now spoke differently. "Now look, Fitz, don't get hot about it. You and me is old friends and union friends at that. But you just *got* to see this my way. Here I am. I got a fund . . . It's a *union* fund. . . . It don't belong to me and it's for *union* affairs. It's for all the union members, for them. Here's a guy who's arrested and gets shot. I ain't saying it ain't a bum rap. Let's say it is. But the guy's only worked here a few weeks and he's never joined the union. If we give him money, we'd give it to anybody, and if we give it to anybody it's all gone. There wouldn't be no picnic next year, and there wouldn't be no strike benefits next year, if we had a strike next year, and if some old-time member gets real sick and his insurance runs out and don't cover him, then we can't help him." Affected himself by these pitiful prospects, Rosa coughed and shook his head mournfully. "It's simply *out of the question.* I've got to look at the broad picture of takin' care of all these thousands of people in the union. I *can't* let sympathy for one guy . . . and he ain't even a member . . . mess up the whole local. I can't do it. Maybe I'd like to, but I can't. That's final, Fitz."

There was silence as Rosa finished. Hogan knew, as he had known in the personnel office, that the last word had been said. He got up and stood over the smaller man. "O.K., Lou. You got the money and I ain't, and I'm too old to take it away from you." Then he turned abruptly to the door.

Hogan walked up the street toward the foreman's parking lot. Behind him Rosa was busy locking up the building. Reaching his car, the foreman absentmindedly got in, started it up and drove into the stream of traffic, still thinking of the injustice of Adam Johnson's circumstances.

Hogan thought about Adam all the way home. Then, reminded by his wife of a bowling date, he forced himself to put the Johnson matter aside. And by the end of the evening, the putting aside was permanent. After all, he thought, the company was probably right, or at least its attitude was understandable. And so was Lou Rosa's. It was real tough on the Johnson boy, but Hogan had done everything that he could. It was just one of those things.

3

WHILE the police waited for a chance to question Adam
Johnson, they continued their investigation. To their surprise, communications with Tennessee police authorities
and a print check at the FBI did not disclose a criminal record. As a matter of fact, the job application at Faultless
Pump apparently contained the straight story on Adam's
background. All of this was learned before the boy was interviewed.

It was not until Monday that Adam was fully conscious.
This was not entirely because of the wound. He had been
given a hypodermic by the ambulance intern as he lay in
the alley on the night of the crime. From then on, drugged

again from time to time, he had been either sleeping or suspended between consciousness and unconsciousness.

Awakening on Monday morning, Adam had a vague sense
of the passage of time and a mixture of impressions—of
being turned over on a surgical table, of bright lights glaring
down on him, of people probing about on his back and of
people talking. He also had semi-recollections of baths, of
nurses and of severe pain. Now awake, he was sufficiently
perceptive to see that he was in a hospital room, in a rough,
cotton hospital gown. The ceilings were very high. Behind
his head were windows, big windows with bars. Everything
was white, including the uniforms of the nurses and the male
attendants moving about, and the bedclothing of all twelve
beds, six on each side of the room. There was only one ex-
ception. At the doorway at the end of the room was a police
officer. He was dressed in blue.

From his surroundings, Adam's confused glance returned
to himself. Slowly he became aware that his bed—he later
was to know it as a Stryker frame—was most unusual. It was
small and narrow and close to the floor, with arm rests. Beside it was what seemed a similar bed, unoccupied. On the
other side, on the floor, was a glass container with a small
rubber hose running from it into the bed. Quite by accident
he discovered that he was wearing a catheter and that it led
to the hose in the glass container.

Still groping toward an understanding of all of these curi-
osities, Adam focused briefly on a man in a nearby bed. He
was a colored man, much older than Adam, and his head
was swathed in white bandages. But his eyes were uncov-
ered and as Adam looked over the Negro said, "Tough luck,
boy. You had a real tough break."

Adam said nothing at first, and then he asked, "What day
is it today?"

As if he understood, the stranger answered, "Monday, and

you been here since Thursday night." Adam hesitated again, trying to understand these facts. But, sick and in pain, he was also hopelessly disoriented and he began to feel a vague sense of panic.

Suddenly he was aware that someone was standing beside him. He looked up and a fat nurse, holding a metal tray of food, said, "Good morning. I've breakfast for you here and you must eat it. You haven't eaten for a long time."

Adam stared blankly at her. She sat down in a chair beside his bed and, opening a confession magazine to read between bites, began spooning food toward Adam's mouth. Although he gagged at the first bite, he finally was able to swallow it and three or four more. He also sipped orange juice and a little milk, sucked up in a glass straw. Then he was finished and the nurse went away.

The nurse returned in a few minutes, followed by a younger nurse carrying a basin of water. The fat one said, "Time for your bath." Seizing the covers, she threw them back unceremoniously.

Adam recoiled at first, but subsided because he seemed rooted to the bed. Ignoring his terrible embarrassment, the women moved in on either side and, amidst a great shuffling of towels and washrags, began to bathe him below the waist.

"O.K., Nell, let's get him over," the fat nurse said.

Before Adam could react at all, one nurse unfastened the catheter. Then they lifted the empty frame from the floor beside the bed and, disregarding Adam's startled apprehension, they lowered it expertly over him. Sandwiched between the two parts of the bed, a padded form circled Adam's face, leaving his mouth, nose and eyes exposed. "Over she goes," said the fat nurse, and the entire contraption revolved, placing Adam face down in what had been the empty frame. The nurses then removed the other frame from his back.

Mystified completely, Adam lay helpless, staring at the

floor through the padded form. The nurses tended to his back.

"Enema?" said the younger woman.

"I guess so," the other said, "although there's nothing much in him. But he did it in bed the second day, so we might as well be safe." Speaking to the younger nurse as if she were a novice, the older woman went on. "I had one of these before . . . *God,* you should've seen the sores he got. The doctor says we've got to keep him clean, and keep the antibiotics going."

The enema was promptly applied, Adam feeling nothing. A penicillin shot was administered, again without Adam's being aware of it. The catheter was put in place and the nurses packed up their paraphernalia. "We'll be back soon," said the fat one, and they left.

In five minutes, the fat nurse returned to Adam's side and lowered her face to talk. But during the five minutes Adam had at last begun to pull himself together. He had found that he could turn his head, and had twisted his face to one side. The side of his head was in the padded hole where his face had been. And it was he who spoke first. "Am I hurt bad?"

"Oh, not really bad, no," said the nurse, but Adam was instinctively frightened by her downcast eyes. Before he could follow up the question the woman said, "Now, you just relax, young man, and keep comfortable. A detective is here and wants to talk to you." She left, and Detective O'Neal walked down between the rows of beds.

"Good morning, Johnson, I'm Detective O'Neal." He brought out his wallet and badge and put them in front of Adam's face.

"Good morning," said Adam.

"I'd like to ask you a few questions, son, if you feel like answering. How about it?"

"Yes, sir," said Adam, reassured by the detective's friendly manner.

"Well, first of all, do you remember last Thursday night? The doctors say that you've been in and out of shock, and I don't want to talk with you if you're hazy. Are you?"

"I'm a little hazy, I guess, still. Thursday was the day all this happened, wasn't it? I mean Thursday night?"

"That's right," O'Neal answered.

"Well, I think I sort of remember . . . I'm beginning to remember right now . . . Yes, I worked Thursday at the plant . . . I remember that."

"What did you do then?"

"I went back to my room and changed clothes first, because I had a date."

"Who was the date?"

"It was this girl at the plant. Her name is Annie, Anne Webster. We went to the cafeteria for supper and then we seen the show. It was . . ."

The detective interrupted. "What did you do after the show?"

"Well, I took her home, of course. We talked and fooled around for a while and then I went home."

"Where does this girl live?"

"She lives with her folks at 1654 on Park."

"What time did you leave her house?"

"I'm not certain, but generally I leave about eleven o'clock or so, 'cause we both work."

"Just what is your relationship with this girl, Adam?"
Adam looked perplexed.

"I mean is she your girl . . . are you engaged, or anything like that?"

Adam colored and said, "No, we're just friends. I've only known her a little while . . . and we're friends."

O'Neal returned to the night of the crime. "All right,

Adam, tell me what happened after you left this Anne's house, shortly after eleven o'clock on Thursday night?"

"Well, I started to walk down Park to go home. I live at Tenth and Central . . . So I started to walk down Park, I remember that . . ." Adam paused. He put one hand to the side of his head and screwed up his face, groping for the scenes of that night. "Yes, I remember walking down Park. It was dark, you know, except by the streetlights. There was lots of noise because of the cars and the people, they had the windows open and the TV sets going. I walked along, and I crossed a couple of side streets. Maybe halfway down this block a car passed me . . ."

O'Neal interposed. "Now, Adam, I want to know your movements a little more definitely. You say you were half-way down 'this block.' I want to know where you were. *What* block?"

Adam hesitated. "Well, I was probably south of Thir-teenth . . . I think I'd crossed Thirteenth. I was about halfway down to Twelfth when this car passed me, going *up* the street. There were men in the car, maybe five or six and they were hollering. They hollered out at me . . . called me a son-of-a-bitch or something lousy, I think it was son-of-a-bitch, and they threw a empty beer can across at me, near me. Well, it made me kind of sore, I guess, because I hollered back, some kind of dirty name. And all of a sud-den the car slowed down, like they were putting on the brakes real quick. But they started up again, going real fast." Adam twisted his head and looked sheepish. "I was kind of scared, to tell you the truth, because I thought maybe they were going to jump me. So I watched and, sure enough, they turned left up at Thirteenth, like they were coming round the block. So I began to go kind of easy down toward Twelfth, watching for maybe this car. And all of a sudden, I saw the car coming up at me very fast and turning over into the wrong lane towards me. So I took off, up into this yard. I was really moving into this yard, it was real dark and, sure enough, I heard them holler 'There he goes.' So I kept going and I ran into a fence in back of this yard, along the alley. So I climbed it and headed up the alley and then these flashlights went on . . . and some more hollering . . . and then they started shooting . . ." Adam's story stopped abruptly. He shook his head and said, "That's all I remember," and looked inquiringly at the detective.

O'Neal surveyed the room once or twice and then looked back at Adam. He had been writing in his notebook, and he wrote a few more lines before he said, "That isn't the way I've heard it, son."

"What do you mean?" Adam asked.

"Well, you're accused of stealing a woman's purse. That's why the police were chasing you, and that's why they fired, when you kept running."

Adam answered firmly, in spite of his condition. "But I didn't steal *nothing*. I've never stole from anybody."

"Well, let's see." Looking as directly at Adam as the boy's position permitted, O'Neal told him Miss Wallace's version.

When he had finished, Adam said simply, "Well, it isn't so. She's lying."

"Well, son, we don't think so," O'Neal said. "Let's go over this story of yours again."

The detective began to probe Adam's account, suggesting alternative possibilities and questioning each fact. But Adam was not shaken and though he made many notes during the cross examination, O'Neal admitted to himself that the substance of the facts that Adam had given had not changed significantly.

Suddenly, O'Neal closed his notebook and stood up. "I have to go. Thanks. I'll probably come to see you again."

"Yes, sir," Adam said.

O'Neal walked to the end of the bed and turned toward the door, but he stopped abruptly at the door and came back to the side of the bed. Looking down at Adam, he lowered his voice. "Son, you're in a pretty bad way, just between you and me, in more ways than one. I can't help you even if I wanted to, because I'm on the other side. But you need some help, plenty of help . . . Maybe I could give some messages for you. Is there anybody you'd like to get in touch with?"

At first the detective thought that Adam had not heard him. He just lay there, his eyes very bright. At last he said, "Well, there's really hardly anybody. Thanks just the same."

Dissatisfied with this, O'Neal said, "What about this girl and your landlady? They both think pretty highly of you."

Adam brightened a little. "Yes, I'd like for them to know about it, if they don't already, and the Abernathys in Kingsway, down home. I can give you their address."

"I've got it, and I'll drop them a note right away," said O'Neal. "I've already told the landlady, Mrs. Davis, but I'll be sure the Webster girl is told."

"Thank you very much," Adam said.

To Adam's surprise, the detective seemed annoyed. "Don't *thank* me, son, *for Christ's sake,*" he said. Then he left.

It was later the same day that Adam was told about his back. Even before then he had become vaguely aware that his wound was serious. Nobody had said so, but the curious pain in the back, the turnovers in the Stryker frame, another penicillin shot and the frequent baths below the waist had somehow implied it. Adam had also become sufficiently acute physically to know that his legs were paralyzed, and there was something in the manner of the nurses that hinted that his condition was critical. Finally, he awakened from one of his fitful naps to find a young physician at his bedside.

"I am Dr. Grubaums," said the man, speaking with a heavy accent. He sat down in a chair beside the bed, waited a few moments and sighed heavily. Then he began. "I seem to have been chosen to tell you something of the nature of your wound."

"Yes, sir," said Adam, tentatively.

The doctor hesitated again. "You are aware that you received a gunshot wound last Thursday night?"

"Yes."

"Well, the bullet entered your back. It . . . it seems to have severed the spinal cord, Mr. Johnson. I should acknowledge that we are not certain of the fact that it was the bullet. It may have been a bone fragment that caused the ultimate harm. In either event, whether it was the bullet or a bone fragment, it is clear that the cord has been severed."

Dr. Grubaums sat back, realizing sorrowfully that his words had not really been understood. Reluctantly, he proceeded, stating in clinical terms the function of the cord, mixing in "vertebrae," "lumbar," "sacral" and other hopeless words. At last he said, "From the point of the severing of the cord, from that point downward, you have lost the use of your body. In your case, this affects the legs, of course, and at least for the time being, your bladder and bowels are involved."

There was silence. Adam turned his face from the doctor, and then looked at him again. "Am I going to die?"

"Oh, no, Mr. Johnson, your life is not endangered. Not so long ago, such an injury frequently led to death because of infection attributable to the malfunctioning of the excretory system. But today the antibiotics usually control infection. The real medical issue is paralysis."

"Can anything be done for my legs, so that I'll be O.K. again?"

Resisting the urge to temporize, Dr. Grubaums said, "No,

Mr. Johnson, I am sorry. Nothing at all can be done. We cannot even remove the bullet. The wound will simply be allowed to heal and then you will be released. The paraplegia will remain."

The doctor stood up. He pressed Adam's arm, turned and walked away.

On the next day, Tuesday, Anne Webster came to the hospital. She had not neglected Adam. She had learned of the trouble on Friday, the morning after it happened, when a fellow employee showed her the newspaper. Startled and frightened, she had telephoned the hospital almost at once, but the police ward was not open to phone calls. At 2 P.M., her supervisor had excused her and she had driven to the hospital.

At the police ward, the officer on duty had been helpful and had even brought a nurse to the door to explain that Adam was unconscious and had been in surgery. But the nurse had added, "He'll be all right," and this had reassured Anne, as had the policeman's promise to call her as soon as Adam could have visitors.

Then on Monday evening, Detective O'Neal had questioned Anne at home. To Anne he had seemed sympathetic and convinced of Adam's innocence. At the end of the interview he had told her that Adam wanted to see her and that she could go to the hospital.

Now Adam saw her coming, walking stiffly beside the nurse, self-consciously ignoring the strangeness of the ward and the stares of the prisoners. She was wearing a party dress and looking intently cheerful. When the nurse turned away, she smiled and finally said, "Hello, Adam."

"Hello, Annie, how are you?"

"I'm just fine, how are you?" she said and sat down in a chair beside the bed. Adam wondered whether he was supposed to say, "I didn't do it," but when Anne finally spoke he saw that this was unnecessary.

"They're wrong, Adam, I know they are. I'm going to help. We'll get a lawyer . . . The detective said you'd need a lawyer. Then you'll be cleared and everything will be all right again."

Adam smiled convincingly, although he knew that this was not so. Everything would *not* be all right again. During the twenty-four hours since he had begun to think again at all, he had been almost unable to think about his situation. He had two terrible problems, and he could not concentrate on solving one without the other's getting in the way. And Anne's comment showed that she knew of only one of the problems. Instinctively, Adam knew that this might be a good thing, so he forced himself to concentrate for the moment on the crime.

Adam knew that lawyers cost money. His gift for small talk was gone, so he raised this question.

Reluctantly, Anne asked, "Do you have any money?"

"Not enough for this. I have about ten dollars, plus my pay check that's coming for the four days last week. That's all."

"Well," Anne said, "I have a litle bit, too. I don't know what lawyers cost, but Daddy will know one, I'm sure, and I'll find out all about it." Pausing, she decided to drop this subject. "You leave that part to me." Another silence fell, interrupted when Anne said, "Everybody at the plant's been very sympathetic, Adam. You have lots of friends."

"That's nice."

"We've got a new IBM machine today, and I may get a chance to be trained on it. The last one we got I couldn't bid for since I was only seventeen. But now I'm eighteen, so I'm eligible."

"I hope you get the job," he said.

After another attempt or two, Anne got to her feet. "I must go home, Adam, and you hurry up and get well. I'll be back now, do you hear?"

Stifling his panic about her assumption that he would get well, Adam thanked her for coming. She smiled, her eyes a little too bright, and quickly walked away.

That night at home Anne and her father talked about Adam's situation. At first they argued, because her father was not as positive that he was innocent. "You hardly know him, child. How can you say that he didn't do it?"

"I'm just *positive*," Anne said, her voice and color rising. "I *do* know. The police made a mistake. They're not always right . . . Even the detective seemed to think he didn't . . ." She began to cry, and her father, either convinced or affected by her tears, decided not to question further that Adam had not done it.

The conversation continued, and Joe Webster conceded another point—that Anne was old enough to do what she wanted with her money. And he also agreed to inquire at work about a lawyer. Then, moving his chair directly opposite hers, the man leaned forward. "Annie, I want you to tell me something, and to tell me the God's truth. Will you?"

"Yes."

Her father took her hands in his. "Are you in love with this boy? . . . If he'd asked you to marry him, would you have considered it?"

Anne looked down at her lap and finally answered. "No, I'm not in love with him. I'm really not . . . But he's a very nice boy and very decent, and a lot of boys aren't that way . . . So I like him . . . as a friend. And, anyway, he's awfully alone, so I'm going to help him through this."

Joe Webster seemed to relax. He sat back in his chair. "All right, that's fair enough. You *should* help him. But don't get carried away with it." Carefully choosing his words, he said, "Young people . . . I mean people younger than your mother and me . . . sometimes overdo things like this. They get involved with situations that really aren't as important as they look like . . . where they really *can't* help very much and where the person really doesn't need their help."

Anne looked up defensively, but he continued.

"What I mean is this. You say that Johnson is alone. Well, he really isn't. People just *aren't* alone anymore, the way they used to be when I was a kid. Now we've got a lot of things to help people who don't have families or money. There are all kinds of welfare things for these people . . . looking out for them. So this boy *will be* taken care of, whether you help or not."

Seeing that Anne was not convinced, her father said, "Now look. He's hurt, and he needed a doctor. So he's in a hospital and he's got doctors and the best medical care he could have . . . All of that happened before you even knew about it . . . And he needs a lawyer. All right, the county or the lawyers' association will get him one . . . They always do . . . Whatever he needs, he'll get. I promise you." Sensing that he was making headway, he said, "That's the way we do things in this country . . . You be his friend. I'd always want you to help a friend, but don't think that he's *dependent* on you. Do you understand?"

"Yes, I do," Anne said. "I've thought of all that, but I do want to help."

Anne Webster went again to the hospital two days later, days marked for Adam by more enemas, more washings, more spoon-feedings, more shots with the needle and almost a dozen turns in the strange revolving bed.

Although she was still stubbornly cheerful, Anne was not

encouraging about the lawyer. Depositing flowers and candy, she said, "I haven't got the lawyer yet. The man that Daddy's boss called wanted to charge five hundred dollars. That's ridiculous, of course. But I'm not done looking yet."

"Good," Adam said. "I mean about keeping looking."

Then they visited, Adam turning aside all questions about his condition.

When Anne left, she spoke briefly to a nurse at the door.

"How's the boyfriend, today?" asked the nurse.

"Well, he's kind of sad, today, sadder than before, I mean."

"Of course, he is. Who wouldn't be?" said the nurse.

"What do you mean?"

"*Well,*" the nurse said knowledgeably, "a paraplegic is a paraplegic, dear. The boy's paralyzed—I'd rather be dead than in a wheelchair all my life . . . But I'd say that *he's* pretty spunky all things considered."

Anne started and stared at the woman. "You mean he can't ever get up . . . and walk?"

The nurse immediately regretted the indiscretion, but she could not retrieve it now. "Well, no dear, he can't, not really, unless there'd be some kind of a miracle . . ." She stammered and said, "I'm sorry to have told you. I thought you knew," and, assuming an injured tone, "he really should have told you himself, if you ask me."

Somehow Anne got to the bus. She got on mechanically, still trying to rationalize the dreadful new information. Oblivious to the people who crowded about her, she drew into one corner of a seat and closed her eyes.

Oh my God, she said to herself, and she shuddered so violently that a fat woman beside her edged away, fearing that Anne was going to be sick.

The more Anne thought the less she seemed to be able to manage the horror she felt. She could not get out of her mind the new picture of Adam, not temporarily hurt, but forever broken and helpless, and the picture absolutely repelled her.

She came to just in time to get off at her bus stop and drag herself home. She went directly to her room. After reassuring her parents that *she* was all right, she avoided dinner entirely and spent the awful evening alone in the room.

During the days that followed, Anne kept the discovery to herself and struggled to maintain her daily routine. Shrinking from the idea of another visit to the hospital, she redoubled her efforts to find a lawyer. But the search for the lawyer did not progress. Following one lead after another, she always ran into the question of money and she was forced ineptly to terminate each conversation.

A week after her conversation with the nurse, Anne finally forced herself to go to the hospital. Arriving in the late afternoon, she smiled firmly and said, "Hello, Adam, I'm sorry that I've missed so many days, but . . . I've been terribly busy."

"That's all right," Adam said.

Anne sat down, carefully fixing her eyes on Adam's face, so as to avoid looking where his legs lay beneath the sheet.

Discomfited by Anne's stare, Adam tried to smile. Finally, he said weakly, "What's new?"

"Nothing," Anne answered, and she began feverishly to think of something to say. She could not ask him how he was, and she did not want to tell the discouraging news about the lawyer. To herself she imagined that anything she said would call attention to his paraplegia. So she said nothing.

Adam was not the one to keep the conversation going, and he turned his head away to avoid her eyes.

The tension mounted until Anne suddenly stood up. "I have to go, Adam. It will be a short visit today . . . I'm in a hurry."

"Sure," he said, rousing himself and turning his face toward her. Seeing her eyes averted, he said quickly, "You will be back?"

"Yes, of course. Goodbye for now."

"Goodbye," he said.

Anne did come back, but the visits, lasting only a few minutes and occurring at less frequent intervals, were strained and unsatisfactory. There was less and less that could be said, as her life went on and his hung suspended on the Stryker frame.

Anne Webster returned to the hospital a total of six more times after the first visits. Late in June, more than a month after the crime, her father met her on the steps of the house and they sat down together.

Joe Webster had learned of the paraplegia. Now he asked, "How's Adam, Annie?"

"Not so good again. He just sort of lies there . . ." She seemed utterly worn out. "I feel so sorry for him, but it's hard to know what to say . . ."

"It's very sad, Annie, but I've told you he'll be taken care of, and he will. That's why we have all of these . . . things." Then, for the first time, he said, "You really can't help him. All you're doing is making yourself miserable and upset, and you're probably making him feel worse . . . to have you there, being as helpless as he is."

Anne looked thoughtfully at her father. "Do you really think that . . . that it makes him uncomfortable for me to drop in like that?"

"I'm sure of it."

But Anne was not entirely convinced, and still wanted to be helpful if she could. Two days after the conversation with her father, Adam received her letter.

June 24, 1960

Dear Adam,

It will be hard for me to come to visit you for a while. I'm getting very busy at work, with some overtime, and Mother needs me here at home a lot, now that summer is here.

I also think that I'm not very good at the visits. I think I may make you unhappy being there. Maybe it will be better for you if I quit coming, at least for now. But, of course, if you *need* me for anything, I'll come right away. Please write me a note anytime you want me to come, and I'll be there.

I hope you feel better.

Love,
ANNE

Adam did not write the note, and he was never to do so.

4

ANNE WEBSTER'S father was right. People are not alone anymore, and the first public interest in Adam Johnson came from an organization that he had surely never heard of. Even as Mueller and O'Neal had scoured the alley on the morning of May 20, the American Civil Liberties Union became involved.

At nine that morning, Harry Hanna, a lawyer who was the paid executive of the local ACLU chapter, unlocked the door of his unprepossessing downtown office. Although in his early thirties, Hanna had adopted a habit of the older liberals in the city. He avoided the morning newspaper, *The Chronicle*, for the sake of his digestion. He had not read of the Adam Johnson episode and was concentrating entirely on his nine-fifteen appointment with Father Patrick Gleason, the pastor of Holy Rosary, commonly known in the city as St. Bingo's Church.

The priest was a member of the Union, and by any standard, an unusual man, most famous for the bingo game that he operated at Holy Rosary. With the profits from this illegal enterprise, he had built a new church, a school, a community building and a number of houses which he rented out for almost nothing. Indeed, the priest and his bingo game had made over an entire neighborhood, converting it from a pitiful Negro slum. Because of all of this, he was one of the city's most controversial figures, regarded by many as a socialist or, worse still, an anarchist.

Hanna did not share the political objections, but he did not like Gleason or admire his work. No civil libertarian could countenance his disregard of the gambling statutes, whether the statutes made any sense or not, and no sophisticated person could ever entirely overcome the feeling that *any* priest represented a superstitious anachronism.

Hanna had barely looked at his mail when the outer office door was cautiously opened and the priest appeared. Extremely tall and gaunt, he was dressed as usual in shiny, frayed clericals. Although surely fifty years old, his unruly black hair was unmarked with gray. And his otherwise handsome dark face was offset by a prominent nose better suited to the face of a prizefighter.

As the priest approached, Hanna went forward to greet him. Gleason smiled and followed the lawyer into the inner office. There he sat down, gathering himself ungracefully into the chair across the desk from Hanna. He was smoking and Hanna saw that his hands were dirty and that his fingernails were chewed down almost to the quick.

"I'm happy to see you, Father," Hanna said.

With blue eyes that were very bright and far away, the priest simply stared at the lawyer. Without any corresponding amenity, he said, "Mr. Hanna, I called you because I want you to answer a question for me. I want your advice."

"Yes," Hanna said.

"I'm asking you this not as a member of the Civil Liberties Union, you understand." The priest suddenly smiled and facetiously said, "Indeed, I hope that I'm still in good standing with the Union. It has occurred to me that I might be expelled any minute because my church fronts on a public street. Sometime you must tell me whether this doesn't threaten the principle of separation of church and state."

Gleason paused to light another cigarette, but Hanna did not respond to his jibe and he went on. "The point is that I'm asking you this question in confidence. Do you understand?"

"Yes, Father, I do. I shall treat it confidentially."

"Do you know Max Gruenwald, my lawyer?" the priest asked.

Hanna was startled. He knew Max Gruenwald, a senior partner in a distinguished law firm, but he had not known that Gruenwald represented the priest. Overcoming his surprise, he said, "Yes, I know Mr. Gruenwald, that is I know who he is. He's a sustaining member of the Union, among other things."

"Well, Max is in Puerto Rico now. He took his wife there . . . she's sick . . . and I don't want to call him, and I'd like to know about this rather quickly." He stopped again, and then resumed. "I've considered a few of the Catholic lawyers, but I'm not close to any of them to tell you the truth and . . . well, they are all very prosperous and I'm never thrown together with them in my work. As a matter of fact" —the priest smiled apologetically—"none of them seems to have any connection with any of the social issues in the city."

"I understand," said Hanna, "and I'm pleased that you've come to me. I hope I can help."

"Well, here's what it is," Gleason said. "Yesterday two men came out to the rectory. They were internal revenue people. They wanted a list from me of the people who have won the games at the church. I didn't give them the list, and they said I had to . . . the law required me to. They suggested that I see a lawyer about it . . . so here I am. My question is whether the law says that I have to give them the list. Do I?"

Hanna was torn between sympathy and amusement at the priest's predicament, and also a little pleased that the question was so easy. Unhesitatingly he said, "Yes, Father, the law does require you to give the list. There's no question about it."

"I'm not surprised, I guess," Gleason said resignedly. He was silent and then leaned forward again. "But what about that writer, you know, the one that was married to the actress. As I remember it, he wouldn't tell the government who his associates were when he was mixed up in some kind of Communist business. Didn't the judges finally excuse him and say that he didn't have to tell?"

"Yes, Father, that's true. But that case was unlike yours in many respects. There the legal questions were . . . well, they were very complicated, but they were different. Your case is clear. The government has a right to make you give this information."

Gleason was obviously distressed by Hanna's views, and he became more and more uneasy, shifting in his chair, smoking nervously and moving his hands about. "I hope you won't feel that I don't believe what you're saying if I ask a few more questions. Will you, Mr. Hanna?"

"No, Father, I'll answer as best I can. Go ahead."

"Well, as you know, no one can ever force me to tell something that I learn as a confessor . . . There is a civil law to this effect just as it is decreed canonically. That is so, isn't it?"

"Yes, it is. Your relations in that respect are privileged."

"Well, isn't there some way that this could be applied . . . I mean couldn't it be worked around that way so that my immunity as a confessor would apply here?"

Hanna could not help smiling. "No, Father. That's very ingenious on your part, but I honestly don't think it would work."

The priest was silent again, his dark face briefly obscured by the smoke from his cigarette. "All right, one more question. You know the authorities in this town. What are the chances in your opinion that they would actually send me to prison . . . it would, of course, be an unseemly business for everybody, but . . . well, you know what I mean. Is it really likely that they'd go through with this and send a *priest* to the penitentiary for this sort of thing?"

Hanna was again secretly impressed with the guile of his questioner. "That's a good question, and I suppose it can't be answered safely. I don't know. As you say, it would be quite a nasty business, and if I were the government I would be reluctant about it. I don't know what might happen, but I do know this—any man is foolish if he decides what to do on the risk that the government won't proceed against him . . . I certainly would advise . . ."

The priest looked up sharply and interrupted. "Oh, Mr. Hanna, that's not my point, really. I've already decided what to do. I will not *under any circumstances* give them the list."

Hanna's surprised expression provoked an explanation.

"To me it is morally reprehensible for one who acquires information of this kind, or any kind, in a confidential sort of way . . . I mean when the other fellow has no reason to be on his guard . . . it is absolutely a sin to betray that kind of relationship. I shall not do it, in *any* event. What I'm trying to do is . . . well, think ahead a little bit."

Warned by the edge that had come into Gleason's voice, Hanna chose not to meet this issue directly. "Well, Father, I won't presume to quarrel with you about what you seem to have decided already, but perhaps you should discuss it with the Archbishop, or the Chancellor, Monsignor Haggerty . . . They may have something to offer . . ."

Gleason smiled, but he was plainly not impressed with this suggestion. "No, I do not propose to do that."

Hanna said, "Well, perhaps you should talk to Mr. Gruenwald. Surely you can stall the question until he's back . . ."

"No, I don't like to stall it. Max will represent me if I'm tried, but he would not try to interfere with my judgment in the matter."

Quelled by this indirect rebuke, Hanna became silent. The priest said nothing either, but he remained seated and again lighted a cigarette. Suddenly, the telephone on Hanna's desk rang. Both men started and Hanna picked it up. The caller was Jack Medlicott, a white man who incongruously worked for *The World,* the city's Negro newspaper.

"This is Medlicott, Hanna," the caller said. "The Keystone Kops have shot another one, a kid named Johnson. Shot him in the back in the spinal column. He was unarmed."

"What's he charged with?"

"Robbery, but if that doesn't work out, the son-of-a-bitches will figure out something else."

"Is he a Negro?"

"No," said Medlicott, quickly. Then he added irritably, "What in the hell difference does that make?"

"Well, I was thinking about the NAACP, but if he's white, that's out. Tell me more about it, Jack."

The reporter rapidly sketched the story and the lawyer began to catalogue the case in his mind. From the standpoint of the ACLU, there seemed to be no specific interest. Taking advantage of a break in Medlicott's narrative, Hanna put in, "Of course, Jack, if a felony was reasonably believed to have occurred, and one did, in fact, occur here, a peace officer has the legal right to use maximum force to impede the escape and effect an arrest."

The reporter exploded. "Christ, Hanna, I've heard that before . . . you know that, but we both know that it means that this shoot-'em-up routine will go on forever."

"Well, that may be, but the law is clear. The cases have said for two hundred years . . ."

Speaking very loudly, the reporter interrupted. "For God's sake, *please* don't tell me about what the cases say. I don't give a damn about that. I *hate* that God damned rubric. It makes me want to puke."

Glancing at Father Gleason and tiring of Medlicott's argument, Hanna sought to terminate the call. "Jack, I don't disagree with any of that. As an original proposition I wouldn't let the cops shoot anybody at any time, unless maybe they were shot at first. But so far as the Union is concerned it's a question of jurisdiction . . . But let's see how it goes. I'm going to Chicago today to this church-state relations meeting. The Union's sponsoring it and I'm on the program because of this suit we filed to get the religious pictures off the walls of the state hospitals. I'll be back tomorrow and I'll call you. In the meantime, get more facts, will you?"

But Medlicott was not easily disposed of. "I've *got* the facts," he said, a note of hostile resignation in his voice. "They're *very* simple. A, the cops think somebody's snatched somebody's purse. B, a guy starts running near the scene of the crime. C, they shoot the poor bastard in the back. D, he's crippled for life. It's *very* simple."

"O.K., Jack, and I'll help if I can, as an officer of the Union." Realizing that he needed help in getting rid of the call, he added, "I have someone with me now. Can't I call you tomorrow?"

To his annoyance, the reporter asked, "Who is it—who's with you?"

"It's Father Gleason from St. . . . Holy Rosary . . . We're talking about Union business."

Medlicott said nothing at first and Hanna thought for a moment that the connection had been broken. "Hello, Jack, are you still on?" he asked.

"Yes, I'm here . . . Please give the father my regards will you . . . Goodbye."

The telephone clicked and Hanna turned back to the priest. "That was Jack Medlicott of *The World,* Father. I'm terribly sorry to have held you up like that . . . Incidentally, Medlicott sends his regards to you."

The priest smiled. "Thank you. I'm pleased to hear from him. Well, Mr. Hanna, my thanks to you. You have answered my questions, and I'm grateful." He stood up and extended his hand.

Hanna took it, and, as the priest walked out, he called after him, "Good luck, Father."

On Monday, the day that Detective O'Neal questioned Adam at the hospital, Harry Hanna and Jack Medlicott met at the lawyer's office. Lowering himself into a chair, the newspaperman looked old and tired, and Hanna wondered briefly about him. He was a small, seedy-looking man, at least sixty years old. Hanna had been to his apartment once, a little hole littered with books and newspapers where the reporter lived alone. Although Medlicott never mentioned them, it was said that he had a wife, or an ex-wife, somewhere, as well as children from whom he was estranged. Perhaps, Hanna thought, this accounted for his terrible melancholy. And melancholy, together with rage, were Medlicott's outstanding characteristics. He was the only totally unphilosophical person Hanna knew.

Interrupting these thoughts and loathing the moment when he would confirm the ACLU's nonintervention in the Johnson case, Hanna was reminded of his discovery of the relationship of Medlicott and Father Gleason. "Say, Jack, before I forget it, how'd an old atheist like you get mixed up with Gleason? He seemed glad to hear from you the other day."

Medlicott colored and said, "Did he really?"

"Yes, he did."

"Well," Medlicott said bitterly, "the bastard was probably being sarcastic. God knows he's got no reason to be my old pal." He hesitated, as if recalling a distasteful experience. "I'll tell you how he knows me . . . it was a helluva chagrining thing, to tell the truth. I'd never liked the guy . . . I don't mean personally, because I've never met him, but I mean the whole damn thing out there . . . I don't know too much about it, but I know enough . . . the bingo, Christ, I've nothing against gambling, but it's against the law and for a God damned church to be running wide open is simply ridiculous. It really puts the cops and the prosecutor in a helluva hole . . . It's so damn phony."

"I certainly agree with you," Hanna said.

Warming to his thesis, the reporter said, "And then all of that big building and slum clearance in that neighborhood. God knows I'm for slum clearance, and as between the whites and the blacks, I'll take the blacks any old time, at least until *they* get all the money and start pooping on the whites. But I don't like the Great White Father stuff, the white man coming with the cross and the beads and bangles, civilizing the natives, converting them to the way and . . . all of that traditional crap . . . Anyway, that's the way I've always felt about Gleason and his whole setup."

Medlicott paused and Hanna said, "I feel the same way. It's a hard thing to take ahold of because of who he is and the things he's done, but it's wrong, and I think that it undermines the bona fide political efforts for liberal reform around here . . ."

"Exactly," interrupted Medlicott, "but I'm the guy who tried to get ahold of it. I wrote this article for my paper. It was pretty cute . . . a feature about how all the games on the Avenue were shut down, but the 'Bingo Priest' . . . that's what I called him, I coined that damn name . . . was running wide open. It was rough. Very snotty stuff about the strange ways that God works. I dressed it up with the usual quotes from unnamed police authorities and community leaders, both of whom were me, of course . . . Well, there aren't any Negro Catholics, not with money anyway, so the story was run." Medlicott hesitated, then leaned forward in his chair. "Well, the God damndest thing happened. My story came out on Friday. On Saturday the guy is rushed to the hospital with a bleeding ulcer. Christ, he almost died. I felt like hell . . . not that the article was responsible or anything like that, but here was a guy bleeding to death and I'd just kicked him in the ass. It really got me down. Do you see what I mean?"

"Sure," Hanna said earnestly. "It's very spooky. I don't blame you. What happened then?"

"Well, nothing, at least as far as I was concerned. The guy got well, of course . . . and I haven't seen him since, but I still feel bad about it. After all he is a human being . . ." The reporter stopped again and then said, "You know, it's a funny thing about that guy. As much as I dislike that business of his, it disturbs me to think of the enemies he's got . . . most of them are the s.o.b.'s of this city. I usually can tell my friends by who their enemies are. Now here's this guy . . . A friend of mine tells me that Gleason and the Archbishop are at odds . . . in fact, I guess that my article got him in more trouble with the Archbishop. He's against the bingo and he's also supposed to be pretty much of a weak sister on the race issue, not a big hater, but dumb as hell and a snob about Negroes . . . So the Archbishop's against him, and I'm damn sure the Archbishop and I would not be chums, so I ought to be for Gleason."

Hanna nodded. "Having the Archbishop against you is a pretty good recommendation, that's for sure."

Medlicott smiled. "Then there's the real estate board. Gleason rents those houses out there for almost nothing. This, of course, is pure Communism as far as the landlords are concerned. They've tried every way they can to horse him around, but he buys land through straw men, and works out all kinds of complicated deals to increase the parish's holdings. If there's any group that makes me want to vomit it's the God damned realtors. You know, twenty bucks a week for one room for a family of five, plus the rats and the roaches, and they've prevented any kind of public housing in this town, and they play along with the ghetto business so that the tenement is all there is . . . they're against Gleason, too, so I ought to be for him . . . The ministerial alliance, the Ku Kluxers . . . by God, it's amazing." Medlicott was genuinely enthusiastic. "The guy has assembled a group of people to hate his guts that anybody could be proud of . . ." The reporter's voice seemed to trail off for a moment. "But, of course, it's still phony . . . although I've often felt fishy about that story of mine."

"Well," Hanna said, "the story was apparently sound in its point of view, it was just the coincidence of the man's being sick that . . ."

Suddenly Medlicott held up his hands. He was reminded of Adam Johnson. "Say, what about the shooting case?"

Parrying, Hanna said, "Are there any new developments?"

"Only that they plan to charge him with *robbery*. I looked up the statute, and he could get from *ten to twenty-five years* if they find him guilty. That would bury the whole thing nicely, of course, so you can bet the prosecution will go heavy on the case."

Hanna frowned. "Anything else?"

"Well, this isn't really new, but the guy's an orphan. He's nineteen years old, just up here from some godforsaken town in Tennessee. He was working at Faultless. Apparently he's got no record." The reporter ran one hand over his eyes. "The whole thing's so God damned sad I can hardly stand it."

"Of course it's sad," said Hanna.

"Well, what are you going to do about it?"

Looking beyond his listener, the lawyer said, "Well, I'm sorry to say that the Union, as such, isn't going to do anything. I checked with the Executive Director in Chicago. The law is clear. With a suspected felon, the cops have the right to shoot to effect an arrest."

Perhaps because he knew that this was to be Hanna's position, Medlicott did not challenge him. Instead, he asked, "Well, suppose this guy is acquitted, what about the cops then?"

"As individuals, they might be liable but, of course, they don't have any money, or at least not enough to do Johnson any good. The city isn't liable, even if the cops were wrong. The law is that a state or one of its municipalities has no liability for tort when it is acting in its political capacities. Police activity is a well established political capacity. But that's beside the point. The point is that as a legal proposition. . ."

Medlicott interrupted impatiently. "O.K., Harry, O.K. . . . I'm always glad to learn a little law, but what about this guy? You can't just sit there and read me the God damned Constitution and Bylaws of the American Civil Liberties Union and forget about it? This guy needs a lawyer."

Nettled, Hanna said, "I didn't say anything about forgetting about it. We'll *get* him a lawyer, but I'm trying to make you understand the Union's position."

"Well, I don't understand it, but so what if I don't. I don't understand anything. Anyway, if you say it's out, it's out. Now who in the hell do we get to represent him?"

"I think I can get Gerry Donahue to do it. He's with Sties, Edison, Behr and Reilly. He was in law school with me and he was a trial deputy in the prosecutor's office before he joined that firm. He thinks the way we do about these things. I *think* I can get him to take it, and for nothing."

"Well, if he's with that firm, he must know something . . . Anyway, we can't be too choosy. Let's get him."

Glancing at his watch, Hanna picked up the phone and called Donahue. The lawyer was in, and in five minutes Hanna and Medlicott were on their way to meet him for lunch at the Bar Association Club.

Gerald Donahue was a few minutes late, but the three men were seated quickly. As soon as a waitress had taken their orders, Hanna introduced the Johnson case, briefly sketching the facts and explaining why the ACLU would not assume the defense. Donahue, whose manner had favorably impressed Medlicott, listened attentively and was not surprised when Hanna finally came to the point.

"That's the case, Gerry, the question is whether you'll take it on."

Donahue answered at once. "Yes, I think I will. I'd like to very much, *if* the firm will give me the time . . . That's the only possible hitch."

"What do you mean, give you the time?" Medlicott asked.

"I mean I'm an associate in the firm, not a partner. I'm on a salary, and I can't very well take a matter like this . . . it will involve a lot of hours . . . unless the firm will let me take the time from the other stuff."

"Do you think they will?" Hanna asked.

"I honestly don't know. Our department is loaded now, and the partner I work for might be behind the eight ball without me. But I'll try like hell. I'd *like* to do it."

After eating, the three men separated. Promising to call Hanna as soon as he knew whether he could take the case, Gerry Donahue headed for his office.

As he walked, Donahue thought about the Johnson case. The truth was that he was unsettled by the opportunity to defend Adam. As a law student, it was exactly what he'd always thought he'd be doing as a lawyer, helping someone who *really* needed help, when the stakes were really significant. Instead, he had spent five years in tax and corporate financing work. He knew that there was nothing wrong with this. He was not that naïve! He respected the clients and they had a right to representation . . . but was it really what *he* wanted to do? As he had told himself many times, if he and his wife could just maintain a stable living standard, he'd someday be in a position to do what he wanted, at least part of the time.

By the time these musings were over, Donahue was at his office. Passing through the walnut-paneled anteroom, he asked at once for Mr. Reilly, the youngest of the four named partners, the one most likely to be concerned with Adam Johnson.

Fortunately, Reilly was in and Donahue went at once into his office. He was relaxed with Reilly, and had no difficulty putting his question.

Reilly answered as Donahue had hoped. "Well, Gerry, it's O.K. with me . . . If you feel as you do about the case, and since the employment's been offered to you, I think you've an obligation to take it. The firm has an obligation, too. After all, we surely make enough money and have enough men to spring one loose occasionally for the commonweal. That's my view anyway." Reilly paused before saying, "I'll take it up with the partnership right away."

"What do you think the verdict will be?"

"We'll have to see. These guys don't always . . . I should

say often . . . agree with me, but maybe they will this time."

An hour later, Reilly came to Donahue's office with the report. Even before he had spoken, Donahue understood that he was not to take the case.

"No soap," said Reilly, defensively. "Sties says he needs you on the Acme merger, and I guess there's no doubt that he really does . . . He thinks that Legal Aid is the answer for this Johnson."

"Legal Aid?"

Reilly sat down before continuing. "The Bar Association supports Legal Aid and it's also part of the United Fund. It was set up to take care of the Bar's obligation to pauper clients. The partners feel that this defendant should be sent there."

"Well, can he get a good defense there?" Donahue had heard of the Legal Aid Society but had not had any experience with it.

"I guess so. In any event, that's what it's for, to keep the pauper cases from interfering with a lawyer's regular practice." Still apparently uncomfortable about what he was saying, the older man added, "I hope you won't feel that this is wrong, Gerry."

Donahue hesitated. He was deeply disappointed, but there was logic in the firm's position and he was hardly in a position to complain. Finally he said, "No, I don't think it's *wrong* for him to have to go to Legal Aid . . . but it isn't what I'd really prefer."

"That's my feeling, too, I think," Reilly said, "but it's apparently got to be that way." He stood up and said, "Sorry, Gerry, but there'll be other chances in the future."

"Sure, and thanks for trying."

After Reilly had left, Donahue called Harry Hanna. "Well, if that's it, there's nothing much to be said," Hanna said, "but I'm not keen on the Legal Aid idea."

"Why not?"

"They're O.K. for domestic relations, and landlord and tenant stuff, and debtors and things like that, but they don't know anything about criminal law. This boy they have now, Sawyer's his name, has probably never been in the criminal courts."

"I'm sorry to hear that," Donahue said. "It's too bad that this state doesn't have the public defender system."

"Yes, it is, but it doesn't," Hanna said. Then he added, "Well, I'm sorry, but we did the best we could. I'll get Legal Aid going . . . Take it easy and thanks to you."

"O.K., Harry, and I wish Johnson a lot of good luck." Donahue hung up the phone and turned to the Acme merger file.

5

Because of the defendant's physical condition, even the preliminary steps of the prosecution in *State v. Adam Johnson* were delayed. But during the first week of July, Paul Willoughby, the Chief Deputy, read the file preliminary to assignment.

To Willoughby the prosecution's case seemed thin. For this reason and because of the shooting of the defendant, he was not surprised to find a note from the Chief of Police, asking the prosecutor's office to call before the case was assigned.

Willoughby dutifully called headquarters. When the chief came on the wire, he said, "Chief, this is Paul Willoughby.

I have your note from this Johnson file . . . the guy who was shot . . . What's on your mind?"

"Oh, yes, Paul, I appreciate your calling. I only wanted to say we're sure Johnson was the guy, and we want the case carefully prosecuted . . . That's all, I guess."

"You mean 'diligently', don't you, *diligently* and carefully?"

"All right, diligently. The point is that he's the guy and we don't want a lot of hollering about shooting innocent people."

"I understand your concern, Chief. I'm glad I'm not one of these officers," Willoughby said. "If it'll reassure you, you can rely on it that we'll prosecute him. That's what we're supposed to do, and we'll do the best we can."

"Well, that's all I meant, Paul. Thanks very much for your cooperation," the chief said, and the conversation ended.

As soon as the telephone line was cleared, Willoughby placed an interoffice call for Harold Rogers, one of the deputy prosecutors. Rogers was a smart aleck, but he was able and imaginative and had enough experience to work independently even on the more difficult cases. In a few minutes, Rogers came to Willoughby's office.

"You rang, sir," he said, with a mock bow.

"Yes, Harold. I've a sticky one here and, of course, that reminded me immediately of you."

"Flattery will get you no place with me, Paul . . . What kind of a case is it?"

"It's robbery, I guess, arising out of a purse snatching . . . it's the case in which the cops shot this boy." Willoughby picked up the file and Rogers took it from him.

"I remember that one, vaguely," Rogers said, opening the file and peering into it.

"Well, I want you to take it. It'll probably go to the grand jury, although you might try for a waiver so that we can go to trial on the affidavit . . . After you've got into it, come and talk to me, will you?"

"Sure. Anything else?"

"No, that's it right now," Willoughby said. "Thanks."

Back in his office, Rogers started through the file. Miss Wallace had signed the affidavit. Her statement and those of Mueller and Sullivan, together with the list of stolen property and the information about where it was found, supported the affidavit. The file also contained Adam's statement, taken by Detective O'Neal and clipped to a medical report.

Rogers began to add the evidence up. For the prosecution there were only two material items, Miss Wallace's identification and the trail of her property in the alley.

"The identification stinks," Rogers said to himself. "Any competent defense attorney would cut it to ribbons . . . brown shoes and brown pants, at night, after being hit in the back and while falling. Jesus!"

He read Adam's statement a second time. It was plausible. He had no record . . . it could surely be sold to a jury. The stolen articles were another matter. If these were strewn in the wake of the defendant's flight, there would be a strong inference that he was the thief. The more Rogers thought, the more the case seemed to depend on this.

Picking up the telephone, Rogers placed a call for Officer Mueller. He was on duty, but the headquarter's switchboard agreed to radio the squad car and tell him to call. Before Rogers could light a cigarette, the phone rang and it was Mueller.

Introducing himself briefly, Rogers identified the case. Then he said, "Officer, I'm concerned about this list of the stolen articles, the purse and so forth, found in the alley by you and the detective."

"Yes," Mueller said guardedly.

"Well, my question is this—were they strung out, one after another, along the alley behind him, so they really led from that back yard to where he fell?"

There was a brief silence at the other end of the wire before Mueller answered, "Not exactly."

Rattled and apprehensive because of this equivocal response, Rogers said, "Well, suppose you tell me where the hell they were."

There was another silent interval. Then Mueller said, "They were all over the place, sort of . . . into the yards . . . and like that."

"Were any of them *beyond* the place where this guy went down?"

"Yes, a little bit . . . the purse was."

"I won't ask you how far beyond, Officer, but I will tell you that this office assumes that you and O'Neal will discuss this case with *no one* but me. Is that clear?"

"Yes, Mr. Rogers."

"All right," Rogers said harshly. "I'll talk to you further later." He hung up the phone and said aloud, "God *damn* the police." To himself he added, "Equipped with .38 revolvers and children's minds." Rustling through the telephone directory, he found the number of the Hal Tobin Cleaners and dialed Miss Wallace. After an undue delay, the woman came to the telephone.

Rogers said, "This is Harold Rogers, in the prosecutor's office, Miss Wallace. I'm in charge of the Adam Johnson case."

"Oh, yes."

"I'd like to see you tomorrow at 9:00 A.M., at my office here in the courthouse. Tell your employer that I've suggested he excuse you. If he won't, call me back. Otherwise I'll see you here at 9:00 A.M. . . . is that all right?"

"Yes, Mr. Rogers. I'll do that, and thanks for calling. I think he'll probably let me come. Goodbye."

Gloomily, Rogers hung up and returned to the file. After a few more minutes of contemplation, he pulled down a book from the shelf and began to outline the elements of the crime of robbery.

Promptly at nine o'clock the next morning, Miss Wallace arrived. At first glance, she seemed a good witness. She spoke clearly, looked directly at Rogers and her hands were still. After a few comments about the heat and humidity, Rogers picked up her statement and began to go over it. When he came to the identification, he looked up.

"Tell me about the shoes, Miss Wallace, what were they like?"

"Well, they were just brown shoes, low shoes . . . as I remember it."

"Have you ever seen shoes like them before?"

"Yes, you see them all the time. They were just brown shoes, the kind men wear, you know."

Stifling an urge to strike his star witness, Rogers turned to the pants. "What about the pants?"

The woman had apparently sensed that Rogers was not pleased with her. Carefully choosing her words, she said, "Well, they were brown, too, kind of a medium brown . . . sort of . . . well, they were cotton, I think. After all it *was* a warm night."

"Have you seen pants like them before, I mean the same color?"

"Yes, lots of times," she said proudly.

"And how were you able to see them, in view of your fall?"

"Well . . ." Miss Wallace hesitated and colored a bit. "I fell down kind of headfirst . . . and looked back between my legs. That's when I saw them, for just a minute, and, of course, it was dark, too."

Satisfied that a Darrow could not prove his case with the pants and shoes, Rogers tried to picture the courtroom and the evidence as the case would develop. He was silent for some time. Then, rising from his chair, he said, "Miss Wallace, you'll have to excuse me for a few minutes . . . I'll be back shortly and I'd like for you to wait here."

"All right, I'll wait."

Rogers walked from the room down the hall to Willoughby's office. The door was closed and he knocked.

"Who is it?" said Willoughby's voice.

"It's Rogers. Are you busy?"

"No, I'm free . . . come in."

Rogers entered and saw that Willoughby was on the telephone. Waving Rogers to a chair, the older man finished his call. Then he stood up, dusted cigar ashes from his suit and poured two cups of black coffee from a thermos on the desk. He pushed enough of the papers away to make room for the cups. Then he said, "What's on your mind?"

Rogers spoke quickly. "This Johnson case, the purse snatcher who was shot, you know the case . . . well, it absolutely stinks!"

Willoughby looked up abruptly, his attention arrested by the tone of his deputy's voice. "How so?"

"We can't prove the damn thing—I'll look like a jackass even trying. We ought to dismiss it, at once. Listen . . ." Rogers quickly sketched the problems in the case.

Willoughby said, "Who's on the other side?"

"I don't know, nobody yet . . . but a man ten feet tall from the circus could beat us, don't you see?"

"Yes, I see the holes in it and I'm trying to think about them . . ." Willoughby paused. "Harold, let me ask you this question—is the case a frame-up?"

"What do you mean?"

"I mean does this woman really believe that the defendant was the guy?"

Rogers hesitated only a moment. "Yes, I really think she does."

"All right. Do the cops think so, too, or were they just shooting at people for the hell of it?"

"Of course they thought he was the guy. That's why they shot him, but the point is that we can't *prove* that he was. As a matter of fact, I'm morally convinced that he wasn't . . . and in any event . . ."

Willoughby broke in. "No, that's *not* the point. The trouble with you is . . . and this isn't our first time about this . . . you don't understand the system. It doesn't contemplate that *you'll* decide who's guilty, or me, or the cops, or anyone else for that matter. It does contemplate that where there's reasonable cause . . . a trial occurs, due process of law, and our job, as the prosecutors . . . our job is to present the case for conviction. That's all there is to it, for us. The defense attacks our case and presents its own case, for acquittal . . ."

It was Rogers' turn to interrupt. "But, Jesus, I know that . . . don't sit there and lecture me with a lot of obvious stuff like that. I don't quarrel with that, but, my God, there's a limit . . ."

"Of course there is . . . a *phony*. I've already asked you that. You don't think it is a phony. Right or wrong, our witnesses *think* that they're right. That's my rule, and it's also what the law happens to say. The system just doesn't provide for guys like you to exercise *your* judgment on the question of guilt or innocence. That's all there is to it."

There was silence now and finally Rogers said, "Paul, you're smarter than I am and you're an older hand at this, but there's more *degree* to it than you acknowledge . . . And even if you're right about the system . . . if that's what it says . . . it's *wrong*. It ought to be changed, at least to knock off the case in which the evidence, on competent examination, doesn't present proof of guilt."

Willoughby smiled. "Well, that may be, but until it *is* changed, your job . . . and I don't like to say it this way because it sounds dirty, which I don't mean it to be . . . your job is to convict this guy if you can, short of falsifying the evidence, bribing the judge or tampering with the jury. That's your job. If you can't do it, I'll reassign the case. But I might as well tell you that I don't want to reassign it and you're dodging if you ask me to."

Rogers leaned forward in his chair and clasped his hands together in front of him. Then he looked up. "O.K., Paul, I'll keep the God damned case and I'll do my best . . . It stinks, but it's mine." He got up and abruptly left the office.

Walking back down the hall, Rogers began to wonder whether Adam Johnson would have competent counsel. When he reached his office, Miss Wallace was waiting. The lawyer smiled apologetically and resumed his seat opposite her. "Miss Wallace, do you believe that this Johnson was the man who pushed you and grabbed your purse?" he asked.

Although obviously startled, she said, "Yes, I do."

"Do you *really* think so?"

The woman seemed puzzled. "Yes, of course."

"All right," Rogers said. "I want you to understand this case. In the first place, you'll be under oath. You'll have sworn to tell the truth . . . You'll be in a big room and a lot of people will be looking at you. And there'll be another lawyer there, and he'll be working for Johnson and . . . against you. Do you see all of that?"

"Yes, I've seen it on TV a lot."

Rogers avoided any comment about this judicial experience. "The point is that you want to be believed, don't you? You want these people to think you're right, and that this man is the man. Right?"

"Yes, sure."

"Well, then, you must speak positively about the facts . . . You can't be the least bit uncertain. If I say, 'Are these the pants and shoes you saw as you fell,' you must say, 'Yes, they are . . .' You must *not* say, 'I think so,' or 'they look like them.' You say *'yes,' period,* is that clear?"

"Yes, sir, I understand."

"And remember this, too. The defense lawyer will probably ask you some questions on cross-examination. If he's inexperienced, he may gamble and ask you something like 'Are you certain that these are the pants and shoes.' You say, 'Yes, I'm certain.' I don't want *anything* which indicates any doubt on your part. Do you see what I mean?"

"Yes, I do. I can be very positive about it."

"All right," Rogers said, "that's fine . . . You may leave now. I want to advise you to discuss this case with no one. I realize that it is a temptation for anybody to tell her friends about a thing like this, but you remember that the prosecuting attorney has told you not to . . . If anyone should come to see you about the case, or ask any questions, you just tell them to see me. You must not answer questions."

"All right, Mr. Rogers. I'll be very careful."

"Fine," Rogers said. He stood up. Miss Wallace rose, too, and they walked to the hall door. "Thank you for coming down. I'll be talking with you again before the grand jury meets and, of course, before the trial. Goodbye."

The woman said goodbye and left.

While the deputy prosecutor was interviewing Miss Wallace, Harry Hanna carried out his chore of enlisting the Legal Aid Society.

The Society's small office was in the new United Fund Building, near the center of the city. The building, made of brick and limestone, was very large and was the city's dream-come-true. It had cost nearly a million dollars. Perhaps a third of this had come from private contributions. The rest was provided by commercial financing from public-spirited capital, principally the banks and locally owned insurance carriers.

Like many of his ACLU colleagues, Hanna's interest was confined to civil liberties matters and he was not a frequent visitor of the United Fund Building. But he approved of the orderliness of a single charitable fund, and housing the agencies together had simplified the Fund's task of unifying and supervising their activities. The completion of the building had accelerated the process of unification. Some few charities still remained outside of the United Fund, but the majority, even those which at first had been able to withstand the boycott of the rich people and closed doors of major industries, had yielded when the building had finally arisen. No longer harassed by separate fund drives, Hanna, like most of the citizens, had supported the United Fund, and it met its quota almost every year.

Arriving at the United Fund Building, Hanna quickly found the Legal Aid office and sat down with its attorney, William Sawyer. He briefly outlined the circumstances of the Johnson case. Bluntly, he asked, "Have you done any criminal work at all, Mr. Sawyer?"

"No, I haven't, frankly. I'm pretty fresh out of school . . . I'm twenty-six and passed the bar last year. I took this job while I look around for a good connection, and, of course, in the meantime I want as much experience as I can get."

Hanna studied the younger man and thought to himself that he looked terribly young. He also seemed to lack the combative aspect of a trial man. Hanna said, "Well, how does this case strike you? Do you feel that you can handle it?"

"Yes, I do," Sawyer said. "You and I know that an experienced man would do it better, all other things being equal, but I'll try hard and I'm really pleased at the chance to get the trial experience." Sawyer smiled. "From what you say I'm elected anyway. Nobody else will take it for nothing, and the defendant surely isn't in a position to choose his own man."

"That's true," Hanna said. "Well, I'm glad you're available, and I appreciate your spirit about it. Good luck!"

"Thanks," Sawyer said. "I think I'll need it." He showed Hanna to the door.

From preliminary inquiry, Sawyer promptly learned of the progress of Adam's wound and the early inactivity of the prosecution. Immersed in other assignments, he was slow to begin work in the case. But in mid-July, with most of the courts recessing for the summer, he turned to the Johnson file.

The lawyer decided that his first step was to interview his client. He went to City Hospital and talked with Adam, taking careful notes of his faltering account of the night of the crime and putting together as complete a biography as he could.

Except for pity, Adam provoked little response from Sawyer. He was bland and laconic, unless the conversation was concerned directly with his guilt or innocence. Only then, as he quietly but firmly denied his guilt, did Sawyer sense any real personality.

At the end of the interview, Sawyer clumsily told Adam goodbye and walked to the end of the ward. As the police officer was about to let him through the door, a man approached. He bowed toward Sawyer and said, "Mr. Sawyer, I am Dr. Abraham Grubaums."

Noting the foreign accent and manner, Sawyer said, "How do you do."

"Very well, thank you, sir. You are Mr. Adam Johnson's lawyer?"

"Yes, I am."

"I wonder if I might speak with you for a minute?"

"Yes, of course," Sawyer said. "Let's step out here into the hall."

The physician followed Sawyer into the hall to a bench in a relatively quiet place away from the police ward. They sat down and Sawyer waited for Grubaums to speak.

After some delay, the physician began. "Sir, I am of the staff here and Mr. Johnson is one of my patients. I . . . ah . . . I have taken somewhat of an interest in him."

"I see."

"Medically, as well as in view of the almost matchless personal tragedy of his situation, I am moved to speak with you about his trial."

"His trial?"

"Yes. You see, sir, in my contacts with Mr. Johnson I have discerned that the trial has become a climactic point for him, medically as well as legally. Do you see?"

"Frankly, I don't, Doctor," Sawyer said in a kindly way. "I am not educated at all in your field, so you'll have to lead me along a little bit."

"Of course. Well, let me see . . . You will understand that the nature of this man's disability has rather severe psychological effects . . . it is an attack on his entire will and his psychological stability."

"I think that I can understand that."

"All right. Now, frankly, we do not know precisely what he was like before this . . . this unfortunate event. We cannot reconstruct his psychological makeup. I have speculated, however, on the basis of the sketchy data available, that he was a . . . a normal, outgoing type, not actually extroverted but well organized and perhaps even demonstrative."

"I see," Sawyer said. "That's interesting."

"Yes. And we both see him now, extremely passive and withdrawn. At first this was the result of shock, but now it would indicate that his situation has, quite understandably, caused an acute degradation of his personality."

"Yes, of course," Sawyer said, although he was becoming impatient and puzzled, wondering why the physician was belaboring these grim facts.

As if he sensed Sawyer's unspoken inquiry, Grubaums said, "My point is this. In the last week or so, in my rather unsatisfactory efforts to communicate with Mr. Johnson, I have discovered that he seems to anticipate the issue of the trial. It has become a crisis for him psychologically."

"Well, I can appreciate that. It is a crisis."

Dr. Grubaums did not smile, but he had a tolerant look, almost a smile. "Yes, Mr. Sawyer, you appreciate it, but I'm not sure you *understand* it. This, of course, is probably because I am explaining it so poorly."

Sawyer accepted the rebuke and waited.

"What I am trying to say is . . . that somehow Mr. Johnson's hope of vindication in the trial has become his raison d'être. It is this hope that is keeping him going, as I think you might say it."

"God!" Sawyer said.

"Precisely! It is not, of course, a necessarily rational thing. If he is found to be innocent, it will not physically affect his paralysis. But it may, at least for the time being, be the guardian of his psychological stability. If the result is otherwise, I would not wish to contemplate his future . . . and I am quite positive that he is wholly unable to."

Having finally said what he wanted to say, Dr. Grubaums stood up abruptly. Sawyer did the same. There was an uncomfortable silence as the lawyer considered what to say. Finally, he said, "Well, Doctor, I don't like to guess about how trials will come out, and I can't estimate Adam's chances in this case. I will, however, do the best I can for him . . . I would have anyway, but I think that it is well for me to understand the significance of the result to Adam personally."

"Then my mission is accomplished, sir. This is why I have spoken. I shall not intrude again. Thank you."

"You're welcome," Sawyer said.

Grubaums bowed again and turned and walked away. Sawyer drove thoughtfully back downtown.

On the day after his visit to the hospital, Sawyer posted a letter to the Abernathys in Kingsway. In addition to telling them of his employment, he asked for more facts about Adam's background and requested the names of character witnesses. He also asked whether they could come north for the trial.

Sawyer was later to hear from the Abernathys—they were to write that they could not make the trip for the trial—and in the meantime he continued to plan for the case. Hoping to shorten the time for preparation, he called Paul Willoughby at the prosecutor's office.

"This is William Sawyer over at Legal Aid," he told Willoughby over the telephone. "I've taken on this Johnson robbery case, and I'd like to know who's got it there in your office."

Willoughby's voice betrayed no surprise at Sawyer's entry into the case. "Harold Rogers has it. Do you know him?"

"No, I don't. Is he in . . . could I talk with him?"

"Sure you can, if he's here . . . I'll tell him to call you. Is that all right?"

"Yes, thank you," Sawyer said.

Hanging up his telephone, Willoughby hurried down the hall to Harold Rogers' office. He burst into the room. "Harold, I've got good news for you!"

Glancing up from a file, Rogers said, "What is it?"

"In your Johnson case, the defense attorney has finally appeared. It's some kid named Sawyer, of the Legal Aid. I'll bet he's never had a criminal matter before."

Rogers smiled broadly. "Good, I also hope he has an I.Q.

of about 27. If he's inexperienced *and* dumb, I'll have it made."

"I'll settle for the inexperience," Willoughby said. "It really is a helluva good break . . . Incidentally, he wants to talk to you. Call him, will you?"

"Sure, I'll call him right now."

Rogers called immediately and Sawyer asked if he could have a meeting with the prosecutor. Parrying this request briefly, Rogers said, "I'd be glad to meet with you, but what's it all about?"

"Well," said Sawyer, "since I'm on this case as a charity, so to speak, I thought perhaps you'd let me see the file. I'm very limited here in my facilities and have a lot of civil stuff going . . . I just thought that maybe you would extend that kind of professional consideration to me."

Rogers hesitated. Then he said, "Well, there's something in what you say . . . You come on over after lunch and we'll talk about it. I'll see what I can do."

"Fine, I'll be there, and thank you very much," Sawyer said.

The prosecutor hung up the telephone and leaned back in his chair. As a practiced advocate, he knew that the interview which had just been arranged was a strategic moment. Turning slowly in his chair, he considered his tactics, picturing as well as he could the young and inexperienced Sawyer, who had somehow seemed apologetic during the telephone conversation.

Suddenly he left his chair and moved to a small, littered typewriter table in the corner of the room. Putting a sheet of paper in the typewriter, he pecked out a memorandum:

RE: State v. Johnson #C 10450
Memo to File

The only issue is identity:

1. The defendant has no alibi—admits
   presence at scene.
2. The prosecuting witness positively
   identifies him.
3. The stolen articles were found along
   his path as he fled.

Guilty plea expected.

Pulling the sheet from the typewriter, he returned to his desk. He opened the file of *State v. Adam Johnson* and placed the memorandum on the top of the other papers. Setting the file aside, he left his office to look up a companion for lunch.

At one-fifteen, William Sawyer arrived at the courthouse and was shown to Harold Rogers' office. The men shook hands and sat down, Rogers waiting for Sawyer to make the first move. Finally, after they had agreed about their ambition for air-conditioned offices, Sawyer began.

"I appreciate your attitude about this case, Mr. Rogers. It's really a little out of my line, and I'm anxious to do the best I can at it."

Rogers smiled. "Well, I want to be cooperative. After all, you're working on a public service basis, and with a bad case at that. That makes it a little different from the ordinary case, to me at least."

"You do think the case is bad, do you?"

"Well, perhaps I shouldn't say that," Rogers said diffidently, "although it is frankly my opinion. You get a kind of sixth sense about these criminal cases when you've had as many as I have, but it's really for you to make your own judgment about it . . . This guy is hardly what you'd call a substantial citizen . . . really almost a vagrant in an untechnical sense, although I'll admit that we haven't turned up his record yet. In a way it's too bad the way these people from the

South come up here like this, sort of a rootless bunch, and our statistics are amazing on the frequency of their criminal activity."

"Well, I suppose that's so," said Sawyer, adding quickly, "about the people from the South, I mean . . . But I've been under the impression that this case was sort of a . . . tough one."

Rogers spoke quickly and earnestly. "Of course it's tough. It's sympathetic in a way. The man's been shot . . . But isn't any criminal case sympathetic? God knows my heart goes out to any guy who's facing the penitentiary."

"Yes, so does mine."

"And it's the shooting that really messes this case up." Leaning forward Rogers said, "Now look at it from your standpoint. Let's suppose the guy was innocent as hell. Suppose it turned out he was John the Baptist in disguise, a saint, who was never near the robbery . . . So you get him acquitted, or we dismiss the affidavit and apologize. Where is he? He's about where he would be if he pleaded guilty and got the maximum. He can't work . . . He has no money. There's no family to speak of . . . He must be put in some kind of institution." Throwing up his hands, the prosecutor concluded. "That's what makes it so lousy, for you and me and everybody else connected with it. There's no real way out of the situation."

Silence followed this remark and the lawyers looked at each other. Depressed by Rogers' analysis and anxious to be done with his errand, Sawyer finally said, "It is a gloomy damn thing, Mr. Rogers, anyway you look at it. But my job is confined to the legal questions, and that's really what I want to ask your help about."

"All right. I'm sorry to have gotten so wound up . . . What you want is to see the file, and to tell you the truth I don't know whether I should do that or not."

Sawyer looked surprised and angry. "Well, I thought . . ."

Rogers interrupted. "On the one hand, I'm disposed to do it, just in the interest of common justice. On the other hand, it seems to me that the same common justice should attach two strings to the file."

"What are they?"

"Well, they concern procedure. As you know, the arrest here was on the affidavit. The charge is a felony, so Johnson's entitled to insist on a grand jury indictment. But this is expensive and time-consuming for us, and it doesn't mean a damn thing for him. So . . . the first thing I wonder is whether you'll waive indictment and try the case on the affidavit."

Sawyer answered at once. "Yes, I'll do that . . . I agree that there's no substantial interest for the defendant, so I'll waive indictment if that's what you want."

"Good. Now the other thing is the trial. You're entitled to a jury. I don't know how you feel about juries, but to me they're a pain in the neck, an anachronism. They're expensive as hell, and we won't have any kind of jury docket till fall, and your man will be stuck in the hospital all that time. I think the jury should be waived, too. Let's try the case to the court . . . what do you think of that?"

Sawyer was unprepared for this question, but he was impressed with the logic and sincerity of the more experienced man. Slowly he said, "Yes . . . I don't see any reason not to go along on that . . . It will speed it up and Adam's chances will be just as good . . . O.K., I agree."

"*Fine.*" Picking up the file, Rogers said, "Here's the file, the whole thing. You take my chair, and I'll go to the library . . . I've some research to do anyway. Make any copies you want, and call the switchboard for me when you're through . . ." As he rose to let Sawyer take his place, he said, "You may want to talk about a guilty plea after you're into the file."

"I'm afraid not, Mr. Rogers. I've talked with the client,

and he's very emphatic about being not guilty . . . I don't see how I can plead him guilty."

"Well, we'll see," Rogers said. "Call me when you're done." He left the room.

Left alone, Sawyer opened the file. He first read Rogers' memorandum and took the trouble to copy it on a pad of yellow paper from his briefcase. Then, taking notes as he went, he carefully read Miss Wallace's statement and the police reports, and examined the list of Miss Wallace's property, "found near prisoner's course of flight" and identified by Miss Wallace. Turning to Adam's statement, Sawyer continued to read and copy, noting as he did that Johnson's story was the same one he had told Sawyer at the hospital. As had been true at the hospital, a twinge of doubt passed through Sawyer when Adam's account told of running when the car approached on the night of the crime.

Sawyer came to the last document, the medical report from City Hospital. Dated five days after the crime, it reported that the prisoner was shot through the spine at the level of the twelfth thoracic vertebra, causing paralysis of the legs, bladder and bowels. There was additional medical data, most of it unintelligible to Sawyer, but he understood a few of the statements: "X-ray findings . . . a large fragmented bullet located in the region of the joint space between the eleventh and twelfth dorsal vertebrae . . . findings conclusive for actual cord injury . . . Prognosis bad. Absolutely against exploration. Removal would not help . . . possibility that harm would result from procedure."

Sawyer shuddered involuntarily and closed the file. He wrote out several final notes and placed the call for Rogers. Only a few minutes passed before the prosecutor returned.

Seating himself opposite Sawyer, Rogers said, "Well, what do you think of it?"

Not prepared to argue the case, Sawyer answered, "Not so good, I guess, although this is only your evidence."

"That's not quite so, Sawyer," Rogers said sharply. "Your man's statement is there, too . . . Surely it's pretty thin."

"No, it isn't so thin. Every kid who's ever grown up in this town has had a similar experience . . . hollered at by some damn fools and hollered back . . . and then have them come after him."

Rogers raised his hand and smiled. "But *they* didn't come after him . . . the police . . ." Suddenly he stopped. Sawyer's face had become slightly flushed and Rogers knew that making him mad might be a mistake. "I'm sorry," he said. "It's useless for us to argue. I'm *sure* he's guilty. You represent him and you're on his side . . . You have to be. Let's let it go at that."

"O.K.," Sawyer said, relieved to end the dispute. "As I see it, I'm to do the best I can with what I've got. And that's what I'll do." He stood up and began to assemble his papers and put them in the briefcase. "I'm grateful to you for your kindness," he said to Rogers, who was also on his feet. "Send me the waiver form on the grand jury question, and I'll sign it . . . By the way, whose court will you file it in?"

"Room 2, I think, Judge Pearce. Is that all right?"

"It's fine with me. He's the best, they say . . . Send me a file marked copy of the affidavit, and I'll enter an appearance and waive the jury."

"Fine," Rogers said, and he courteously escorted Sawyer to the door.

As he hurried back to his office, Sawyer was diverted from his misgivings about the case by thoughts of Judge Pearce of Criminal Court, Division 2. To a young lawyer, the judge seemed especially illustrious.

"Public spirited" was the term frequently applied to Clifford Pearce, and it struck Sawyer that in the judge's case it did not mean that he had devoted his life exclusively to his own interests. The judge had practiced law for more than thirty-five years, advancing finally to the senior partnership in his own large firm. Lawyers, at least—all of them, the young ones and the old ones—were impressed by the fact that he had, in his prime, regularly earned in excess of $100,000 a year in attorney's fees.

But the more remarkable thing about Pearce was the way he had practiced liberal political and social views, in plain sight of his clients. Most lawyers in the community knew better than this. Sawyer was already convinced that it was not the high road to success. It seemed obvious that the NAACP, the American Civil Liberties Union and other such organizations were barren as client sources. But Pearce had bypassed the usual community activities, like the symphony and art association boards, and had allied himself with the unpromising groups.

Pearce's final quixotic moment, at least Sawyer had heard others call it that, had come in 1958. Withdrawing from his firm, he had accepted a nomination for the judgeship. Elected that fall, he had gone to the court and it was generally acknowledged that his tenure had been unmarked by the lack of confidence which frequently surrounded the local courts.

Sawyer found that he was both concerned and pleased that his maiden trial experience would take place before Judge Pearce. The man would spot a false or sophomoric move, but if he were impressed, it would be to Sawyer's advantage, and this was another reason to take Adam Johnson's case seriously.

Before presiding in *State v. Adam Johnson,* Clifford Pearce had another public duty. With the trial only a few weeks away, he was scheduled for July 30 as the speaker at the annual dinner of the United Fund. The judge was a logical choice for this event. He had his detractors—there were many who would never forgive him for his radical associations —but even they felt he was about right for United Fund dinners.

The dinner, held as usual in the air-conditioned Empire Room of the Warmoth Hotel, was to be a happy affair, the annual one night truce among the factions in the city which warred on each other throughout the year. The businessmen were there, along with their Chamber of Commerce spokesmen. They ordinarily described their service to the public as making jobs and wages—and, incidentally, profits—available, but they were loyal to the United Fund. Trade union people were also present, apparently grateful for this once-a-year acceptance. Represented, too, was the clergy, "of all faiths" as the newspapers phrased it, and ministers, priests, and rabbis could be seen mingling self-consciously. Even the "Negro Community"—again the idiom of the press—was represented, by several leaders who were a credit to their race and by others, the militant ones, who somehow seemed not to be. And the newspapermen themselves were on hand, to cover the event for their papers as the guests of the United Fund.

Among the agents of the press was Jack Medlicott, the recipient of one of the free tickets issued to *The World*. Arriving during the cocktail hour, the reporter wished at once that he had not come. A cursory survey of the large crowd showed almost no one for whom he had the slightest regard. He was on the point of turning to go when he recognized a cluster of Negro clergymen crowded into one corner of the room, apparently separated from the college reunion conviviality of the others. Medlicott elbowed his way toward them and was soon at ease.

After half an hour of standing about, the crowd began to drift to the dining room. Medlicott's composure was suddenly upset by the appearance of Father Gleason who had approached the group because he knew several of the ministers. With Gleason was another priest, a young Negro who assisted at Holy Rosary.

Introduced to Medlicott by a Baptist who once had been president of the local NAACP, Gleason shook hands cordially and the discomfited reporter thought at first that he had not been identified. Before he could recover himself, dinner was announced and the dense crowd moved en masse toward the tables. The aimless maneuvers of others in the party resulted in Medlicott's assignment to a chair between Gleason and the young Negro priest.

A too long grace was finally pronounced from the speakers' table and the crowd was seated. At once the Negro priest turned to Medlicott. "I missed your name, sir, when we were introduced."

"Medlicott, Jack Medlicott," the reporter said, and he noted immediately that the young man had associated him with the St. Bingo's article.

The priest recoiled and, leaning forward, spoke with a snarl to Father Gleason. "Do you know who our companion is, Father?"

"Yes, I know him, and I'm glad to see him," Gleason said. "Mr. Medlicott is entitled to his own opinion about our parish. There are a good many others who feel as he does."

Although it seemed clear that Gleason did not wish to discuss the issue, something—perhaps his unwillingness to be simply lumped with Gleason's other critics—nettled the reporter. "I hope that you are discerning enough to see that my criticism is a little different from that of the others, Father," Medlicott said unpleasantly. "My basic concern is with the . . . the word that strikes me is 'dishonesty' . . . of your program . . . I, for one, don't accept the idea of special immunities for churches or priests." The reporter smiled archly. "Of course, I may simply be benighted."

Gleason looked darkly at Medlicott. "Yes, Mr. Medli-cott, you may very well be benighted." He turned to his grapefruit.

Feeling worsted, Medlicott said, "How do you like your new church, Father? I've not seen it, but I'm told that it's very fancy."

The priest swallowed a grapefruit bit and answered slowly. "We like the new church a great deal. We think that it's beautiful . . . 'Fancy' is not quite the word I would have thought one would apply to it." He smiled. "It is different, as you may have heard. Since we paid for it ourselves, we were not required to follow the Archbishop's all-purpose, uniform architectural plan. The church is of modern style, very simple and, as I have said, quite beautiful . . . No Infants of Prague or bleeding plaster casts . . . Very simple and plain."

"Perhaps 'fancy' was not the precise word I should've used, Father," Medlicott said. "I think 'elaborate' is the word I've heard from those who are critical . . . I've heard it said that in a neighborhood where food and a roof over the head are so important it seemed . . . unrealistic to spend so much money on a church."

Glancing at the priest from the corner of his eye, the re-porter saw that at last he had drawn blood. Gleason colored perceptibly. Carefully putting his spoon down, he said, "I've heard that sentiment expressed, but I am not persuaded by it . . ." Apparently feeling that he had to explain, he con-tinued. "As you may know . . . I think your own article referred to the fact . . . we are *trying* to do something about the food and the houses, and everything else, for that matter. We built our school several years ago . . . it is, incidentally, a free school and open to all who wish to come . . . and also the community center and the playgrounds. These were done *before* the church." The priest seemed to have finished but was displeased with what he had said. He started to speak again. "I should say, too, that the church is not *last* on the list . . . and I don't think that it should be. Entirely apart from religious grounds, the church is a work of art . . ." The priest hesitated. "And beauty. I think the social psychologists are right when they say that *beauty* . . . a beautiful painting or a beautiful building . . . dignifies the human spirit. This is the point of a beautiful Holy Rosary, at least from a secular standpoint. There is an integrity to our plan . . . food, a roof, beauty and . . . if you will excuse the term . . . *grace* are all involved."

Disarmed but unwilling to quit the contest entirely, Medlicott dropped his baiting tone. "I can see that, Father, from *your* standpoint. My trouble is, I suppose, that I am not blessed with the spirituality, or fantasy, that orthodox religion seems to require. It is a cliché, I know, but the ceremony . . . all of the trappings of your faith . . . are a little beyond me. So I have difficulty with the idea of an elaborate church . . . not only one of yours, of course, but any kind."

The priest could not at first respond to this as a waiter moved between them, exchanging a veal cutlet for the grapefruit. When the waiter moved on, the priest said, "As you say, concern with the ceremony of the Catholic Church, or any other, is a cliché, Mr. Medlicott. And it also seems to me to beg the question."

"How so?"

"I mean simply that if Gleason and Medlicott are the *only* ones in the church, only a damn fool would burn any incense or bow his head . . . But if God is there, too, only a damn fool wouldn't." The priest paused and added impatiently, "I was told that years ago, I think, when I was a sophomore, which was about the last time that I argued with anyone about his religious beliefs . . . or disbeliefs." The priest's manner suddenly changed, and he smiled in a most agreeable way. "I'd like you to see the church, Mr. Medlicott. Come out and see it. I'll show you around, and I promise that I'll invoke no hocus-pocus."

Before Medlicott could answer, the priest turned purposefully to the man on his other side and began a conversation. Annoyed and unwilling to try to break the ice with Gleason's ally to his left, Medlicott lapsed into silence and ate.

As soon as the dessert was finished, the program began. The master of ceremonies, an executive of the United Fund, began to introduce those who had made the dinner possible, interspersing poor jokes along the way.

A special award was announced for the publisher of *The Chronicle*, because of the space it had given to the United Fund's campaign. *The Chronicle* was preoccupied with attacking the "double-domes," "eggheads" and "pinkoes" who were responsible for the frills in public welfare, but it did go all out for the United Fund. Accepting the award, the publisher spoke briefly in behalf of the Fund, "the bulwark, perhaps the last rampart, in the defense against communism, the welfare state and confiscatory taxes." He retired to the loud applause of most of the audience.

At last Judge Pearce was introduced. His speech—he called it "The Good Society"—began with a series of quotations from French and English history describing the widespread, grinding poverty of former days. From Victorian England he crossed the Atlantic and, still quoting authoritative sources, focused on Hell's Kitchen in the late nineteenth century. Gradually he moved inland to his youth in the city and told of the beggars, often crippled and blind, who had infested the sidewalks.

Leaving his youth, the judge jumped to 1960, to the present and the United Fund dinner. Saying nothing of the fact that the city had removed whatever beggars remained by the simple expedient of clapping them in jail, he catalogued the city's charitable facilities. There were fifty-nine agencies affiliated with the United Fund with an annual budget of

$3,940,575. The County Welfare Department spent an additional $6,742,740 each year and the township trustees in the county had an annual relief budget in excess of $1,000,000.

Approaching the conclusion of his remarks, the judge proclaimed, "As human beings, we may be charged with many failures. But we are reaching for 'The Good Society.' This, I take it, is why we are together tonight, because the United Fund is a symbol of that society."

The judge sat down, warmly applauded, and the master of ceremonies again rose. In perhaps five minutes he summarized the judge's speech, complimenting it with fulsome praise. It was, he said, the best speech he had heard in a long time. Then he resumed his introductions of others in the audience, persons he had previously overlooked but without whose help the dinner could not have taken place. After another prayer, the evening was adjourned and the crowd stood up to go.

Because of their location, those at Father Gleason's table could not make a rapid exit. They stood waiting until the way was cleared and then shuffled in silence toward the door.

In the lobby, Father Gleason suddenly turned and extended his hand to Medlicott. "I've been unpleasant to you, Mr. Medlicott . . . and I apologize. I . . ." The priest stopped momentarily. "I have no excuse, but would be grateful if you would forgive me."

Taken wholly by surprise and still resentful, Medlicott did not unbend. "Yes," he said coldly, "of course I will forgive you."

"Thank you, and remember my invitation. Come out and see me and the new church. I mean it. It would be very nice to have you."

"Thanks, I will sometime," Medlicott said, and he hurried off into the night.

6

Adam's trial was set for 10 A.M. on August 20. He was awakened at the hospital at six. Because his wound was healed and the danger of further spinal damage was passed, he was now in an ordinary bed instead of the Stryker frame. As soon as his enema and bath were over and the catheter changed, the nurses put him in a clean gown, propped up his head and brought in his breakfast. Adam fed himself and then shaved with an electric razor. He was then turned over onto his stomach and lay quietly, waiting for his lawyer.

William Sawyer arrived at eight o'clock, to talk briefly with his client and try to cheer him up. Adam became increasingly nervous as the time for the trial approached and

Sawyer did not succeed in his efforts to reassure him. Seeming as tense as his client, the lawyer insisted that Adam go through his "version of the facts"—this was Sawyer's term—and Adam was further disconcerted by frequent suggestions about the words he should use.

At last at 9 A.M. two orderlies came down the aisle with a stretcher on wheels. Behind them walked a familiar nurse and a strange police officer. Mumbled "good mornings" were exchanged and the orderlies unhooked the catheter and lifted Adam from his bed and placed him on the stretcher.

"Put him on his back," the nurse said. "It's time for a change."

The orderlies turned Adam and one of them fitted him again with the catheter, placing the waste jug under the sheet.

The nurse crooked a finger in Sawyer's direction and he went to her. Nodding toward the policeman, she said, "He's supposed to remember this, but I'm telling you, too . . . The boy is supposed to be turned over every two or three hours. It's important. If you don't do it, he'll get bedsores, they're *awful* . . . He's only had one so far and it's all healed up, but don't forget, just roll him over onto his stomach . . . Will you remember?"

"Yes, I surely will," said Sawyer, making a firm mental note. "I'll be careful."

"Good," said the nurse.

While Sawyer and the nurse had been talking, the orderlies had turned the stretcher so that Adam's head was at the front. Then they began to push slowly down the ward toward the door. Sawyer and the policeman, followed by the nurse, walked behind in silence, but several of the prisoners called out to Adam.

"Good luck, boy," said a man whose leg was suspended in a cast.

An older man, a newcomer to the ward, shouted, "Don't let 'em get you down, son."

Adam raised his hand at each greeting, but he was too preoccupied to say anything back.

At the end of the ward, the police officer spoke with the guard and exchanged pieces of paper with him. The doors of the ward were unlocked and swung open and the procession moved into the hall.

Adam had been in the hall three months previously, on the night of the crime, but he had been unconscious then. Since that night, he had not left the prison ward and his attention was now drawn to the new sights and sounds as he was rolled down the hall. Faces suddenly appeared and disappeared, each one looking down at him with curiosity. He saw white steel tables and chairs and the legs of the nurses, also white. Above him was the ceiling, a kind of pale green, occasionally marked with large fluorescent light fixtures. At length he saw ahead of him an open doorway. Sunlight was streaming in and as he was moved outside, it flashed into his eyes with blinding effect. Squinting his watering eyes, trying to adjust to the daylight, he realized that he was being lifted up.

"Easy, easy," the police officer said.

The front wheels of the stretcher struck something solid, and it was pushed slowly into the van of an ambulance. The bright sky overhead gradually gave way to the plush interior. The stretcher stopped. There was a clicking noise and Sawyer and the police officer climbed in and sat uncomfortably on jump seats, the officer behind Adam's head, the lawyer at his feet. The motor started up and the ambulance pulled quickly from the curb.

From Adam's position, he could see little of the trip. There were windows, but they were too high up to allow him to see anything but the second stories of the buildings that passed by. He began to sweat heavily as the ambulance proceeded, stopping now and then as the traffic swirled about, horns honking and engines whirring. These sounds were welcomed by Adam, because there was dead silence in the van. Sawyer and the officer smoked and looked out the window. No one spoke until the ambulance stopped and the motor was turned off.

Sawyer said, "Here we are."

The door behind Adam's head was opened. He heard the officer talking, and then the stretcher was moved backward and the bright sky again came into view. Adam saw several more policemen and, as the stretcher swung from the van and was placed on the sidewalk, his face was turned toward a large, dirty building. The stretcher began to move again, and another parade of curious faces began.

Inside it was dark and cool. The walls were a strange greenish brown, and were occasionally broken by large doorways leading into the hall, each with a sign above it. Adam read the signs as he moved along—INHERITANCE TAXES, MORTGAGE EXEMPTIONS, AUDITOR—and then the stretcher stopped at an elevator door. The door opened to disclose a number of people packed together.

One of the officers said, "You folks will have to get out for this trip. We got a prisoner here on a stretcher. Please step out."

The passengers looked at Adam and shuffled out. The stretcher entered the elevator and the door closed. As it began to move, Adam saw that he, Sawyer and four policemen were the occupants.

When the elevator stopped, the doors opened and the stretcher was pushed into the hall. It then moved along to a door marked CRIMINAL DIVISION, ROOM 2. This door was opened and Adam was moved through it, across a floor and through a small, swinging gate. Inside the gate, the stretcher stopped beside a long table. Sawyer placed his briefcase on the table and sat down in a chair next to Adam's head.

Adam looked cautiously around the courtroom. In front of him was a large wooden dais, its top perhaps ten feet above the floor. On one side of this was the witness stand, a slight platform with a chair, enclosed by a wooden railing. To Adam's left was another long table and beyond that was an enclosed space containing twelve chairs. To the right, beyond the long table where Sawyer sat, was another enclosed area with several desks. Seated at these desks and lounging across them were a number of people, perhaps six or eight men and women, including the police officers who had come up on the elevator. The group had suddenly become quiet when Adam was wheeled in, but now they resumed their talking and laughing.

Looking straight up, Adam saw a painting on the ceiling. A number of people and things were in the painting. Adam recognized George Washington holding a sword in one hand and a piece of paper in the other. Behind Washington was an Indian woman, naked to the waist and with full headdress. Another figure seemed to be a pioneer, with a leather shirt and coonskin cap and a gun. Hovering above the group was a woman with a crown on her head and a branch in her hand. She wore what looked like a nightgown and she seemed to be flying.

Other things were in the picture, too, a log cabin, an old riverboat and a church. But Adam's study was interrupted when a man carrying a briefcase with a suit box under his arm walked up to Sawyer and shook hands. Adam heard them say good morning, and then they came around to the side of the stretcher.

"Adam, this is Mr. Rogers, the prosecuting attorney," Sawyer said.

Adam said, "Hello."

"Glad to see you, Adam," Rogers said, and then he quickly turned to the other long table and put the suit box and brief-case down. He opened the briefcase and began piling stacks of paper on the table. This done, he walked back toward Sawyer's chair and the two men stood behind Adam's head.

The prosecutor asked, "Any chance of a guilty plea, Bill?"

"No, I think not." Sawyer lowered his voice. "He says he didn't do it . . . We'll have to try it."

Suddenly Adam said, "I *didn't* do it."

Adam said this very loudly, and he was surprised himself that he had. The lawyers also seemed to be surprised. They walked around beside Adam and looked down at him. Both were silent for a minute.

"Okay, Adam, I didn't mean to upset you," Rogers said softly. Putting his hands in his pockets and crouching down close to Adam, he added, "I'm sure you know that this is my job . . . It's just my job . . . as a prosecuting attorney."

Adam said nothing and Rogers stepped away nervously and began to examine some papers he had taken from his briefcase. Adam resumed his study of the room and became aware of activity behind him, on the other side of the swing-ing gate. Because of his position, he could not see what was going on, but the noises indicated that other people were coming into the courtroom. As he turned his head to try to see, a small man in a rumpled suit pushed through the gate and walked hurriedly over to Sawyer and Rogers.

"Which of you guys is William Sawyer?" the man asked. Sawyer looked up. "I am."

"Well, I'm Jack Medlicott, from *The World*."

"Yes . . ." Sawyer said, tentatively. He waited for Med-licott to state his business and finally asked, "What do you want?"

The reporter, apparently not quite certain what his er-rand was, stammered briefly. "Well, I'm a . . . I'm interested in this case, not for the paper . . . I'm a friend of Mr. Johnson's." He looked toward Adam, who had overheard and was studying Medlicott trying to identify him. He was sure that he did not know him at all.

Although surprised that his client had a friend he had not been told about, Sawyer for the moment was satisfied with Medlicott's explanation. "Well," he said, "it was nice of you to come. If you'd like to talk to Adam before court begins, go ahead."

Sawyer returned to his conversation with Rogers, and Medlicott walked over to Adam. "I'm Medlicott," he said. Sensing that Adam was disconcerted by his claim of friendship, he added quickly, "I really am a friend of yours, though I guess this is the first chance we've had to meet."

Adam nodded, but said nothing.

"I'll . . . be here during the trial, Adam, . . . just for luck, and so you'll know someone is pulling for you. Is that all right?"

"Yes, sir, it is," Adam said, and Medlicott clumsily backed away and sat down in the first row of chairs beyond the gate.

The interview with Medlicott was barely over when a door to the left of the dais opened and Judge Pearce, clad in a black robe, walked in. The bailiff struck his desk with a gavel. The sharp crack frightened Adam, and he was further unnerved by the fact that everyone jumped to his feet. The judge quickly mounted the bench and sat down. The others were seated, too, and the room became very still. The judge's head and shoulders were visible to Adam, and he saw the judge look intently down at him.

The judge picked up a piece of paper from the bench. Clearing his throat, he began to talk. "This is the case of *State v. Adam Johnson*. The affidavit charges robbery committed against the person and property of one Josephine Wallace on the night of May 19, 1960. The file shows waiver of indictment, a not guilty plea and waiver of trial by jury. Mr. Sawyer, you are the attorney for the defendant? Good morning."

Sawyer stood up and said, "I am, Your Honor . . . Good morning to you."

"Are you ready to proceed to the trial of this cause?"

"I am, Your Honor."

Turning toward the prosecutor, the judge said, "Are you ready, Mr. Rogers?"

"Yes, Your Honor."

After shuffling several papers on the bench in front of him, the judge looked up. "I have a question . . . What is the reason for the defendant's being on this stretcher?"

There was a slight pause and then Sawyer said, "Well, sir, because he was shot in the back by the police. His spinal cord was severed."

Barely changing his expression, Judge Pearce said, "Oh . . . I see . . . Well, is he well enough to stand trial?"

"Yes, Your Honor," Sawyer answered. "It seems that he's. as well as he'll ever be."

The judge took off his glasses and swung them in front of him. Leaning forward very far, he said, "You understand what I'm talking about, do you, Mr. Sawyer? Is he competent . . . physically . . . so to speak, to defend himself?"

"Yes, he is, sir."

"Well, all right. Let's proceed. Mr. Prosecutor, do you have an opening statement?"

Rogers again got to his feet. "I do, Your Honor."

"You may proceed," said Judge Pearce.

The prosecutor began. Prefacing his remarks with the statement "Our evidence will show," he recited the police version of the crime. Adam listened and was acute enough to react in his stomach to such phrases as "positive identification" and "when the police shouted to him to stop, he ran instead, the traditional conduct of the guilty man."

When the prosecutor had finished, Sawyer rose. He told the judge what Adam had told him, about the gang in the car and the reason he had run. He also pointed out that Adam had never been in any trouble before, and said the identification would prove to be very weak. The defendant's evidence, Sawyer said, would prove that the police had shot down an innocent man.

When Sawyer finished, the judge said, "All right. Mr. Rogers, call your first witness, please."

Rogers turned toward the back of the courtroom and called out the name of Josephine Wallace. She passed through the gate and walked up to the witness stand beside the bench. An elderly man carrying a worn Bible stepped from behind the railing and Miss Wallace took the oath. She sat down mechanically and the prosecutor began his examination. Adam became aware of a man at a table close to the bench recording the trial on a stenotype.

Miss Wallace first told of the robbery and of her view, as she fell, of the legs and feet of her assailant. Without any prompting, she stated that she "had a good look at them in the light from the streetlight." Then she told of walking up the alley with Sullivan and seeing the defendant on the ground.

"Did the officers ask you whether the man on the ground was the man who had robbed you?"

"Yes, they did."

"What did you say?"

"I said he was the man, because of the same pants and shoes."

"How could you see these in the alley?"

"Well, the policemen had their flashlights and showed them on his legs."

Rogers turned and opened the suit box on the counsel table and took out a pair of brown cotton pants and a pair of brown oxfords. Turning to Sawyer, he said, "Will counsel stipulate that these are the defendant's property and that he was wearing them on the night of May 19, 1960?"

Although taken unaware, Sawyer stood and picked up the pants and shoes. The pants were stiff in the back, above the seat, discolored by a dark brown stain. Crossing to Adam's stretcher, Sawyer held out the articles.

"They're mine," Adam said.

"Yes, the defendant will so stipulate," said Sawyer.

Rogers took the pants and shoes from Sawyer and walked over to the court reporter and had him mark a tag attached to the pants and a tag attached to the shoes. Holding up the pants before the witness, he said, "These are marked as State's Exhibit A, Miss Wallace. What are they?"

"They're the pants he was wearing when he grabbed me and my purse and hit me. He was still wearing them in the alley on the ground."

"And what of these, marked State's Exhibit B?"

"They're his shoes. I saw them when I fell and again in the alley."

Looking up at the bench, Rogers said, "I offer State's Exhibits A and B, Your Honor."

"No objection," Sawyer said, and the clothing was admitted into evidence.

Rogers turned graciously to Sawyer. "You may cross-examine."

Sawyer walked uncertainly toward Miss Wallace. The truth was that he could see no way to attack her testimony by cross-examination, but he felt that he was expected to say something to her. There was a brief and embarrassing silence. Finally, although still at a loss, Sawyer decided to try.

"Miss Wallace, you are aware, I take it, of the fact that this man is charged with a serious crime. Are you aware of that?"

"Yes, I am."

"Having that in mind, are you positive of your identification of these pants and shoes?" Almost before he finished his question, Sawyer realized he should not have asked it. But it was too late, and he could only accept the woman's categorical response.

"Yes, I'm absolutely positive," she said.

Deeply chagrined, Sawyer turned away from her and said, over his shoulder, "I've no further questions."

Rogers was on his feet quickly. He signaled to John Mueller who was sitting anxiously in a seat just behind the gate. The policeman came forward, climbed into the witness stand and was sworn. He sat down warily and Rogers' questioning began.

At first the questions and answers identified John Mueller and his record on the force. Then the officer told of how he and Officer John Sullivan had been cruising up Park toward Twelfth Street at approximately 11:30 P.M. on May 19. A number of people were on the sidewalk at the intersection and on the northwest corner people were shouting. Mueller said that he had pulled across the intersection and had seen a woman on the ground near the curb, north of the intersection. Mueller and Sullivan had left the car, and had been told of the robbery. Within minutes, they were back in the car driving up the street.

"Tell us what happened then, sir," asked the prosecutor.

"Well, as we got toward the middle of the block, we saw a man on the sidewalk. He was sort of standing back in the shadows from the trees, on the left side of the street."

"What did you do then?"

"We started to pull over into the left lane, getting ready to stop."

"Then what?"

"Well, this man began to run up into this yard there and we, John and I, we stopped and jumped out."

"Now, Officer Mueller, I want you to answer this question

carefully, because it is most important. Did you call out to the man?"

"Yes, sir."

"What did you call out?"

"I said, 'Stop—we're police officers' . . . I always say that at a time like that."

At this Bill Sawyer rose from his chair. "Objection, Your Honor, to what he always does."

Judge Pearce glanced down at Sawyer. "Your objection comes too late, Mr. Sawyer. The witness has already answered the question."

Sawyer colored and began to sit down, but he checked himself, stood up and said, "I move that the portion of the answer having to do with what the witness always does be stricken as unresponsive to the question and immaterial. The issue here is not what the witness may have done in other cases."

"I'll grant that motion," said the judge. "The reporter will please strike the statement 'I always say that at a time like that.'"

Rogers, who had been silent during this colloquy, said, "Your Honor, I'd like to be heard on that ruling . . ." and then, with a mock show of the magnanimous, he added, "Oh, well, let it go." Turning again to the witness, he asked, "All right, Officer, when you called out was the man still in sight?"

"Yes, he was. We could barely see him, but he had on a white shirt and was maybe halfway back into the yard . . . and I called very loud."

Sawyer stirred in his chair at this gratuitous remark, but he decided to let it pass.

The examination proceeded as Mueller described the race through the yard, and the chase up the alley. He sprinkled the narrative with statements about shouting "Halt" and "Stop" as the chase continued, and then told how the man had been picked up by the beams of the flashlights.

"And then what, Officer?" asked Rogers.

"Well, I began to fire, aiming over the man's head. Sullivan fired, too. I fired four shots and Sullivan fired six. Apparently, a bullet richocheted off a fence or something, because the man was hit and fell. Sullivan and I ran up to him."

"Who was the man, Officer?"

"It was the defendant here, Adam Johnson."

Mueller then described the arrival of Miss Wallace, brought along by Officer Sullivan.

"When she arrived, what happened?"

"Well, I asked her if she could identify the man. She said yes, that he was the one."

Rogers picked up the pants and shoes from the counsel table and turned again to the witness. "Are these the pants and shoes which the defendant was wearing when he was . . . taken . . . in the alley, Officer?"

Mueller said that they were.

"Did you later return to the scene of the pursuit of the defendant, Officer?"

"Yes, I did. Detective Terry O'Neal and I went back the next day to look for the woman's property in the alley."

Turning to the counsel table, Rogers picked up a piece of paper and handed it to the court reporter, asking him to mark it as State's Exhibit C. This done, he advanced to Sawyer's chair and showed him the paper. Then he walked to the witness stand and gave it to Mueller. "I hand you what has been marked State's Exhibit C, Officer. Tell the court what that is, if you please, sir."

"It's the list of things we found . . . just like it says, near the prisoner's course of flight."

"Were these things later identified by Miss Wallace, the prosecuting witness?"

"They were, yes, sir."

"Please turn the exhibit over, Officer."

Mueller turned it over and noted Miss Wallace's signature and described how he and O'Neal had obtained the identification from her on the day after the crime.

Rogers took the piece of paper from Mueller and handed it up to Judge Pearce. "I offer State's Exhibit C, Your Honor."

The judge glanced down at the defense table.

Sawyer said, "No objection."

"It is received," Judge Pearce said.

Rogers had by this time returned to his table. After glancing at his notes, he said, "Thank you, Officer Mueller." With a nod in Sawyer's direction, he added, "You may cross-examine, Mr. Sawyer," and sat down.

During the concluding portions of Mueller's testimony, Sawyer had become acutely uncomfortable. He had thought many times before the trial about the prosecution's identification testimony. In spite of Miss Wallace's positiveness, he knew that the judge would recognize the weakness of the identification because of the commonplace character of the pants and shoes and the circumstances of Miss Wallace's fleeting view of them. It had now occurred to him that he had not made any effort to investigate the finding of the stolen articles. He had simply accepted what Rogers' file showed about this, and now it was in the record. He considered briefly what he could do about this without looking foolish and incompetent. Then he forced himself to put the problem out of his mind so that he could at least begin his cross-examination.

Rising, Sawyer looked quickly at the notes he had taken during Mueller's testimony. He cleared his throat and, with a slightly quavering voice, asked his first question. "Now, Officer, as I understand it, you arrived on the scene after Miss Wallace had been robbed?"

"That's correct, sir."

"Do you know how many minutes had passed between the robbery and your arrival on the scene?"

"I don't know exactly, but probably from three to five minutes, from what she said."

"And how long was it from your arrival until you started to drive up the block, having in mind that you and Sullivan got out of the car, talked with her and the people and got back into the car?"

"I'd say approximately a minute or two."

"All right, that means, does it not, that from five to seven minutes passed between the time you arrived at the corner and the time you first saw the defendant?"

In the moment that Mueller hesitated, Rogers said, "Objection, Your Honor. The question is entirely leading and suggestive. Counsel is arguing with the witness."

Before Sawyer could respond, the judge said, "Overruled. You may proceed, Mr. Sawyer."

"Will the reporter please read the question?" Sawyer asked.

The reporter read the question.

Mueller said, "I think the times I've used are a little long . . . I don't think it was that long."

"Well, I won't quarrel with you, Officer. You acknowledge that it was several minutes?"

"Yes."

"All right. Now, Officer, does it seem curious to you as a police officer that a robber would commit his crime and then stroll leisurely up the street?"

Rogers again interposed. "Objection, Your Honor. This is surely argument."

Judge Pearce said, "Sustained . . . Mr. Sawyer, your point is in the record from the facts. You need not belabor it through the witness."

"Yes, Your Honor," Sawyer said apologetically. Then,

looking again at his notes, he said, "Now, Officer Mueller, you've also said that when you first saw the defendant he was standing still. Is that correct?"

"Yes, he was sort of standing still."

"In any event, he wasn't running?"

"That's correct, but he started to run when we drove up."

"Now, I've another question, Officer. You've told us there were several people with Miss Wallace. Is that right?"

"Yes."

"Were there other people hanging around the corner?"

"Yes, sir. It's a busy corner even at night. Lots of people."

"Were there other people along the sidewalk on the *right-hand* side of the street when you drove up?"

"I don't remember seeing any."

"Well, are you saying that there weren't any?"

"No, sir. I said I don't remember them."

"What about the sidewalk on the left side of the street?"

"I didn't see anybody but the defendant."

Sawyer then turned briefly to other phases of the testimony, requiring Mueller to repeat several portions of it. As Mueller answered, Sawyer tried to decide whether to ask him anything about the stolen articles in the alley. The trouble was that he did not know what the facts were and he now recalled an axiom from his law school course in evidence: Don't ask a question on cross-examination unless you know what the truth is and can prove it. He had overlooked this rule with Miss Wallace and had been made to look silly as a result. He desperately wanted Judge Pearce and Rogers to think that he was capable. And surely, he thought, Rogers, having been so cooperative and helpful, would not take advantage of him.

As Mueller answered his last question, Sawyer decided to ignore the issue of the stolen articles in the alley. Relieved, he thanked Mueller and returned to his table.

Having gotten past a critical part of his case, the prosecutor was quick to take advantage of the state of the record. He rose and turned again to Sawyer. "In order to save the court's time, I wonder if Mr. Sawyer will enter into a further stipulation. Will you stipulate that Officer Sullivan and Detective O'Neal would testify consistently with Officer Mueller? You will note that I am not asking for a stipulation of *facts*. I seek only a stipulation as to what their testimony would be, and only to the extent that they have competent knowledge of the facts."

Taken off guard, Sawyer did not immediately answer. But he could not think of any good reason not to join in the stipulation and, glancing at the judge, he sensed his desire to avoid tedious repetition. Finally, he said, "Yes, the defendant will so stipulate."

"Thank you, Mr. Sawyer," Rogers said. "The State rests, Your Honor."

"All right," said Judge Pearce. "There will be a ten-minute recess." He left the bench, disappearing behind the door he had entered earlier.

Taking advantage of the respite, the prosecutor strolled to the back of the room to chat with the police. But Bill Sawyer remained in his chair. He was still rattled by Miss Wallace's positiveness about the pants and shoes and his doubts about the stolen articles in the alley. He was convinced that the State had surely made a prima facie case. Still, it was difficult to think that the pants and shoes were enough to send a man to prison. Reading quickly through his notes, he tried to think whether he was missing anything. He felt that he had at least damaged the prosecution's theory, because of the time lapse between the robbery and the chase. Surely, he thought, this would credit Adam's testimony.

The judge returned to the bench precisely ten minutes after his departure. "All right, Mr. Sawyer," he said. "We are ready for the defendant's case."

Sawyer said, "Your Honor, I should like to move for a directed verdict."

Unhesitatingly, Judge Pearce said, "Your motion will be noted and denied. I will not hear argument, if you don't mind, because I'm convinced that a prima facie case was made. Now please proceed."

Looking down at Adam, Sawyer said, "Your Honor, my witness is the defendant. He will have to testify from where he is.

"Of course," said the judge. "Will the bailiff please swear the witness."

The old man moved to Adam's side and stooped to hold the Bible to him. Adam repeated the oath and the questioning began. At first he gave his name and age and the rooming house address. Then the questions turned to his childhood in Tennessee. He was vague about his parents. His father "had not returned" from the war and his mother had died "when I was a kid, very young." The spectators in the courtroom seemed to share his embarrassment at knowing so little about himself.

Adam brightened when he spoke of the Abernathys, and of his schooling and his job at the grain elevator. He had been paid fifty cents an hour at the job and supported himself, paying the Abernathys ten dollars a week for room and board. After graduation from high school, he had worked full time at the elevator, but at Christmastime he had decided to come north, because he'd been told that there was more opportunity. He had saved his money and finally had enough for the trip and to tide him over until he could get a job. Arriving in the city early in April, he'd rented his room and looked for work.

"And did you find a job?" asked Sawyer.

"Yes, sir. It wasn't as easy as I thought, but on April 23 I got on out at Faultless."

"What kind of a job did you get, Adam?"

"I was in the warehouse, a good job that paid $1.87, plus, an hour . . . It was regular, too. I didn't miss a day the whole time."

Sawyer had thus far been standing beside Adam. Now, with an apologetic glance at Judge Pearce, he pulled his chair toward the stretcher and sat down. After a glance at his notes, he continued. "Now, Adam, I'd like to ask you if you have any relatives."

"Well, really not, sir . . . The folks I lived with, I called them 'aunt' and 'uncle,' but they was really just friends."

"Did you try to contact these people after you were arrested?"

"Yes, I wrote the Abernathys. They sent me a little money, all they could spare, I think, but they couldn't come here because Mrs. Abernathy isn't healthy . . . she's kind of old . . . and the mister couldn't really spend the money." Adam hesitated and then blurted out, "They said I was a good boy and they knew I was a good boy and that I wouldn't do this thing they say I've done . . . but then they couldn't do much for me, especially with me hurt like this."

Rogers had tentatively leaned forward in his chair, preparing to object to the hearsay report of the Abernathys' views, but he couldn't quite bring himself to. He subsided and concentrated on the file on the table before him.

"Now, Adam, have you ever been in any trouble with the police?" Sawyer asked.

"No, sir, I haven't. I've never been in any trouble with anybody."

Sawyer rose and advanced to the bench, glancing at Rogers. In his hand was a sheaf of letters. "Your Honor, and Mr. Rogers, I have here some letters from people in Kingsway who know this boy. His schoolteacher, the school principal and the man he worked for at the elevator. Also, the Abernathys have written. All of these people vouch for him. I'd like to introduce the letters into evidence."

The judge looked at Rogers, who said, "I'm sorry, Judge, but I can't let that kind of stuff into the record. Mr. Sawyer knows that . . . it's the rankest kind of hearsay . . . and it's also really immaterial. If I let it in here, I'd have to let it in in any other case. I just can't do it. I object to it."

The judge thought for a minute before speaking. Looking sympathetically at Sawyer, he said, "My situation is much like Mr. Rogers'. I think that it is probably relevant and material, but it is hearsay, and if I accept it from this defendant, I'd be haunted by it in another case." Passing his hand over his forehead, he said, "I realize the practical problems of your case, Mr. Sawyer, but I must sustain the objection."

Mumbling that he understood, Sawyer returned the letters to his file. After a brief silence, he said, "Now, Adam, tell us in your own words about the night you were shot."

Adam first mentioned Anne Webster. He told of taking her home and starting down Park. He described the gang's passing by, shouting and throwing the beer can at him, and said that he had called out to the car. He had watched the car continue up the street and turn left. Then he told of seeing the car approaching from the south, and of the chase and the shooting.

"Adam, why did you run?" asked Sawyer.

"Because I thought it was these guys coming back."

"Did you hear anyone call out anything about the police?"

"No, sir."

"Did you hear shouting at all?"

"Yes, I heard some hollering behind me . . . I heard someone holler 'There he goes' . . . I thought it was these guys, so I kept going."

"Now, Adam, I'll ask you one final question. Did you rob this woman . . . did you do the things which you are accused of here in this court?"

"No, sir, I did not. I'm not guilty."

Sawyer turned toward the prosecution. "Your witness, Mr. Rogers."

Rogers got up slowly and began his questioning. "Adam, according to the police reports, there was three dollars in your wallet when you were arrested. Is that about right?"

"Yes, sir, plus a little change in my pocket."

"Do you have a car?"

"No, sir."

"Was your rent paid up?"

"Yes, sir. I pay by the week, and I'd just paid eight dollars for a whole week."

"Did you have a bank account?"

"No, sir."

"Did you have any money besides the three dollars?"

"I had about ten more dollars . . . nine dollars . . . in my room, in a drawer. The police found it and kept it for me . . . And the money order from the Abernathys. That was for seven dollars and I've saved it, too."

"What about clothes, Adam, what clothes do you own?"

"Well, I had a suit. I'd just got it and another pair of shoes, black ones, and some pants and shirts, underwear and socks, and I had my own razor and things like that. They was all bought and paid for by me."

"Is that all of your property?"

Adam looked puzzled. "I don't know what you mean."

"Well, let me put it this way. You described your twelve or thirteen dollars and the money order, and your clothes, your one week's rent paid in advance and your toilet articles. I'm asking you if that is all you owned?"

"Yes, sir. That's all."

"Now, one more question. I don't like to ask this, but I think the court should know it. What do the doctors say about your condition? Will it improve?"

"No. They say they can't do anything about it."

"I have no further questions," Rogers said and he returned to his chair.

Although uncertain about the meaning of Rogers' questions, Sawyer said that the defense rested and Rogers immediately stated that the prosecution had no rebuttal evidence.

"All right, gentlemen," said the judge. "We'll recess again, for five minutes this time, and I'll be ready for argument when we resume."

The judge left the bench and the courtroom became informal.

7

DESPITE the conversation in the courtroom behind them, Rogers and Sawyer remained at their tables, putting the final touches on notes for the closing arguments. At the end of the five minutes, Judge Pearce returned, the room became silent again and, responding to the judge's nod, Rogers stood up to begin.

"Your Honor," he said, "for my own sake, I'd like to say at the beginning that this case is very painful for me, and I wish that someone else had my job today. But it should also be said that sympathy is beside the point in a court of law. Granting that all of us here feel deeply the personal tragedy of this young man, the question . . . the only question . . .

is whether he did or did not commit the crime of which he stands accused.

"It may be anticipated that the defense will attack the identification by the prosecuting witness. This attack will be based on Mr. Sawyer's imagination, because the record shows a positive and categorical identification, unimpeached and unanswered by the evidence. Still, the attack will be made. At the outset, therefore, let us set aside the identification entirely. Let us act as if there were no identification testimony. Even without that aspect of the case, the picture of guilt is clear. This guilt arises from the coincidence of three *undisputed* . . . please note that I say undisputed . . . facts: motive, opportunity, and the place where the stolen articles were found. I should like to discuss each of these in turn.

"First, what of motive? It is surely *not* my contention that poor people are presumed to be guilty. The court and Mr. Sawyer will give me too much credit to accuse me of that. At the same time, I *do* say that this man's economic situation, and his sociological circumstances, are wholly consistent with the *type* of crime committed here. He is not a desperado. He apparently has no criminal record. But he is rootless, and marginal in terms of money, and a purse snatching is the type of petty, mildly violent offense that such a person often commits. Thus, I start out with the proposition that motive exists here.

"What of opportunity? This, I think, is the basic weakness of the defendant's case. Thus, it is admitted on all sides that this man was at least a half block . . . a few hundred yards . . . from the scene at the precise time that the crime was committed. We are not concerned here with any far-fetched, strained hypothesis. We are concerned with a man with a motive who admits that he was at the *right* place at the *right* time, but who denies that he committed the act. It may be noted that he has no alibi at all. His story of walking halfway down the block but not all the way to Twelfth Street is self-serving and unsupported. His story about a carload of toughs is inherently unbelievable and is wholly discredited by the police testimony that they called out that they *were* the police. In short, Your Honor, this man with a *motive* also had the *opportunity*. He was right there at the time.

"And what of the place where the stolen articles were found? This, I contend, is the ultimate incriminating fact. This man's course of flight and the location of the victim's property are undisputed. Is this court prepared to say that it is simply a coincidence that Miss Wallace's property was strewn in the wake of the defendant's flight? Of course it was not a coincidence. And this means that the man with the motive, the man who was at the right place at the right time . . . who had the opportunity and has no alibi . . . also left a telltale trail as he was pursued down the alley.

"And all of this adds up to one thing—the guilt of this man. And with these undisputed facts in the record, now please look at the identification. Would it not be straining the bounds of credulity to say that the man with the motive, the man with the opportunity and without an alibi, the man who marked his path with the stolen articles, *which man was also identified* . . . isn't it really too much to ask this court to find this man not guilty? The prosecution submits that it is too much. If the *evidence* is to decide this case, and this is what the law says must be, this man must be found guilty."

Rogers turned to his chair and sat down. He knew that he had made an effective argument. He had watched the judge and could tell that he had made notes of the key points of the prosecution's case—motive, opportunity, the stolen articles and the identification. He sensed that he had affected the judge. He had been just right. He had said enough, but not too much.

The judge now turned to Sawyer and thoughtfully asked

him if he wanted a recess before summing up for the defense. With unbecoming eagerness, Sawyer accepted and a few minutes was allowed. Again the judge left the bench and Sawyer, his head spinning from the force of Rogers' remarks, began feverishly to rewrite his argument.

The truth was that Sawyer had concentrated in his own mind on attacking the identification, and now Rogers had deftly outmaneuvered him, discarding this as the cornerstone of the State's case. Sawyer's ears rang with the logic of motive, opportunity and stolen articles. He could not, in the brief time available, think clearly of a way to meet this. But he did scribble a few random notes before the judge reappeared and nodded to him.

Sawyer rose and began. "I should like at first to say that the prosecutor has a rather loose notion of the concept of motive. Although he asks that I credit him with not attacking this man because he is poor, that, Your Honor, is exactly what he has done. If his motive contention means anything at all, it means that if this man had money in the bank he would not be accused of this crime. Since he does not have money in the bank, he is 'a little bit guilty' at the outset. I contend that this is not an argument which should be listened to at all, because it can only mean that a poor man has one strike on him for that reason, so the prosecutor needs to find only two more to put him out. I will not belabor this point, but I ask the court in the name of common justice to disregard the so-called motive argument.

"With regard to opportunity, I concede that this defendant was *near* the right place at *nearly* the right time. But does this prove anything? Perhaps a hundred others were near the place at nearly the time. The prosecutor is simply pulling himself up by his bootstraps, and practically mis-stating the evidence at that, when he says that this defendant was *at* the scene of the crime. I contend that the fact that this defendant was one of *many* people *near* the scene is no evidence of his guilt of the crime.

"As to the articles in the alley, this again is bootstrap reasoning. We all concede that this woman was robbed and that the robber fled. The articles prove that the robber fled up the alley, but they do *not* prove that this defendant was the robber.

"When all is said and done, Your Honor, the prosecutor is cleverly kidding us when he says that he need not and does not rely on the identification by Miss Wallace of the pants and shoes. The truth is that this is still the heart of the prosecution's case, but the prosecutor knows that it is also pretty weak stuff so he would gloss over it now. But think for a minute. If the so-called identification was not the basis of this prosecution, why did the police bring this woman up that alley on the night of the crime? She had been knocked down. She was admittedly hurt and unsettled, but the police walked her up that alley because they knew that they might or might not have shot the robber, depending upon Miss Wallace's identification. But on what basis? On the basis of a momentary, fleeting view of pants and shoes as she fell to the ground. And what about the pants and shoes? At least a thousand working people in this town wear this kind of pants and this kind of shoes. The so-called identification, Your Honor, is outrageous. It is the prosecution's real case, and surely you will not send a man to prison on that kind of evidence.

"In short, Your Honor, let us reject the identification entirely. I insist that the 'poor man' motive argument also be rejected. What does this leave? It leaves the fact that the defendant was one of many *nearby* at the time, and the fact that the robber fled up the alley. But do these prove the guilt of *this man,* beyond reasonable doubt? I say they do not.

"And I would add one final comment. The prosecution's

hypothesis—its line of inferences based on inferences and leading to more inferences—requires you to believe one strictly unbelievable thing: that this defendant robbed this woman, setting up a great hue and cry of neighbors and passersby which attracted the attention of the police, and then calmly strolled up the street with the purse under his arm so that he was right there on the premises when the police arrived. Will you believe this, Your Honor? I think not. I submit that not guilty must be your verdict."

Sawyer sat down. His throat was very dry, as if he had spoken for an hour instead of a few minutes. He was too excited to have any feeling about the effect of his presentation, but suddenly he saw Adam Johnson out of the corner of his eye. He had almost forgotten the boy, but now he became acutely conscious of him. He had screwed himself around and risen on one elbow. He was looking straight at Sawyer and there was color in his cheeks, the first that Sawyer had ever seen. His usual blank expression was gone. His face was animated and he actually seemed to be smiling, for the first time in Sawyer's recollection. Without meaning to, Sawyer reached out with his left hand. Adam clumsily but firmly gripped it with his right. Then the hands withdrew. All of this took only a moment and while it was happening Rogers began his rebuttal.

Assuming a convincingly petulant tone, Rogers said, "If the court please, I frankly resent the implication that I have misstated the record. I have *not* misstated the record, in this case or any other case, for that matter. I would also point out the curiosity which *defense counsel* presents in telling the court what the *prosecution's* real case is . . . But this is not a game between lawyers. I am not interested in debating with Mr. Sawyer or matching wits, or insults, with him. This is a legal proceeding. The question is the guilt or innocence of this man, and this turns not on how I characterize the case, or how Mr. Sawyer characterizes the case, or how either of us characterizes the other. The question of guilt or innocence turns *on the record.*

"A crime has been committed. This is admitted. Whether this man did it depends on what *the record* shows linking him to it. And he is linked by the elements of *time, place,* and the telltale *tracks.* I have incidentally noted that the crime is surely not inconsistent with the circumstances of this man. I have called this motive, but by any other name the court surely understands what I'm talking about. Finally, there are the pants and shoes.

"And against all of this there stands but one single thing—the defendant, standing alone and uncorroborated in the record, says that he didn't do it. *Of course* he says he didn't do it, but this is why we have trials in our legal system and this is why we look at all of the evidence and don't just take the word of the accused. Look at that evidence, Your Honor. This man *is* linked to the crime, as only the guilty man could be."

Rogers bowed slightly and backed into his chair.

Judge Pearce looked at his watch and said, "Gentlemen, it is now just past noon. I would like to adjourn for lunch and reconvene at one-thirty. By that time, I will have gone over my notes and I may have a question or two. After the reconvening, we will adjourn and I'll take the case under advisement and call you back when I've reached a verdict. Is this agreeable?"

The lawyers unhesitatingly agreed and Judge Pearce, gathering up his file of notes, left the bench.

As soon as the judge had disappeared, Rogers, his hand extended, walked over to Bill Sawyer. "Nice work, Bill, you gave your man a run for his money . . . I think it could go either way."

Although he was actually annoyed at Rogers' references

to Adam's financial situation, and was also more concerned than Rogers about his own performance, Sawyer relaxed at Rogers' show of professionalism. "Thanks, Mr. Rogers . . . I hope I did all right . . . Your presentation was very effective, so I congratulate you, too."

Rogers smiled. "How about lunch?"

Sawyer hesitated. "Well," he said, nodding toward Adam's stretcher, "perhaps I should . . ."

Rogers interrupted. "He'll be O.K. The cops'll take care of him."

"All right," Sawyer said, obviously relieved. "I'll go with you. Just a minute." He turned to Adam. "I'll be back soon, Adam, and the police will get lunch for you . . . Is there anything I can do for you before I go?"

"No, thank you," Adam said.

Sawyer began to organize his papers and was putting them in his briefcase when Jack Medlicott passed through the gate and came up to where he was standing.

"Sawyer," Medlicott began, "I'll stay with the boy if you're leaving."

Sawyer turned to the reporter. "All right, that would be fine." Having finished packing, he said, "Goodbye, Adam, see you shortly," and left with Rogers.

Medlicott sat down in Sawyer's chair, turning it around so that he faced Adam. Shifting about in the chair under Adam's inscrutable stare, the reporter was silent for several minutes.

Suddenly he said, very loudly, *"Jesus Christ . . ."* Then he lowered his voice and leaned over to Adam. "What about something to eat, Adam? I'll get you a sandwich and we'll eat right here. What do you want?"

"I'm really not hungry, sir."

"Well, I'm not either, but we ought to eat something. Come on, I'll get you a hamburger and a carton of milk. Please."

"All right, I'll try."

Medlicott got up and walked toward the gate which separated him from the back of the courtroom. Miss Wallace and most of the spectators had gone, but the policemen were still there and Mueller was detailing one of them to maintain custody of the prisoner. Medlicott pushed through the gate and walked into the midst of the policemen.

To the man assigned to guard, Medlicott said angrily, "Stay back here, away from him. I'll buy his lunch!"

Surprised, the officer turned inquiringly toward Mueller.

"That's O.K.," said Mueller. "Just stay back here."

Medlicott left the police, passed into the corridor and walked downstairs to a lunch counter. After a brief wait, he bought two hamburgers and two small cartons of milk and returned. The courtroom was empty now, except for Adam and the policeman. He was sitting toward the back reading a newspaper.

Medlicott walked to the table beside Adam and put the food down. He unwrapped the sandwiches and handed one and an opened carton of milk to Adam. Adam raised up on one elbow and began to drink the milk, nibbling at the hamburger between swallows.

The sandwich was absolutely tasteless, but Medlicott choked his down anyway, finished his milk and began to smoke. He offered a cigarette to Adam, but the boy shook his head. They sat there then, in silence, for what seemed like a long time, Medlicott thinking all the while of some conceivable comment.

Finally, it was Adam who spoke. "Sir . . ."

"What is it?" Medlicott asked as Adam stammered and again became silent.

"Well . . ." Adam started again. "I'm . . . I don't like to ask you, but I need some help . . . I'm afraid if I don't . . ." He stopped again and, studying his face, Medlicott saw that he was about to cry.

Leaning forward, his hands on the stretcher, the reporter spoke as gently as he could. "For God's sake, Adam, please tell me what you want . . . *I want to help you* . . . Jesus, boy, please give me the chance."

Adam seemed to settle down at Medlicott's statement. The trace of tears left. He swallowed and, carefully choosing his words, said, "Well, I really should be put over on my stomach . . . Mr. Sawyer just forgot about it, and that's all right . . . but if I don't, I'll get a terrible sore on my . . . back. I had one already . . . Will you . . . please turn me over?"

Medlicott had risen from his chair. Following the boy's lead, he placed one arm under his buttocks and grasped his legs at the knees with the other. Straining mightily and holding the catheter tube with one hand, Adam dug an elbow into the stretcher and began to turn. Medlicott forced the rest of his body over and finally Adam lay on his stomach. An adjustment of the legs, performed by Medlicott, completed the turn.

For a few minutes both men were silent after their exertion. Then, perhaps warmed by the physical intimacy, Adam said, "Mr. Medlicott . . . what do you think?"

Instinctively the reporter knew that Adam was talking about the trial. He fought off the temptation to reassure him and said simply, "I don't know, son. I'm afraid to think about it."

His voice rising, Adam said, "Me, too, but *God* . . . I'd like to be let loose."

He spoke with such feeling that Medlicott almost expressed the questions in his mind—what's the difference, what will you do if you are acquitted?—but he did not. Instead, very quietly, he said, "We'll just have to wait and see."

Shortly before one-thirty, Medlicott's cheerless vigil ended.

Sawyer, Rogers and other court officials and spectators began to drift into the room.

Noticing that Adam was on his stomach, Sawyer was reminded of his responsibility to turn him. "How'd you get over, Adam?" he asked.

"Mr. Medlicott helped me."

The reporter had stood aside as Sawyer resumed custody, but the lawyer drew him back and thanked him for helping out.

At one-thirty Judge Pearce returned to the bench and Medlicott scurried through the gate to his chair. After the bailiff had sounded his gavel and the people in the courtroom sat down, the judge put on his glasses and slowly perused several yellow, legal size pages on which he had made notes. He looked up. To the lawyers he said, "I have only one question, I think, gentlemen. It concerns these possessions of Miss Wallace. I've examined State's Exhibit C, captioned 'Found near prisoner's course of flight' and listing the pocketbook, lipstick, etc. I'd like to be refreshed on what the transcript shows about this exhibit . . . the testimony of Officer Mueller at this point in the record."

Rogers said, "You mean, what Mueller said about the place that the things were found?"

"Yes."

"I took a note of that, Judge," Rogers said. "I handed him the exhibit for identification and he said, 'It's the list of the things we found, just what it says, near the course of flight.' That's the testimony."

The judge looked over at Sawyer.

Glancing up from his file, Sawyer said, "That's about it, Judge. It may not be verbatim, but that's the substance of the record."

"All right," Pearce said. "If you are agreed I need not ask the reporter to read it back. That's all I have . . . I don't wish to set any time limit on myself, but I will surely have decided before five. I'll have the bailiff call your offices and the prisoner." Rising, he added, "Thank you both. You were courteous and professional and presented a clean record. I congratulate both of you on your presentations." With a slight bow, the judge withdrew.

As the spectators behind them began to leave the room, Rogers again walked over to Sawyer. "Well, Bill, that's it . . . can I buy you a drink?"

Apparently uncertain about this invitation, the younger lawyer hesitated.

"C'mon, boy," Rogers said. "You can't sit around in courtrooms all your life waiting for the damn verdict . . . Let's go . . . the bailiff'll call us."

"Well . . ." Sawyer began, looking down at Adam. "I suppose it's O.K. . . . we could come back here then, couldn't we?"

"*You* could. I'll just go to my office . . . but let's get a drink first."

"All right." To Adam, Sawyer said, "I'll be back shortly."

As the lawyers left, Medlicott came forward again to Sawyer's chair to resume his self-appointed role. The reporter and the defendant and the policeman were again the only occupants of the room. Medlicott said nothing to Adam and he was also silent. He seemed utterly withdrawn. His eyes were lightly closed and only his breathing showed that he was alive.

After smoking several cigarettes, Medlicott got up and strolled over to a window and looked out. Then he crossed to the wall where a calendar was hanging. He studied the calendar, although it was perfectly plain, for perhaps ten minutes before returning to his chair. At the table, he read over several old letters taken from his inside coat pocket.

Then he walked again, this time from the front of the court-room to the rear and back again, glancing occasionally at Adam who remained perfectly still except for the rise and fall of his chest.

An hour finally passed, and then another fifteen minutes. Suddenly the bailiff walked briskly from a door to the right of the bench. He picked up the telephone from a desk and dialed. "Harold," the bailiff said, "the judge's ready. Come on over . . . Is Sawyer with you? . . . Good . . . bring him along."

It did not take the lawyers long to reach the courtroom. They strode in, followed by several policemen and specta-tors. Medlicott again left the counsel table and, satisfied that the room was in order, the bailiff disappeared at the judge's door. Then he re-entered the courtroom and Judge Pearce came in and sat down at the bench.

Without even looking up at the lawyers, the judge put on his glasses. In a wholly unnatural tone, he read from a piece of paper, "I find the defendant guilty as charged." Then he removed his glasses, looked at Sawyer and, in a more conversational voice, said, "Under the statute, I have no discretion with respect to the penalty, Mr. Sawyer. The statute mandates a sentence of ten to twenty-five years in the penitentiary, and calls for disenfranchisement for twelve years. Do you understand that?"

Sawyer, who had risen from his chair, answered, "Yes, Judge, I know that's what the statute says."

There was an uncomfortable silence for several moments. Then Judge Pearce motioned to Sawyer and Rogers to come up to the bench. Leaning toward them, he said, "Gentlemen, I'm frankly at a loss as to what to do at this point . . ." He cleared his throat. "If there were to be a motion for new trial as a step prior to appeal, I would, of course, withhold the sentence . . . but . . ." He looked at Sawyer. "Under the circumstances, I doubt if there will be an appeal . . . In any event, I assume he couldn't make bond, since he didn't make it after the arrest. As a matter of fact, I couldn't even find where bond had been set at the time of his arrest, because of his condition, I guess. But I'd be glad to withhold sentence or set a bond to stay the sentence pending appeal. Mr. Sawyer, what do you think?"

Sawyer said, "I hadn't thought about it at all, Judge, and now that it's over with I can admit I really don't know much about the procedure at this point."

The judge said, "Well, the man's entitled to appeal if he wants to, and a bond would stay the sentence, of course. But he can't go free anyway because of his legs. So my idea would be to sentence him and even to sign the commitment right away. This would begin the running of his term and get him into the hospital at the prison . . . It wouldn't stop any appeal, you understand. If an appeal were successful, he'd be released. The only real issue has to do with interim custody and with his defect that's a pretty moot question."

"If you commit him now, he goes right to the prison, today?" Sawyer asked.

"Yes. The sheriff will take him there, in an ambulance, of course, today . . . this afternoon. But what's the alternative . . . ? There really doesn't seem to be anything else to do. Is there, really?"

"No, I guess not," Sawyer said. "All right, Judge, go ahead. I'll try to explain it."

Sawyer returned to Adam's bed. The boy was lying quietly, arms at his sides and eyes closed. Sawyer knelt and touched his shoulder. "You heard the verdict, Adam?"

"Yes, sir." The boy had opened his eyes, but he did not look at Sawyer.

After a pause, Sawyer said, as evenly as possible, "Well, it looks as if they'll take you to the prison today, to the hospital there . . . to see if they can do something about your back."

"Yes."

Although it seemed especially hard going, Sawyer continued. "Well, now, you've got a right to appeal, Adam . . . You can go to a higher court and ask them to review the verdict here . . . to say whether this judge was right or wrong. Do you understand that?"

"Yes, sir," Adam said, and then he asked the logical question which Sawyer had hoped he would not ask. "What would my chances be in the other court?"

Sawyer stammered at first, but he finally said, "Well, it's kind of complicated to explain. But the higher court simply reviews questions of law, like an error on what evidence was admitted in this trial . . . or something like that. Or it could reverse this court if it felt there just wasn't any evidence that tended to prove you were guilty."

Still looking straight ahead, Adam said, "What do you think my chances would be?"

Checking an urge to avoid this question, Sawyer said, "I hate to say this, Adam . . . as a matter of fact, I hate the whole God damned thing, but truthfully I don't think your chances would be any good at all."

The boy hesitated a moment and then quietly said, "Well, then, I guess there's no use to appeal."

Although vastly relieved, Sawyer said, "You don't have to decide that today. You've got thirty days to decide that. I'll give you my card and if you want to appeal, I'll do it for you and do the best I can."

"All right."

Sawyer rose, rubbed his knee and returned to the bench. "Well, Judge, he's ready to go, I guess. I tried to explain the appeal business to him, and said I'd take it for him if he wants to do it."

The judge said, "Well, I guess that's that . . . I'm sorry,

Sawyer. This has been a trying day for all of us. If it's any consolation to you, I'm not convinced that the boy would be better off if he were innocent. And you did a fine job, an excellent job."

"Thank you, Judge. How soon will the sheriff's men be here?"

"I'll have them called right away and expedite the transfer." The judge gathered his papers together and, almost as an afterthought, reached over and shook Sawyer's hand. Then he hurriedly left the room.

Rogers and Sawyer turned from the bench and, as if reluctant to go near Adam, walked slowly to the prosecutor's table. Sawyer stood there as the prosecuting attorney closed his briefcase.

At last, cocking his head toward Adam, Rogers said, "Bill, if they're going to drive him to the prison today, it'll take about two hours . . . I've been . . . wondering. Has he been to the toilet all day?"

"No, he hasn't," Sawyer said. "But that's all messed up, too. He's got some kind of a contraption on to keep him clean. He can't . . . take care of himself."

Rogers grimaced, as if this was the last straw. He shook hands limply with Sawyer and, avoiding Adam, left.

Sawyer was now uncertain what to do. In any professional sense, his role was ended, but he somehow found it difficult to follow the prosecutor from the room. Uncertainly, he sat down as the courtroom emptied and watched the police officers who gathered about the telephone at the bailiff's desk while one of them summoned the sheriff and arranged for Adam's journey.

But Sawyer was not the only one waiting. Looking unusually woebegone and unsure of himself, Jack Medlicott also lingered and finally came forward toward Sawyer. With a glance at Adam, he asked, "What now, Sawyer?"

"Well," Sawyer began, "the sheriff will be here soon and they'll take Adam to the penitentiary . . . The case is over."

Medlicott had realized that the case was over and suspected that the transfer to the penitentiary was being arranged. He said nothing, but stood helplessly for a minute, looking all the while at Adam. Finally, he crossed over to Sawyer's counsel table and slumped into an empty chair.

Another minute or perhaps two passed before the lawyer spoke. Self-consciously clearing his throat, he began tentatively. "Mr. Medlicott . . . it seems to me, quite frankly, that there is really not much more for me to do at this point . . ."

Medlicott looked directly at the lawyer but did not assist him at all.

"My feeling is," continued Sawyer, "that I really may as well excuse myself here . . . and go back to my office to see if there's anything for me to do there."

"Maybe so," Medlicott said.

"Well, then, . . . since you're a friend of Adam's, maybe you could stand by here until the sheriff arrives . . . What do you think?"

"Yes, I'm going to stay."

With almost startling haste, Sawyer was on his feet. Briskly, he picked up his briefcase and swung it to his side. Then, after a moment's hesitation, he walked directly to Adam's bed. "Adam," he said, as the boy opened his eyes, "I . . . I must leave now." Sawyer groped in the pocket of his coat and produced a professional card. "Here's my card . . . Write me, if I can do anything . . . I'm terribly sorry that we lost today."

Adam extended his hand and took the card. "Thank you . . . I'm sorry, too."

Sawyer started to turn away, but stopped again. Leaning forward, he reached for Adam's hand and shook it. Reassured by the unexpectedly strong grip from the helpless boy, Sawyer said, "Goodbye and . . . good luck." Then he walked quickly from the room. Although his spirits rose immediately as he reached the hall, the feeling that he had done a competent job could not overcome his depression at the plight of his former client.

As soon as Sawyer disappeared, Medlicott moved a chair over to Adam's bed and again was seated. Leaning over, he said, "Adam . . . is there anything, . . . I mean *anything* I can do for you?"

"I don't think so."

The reporter sat back and then leaned forward again. "Well, will you do something for me?"

Adam shifted his head and looked at Medlicott, an expression of surprise in his eyes. "Yes?"

"All right . . . here's what I want you to do for me . . . Don't give up. *Don't give up.* Don't let this unspeakable . . . God damned business break you . . . Do you promise?"

Without changing his expression, Adam said, "Yes, sir."

The boy had hardly spoken when a commotion behind them announced the arrival of the sheriff's men. With scarcely a glance at Adam and his companion, the officers, in brown uniforms with brown campaign hats, walked to the bailiff's desk and greeted their counterparts from the police department. Papers were exchanged and the deputies accepted custody of the prisoner. Then they diffidently approached Adam.

Looking inquiringly at Medlicott, one of the deputies spoke to Adam. "Mr. Johnson, I'm Asa Carlson from the sheriff's office . . . We're going to take you to the prison . . . It's quite a drive, so we'd better get moving. Are you ready?"

"Yes," Adam said.

Medlicott stood up and, as the sheriffs began to maneuver the stretcher, he began to walk slowly beside it. The police fell in behind and the procession moved out of the court-room, down the hall, to the elevator and, finally, to the street. At the ambulance, a different one from that used in the morning, Adam was picked up and transferred to another stretcher. His catheter was rearranged and he was raised into the ambulance.

Just before the doors were closed, Medlicott stepped for-ward. "Adam, don't forget your promise to me."

"All right," Adam said, but he looked entirely blank as the doors were shut and the ambulance drove away.

Long before Medlicott had said goodbye, hopelessly and bitterly to walk back to his room, another of Adam's com-panions of the day had expressed himself. Having at first sat staring at his desk, Harold Rogers had sought out the Chief Deputy, Paul Willoughby. Entering his superior's office, Rogers said, "Well, Paul, you can congratulate me. Johnson was convicted."

Without the slightest exultation, Willoughby said, "So I understand . . . You apparently did a good job."

"Yes, I did." Then, in a different and louder voice, Rog-ers said, "We *all* did a real good job. First, we cut his spinal cord, and now we lock him up for twenty-five God damned years . . ." The lawyer's voice grew even louder. "And I'll bet you a bottle of gin he's innocent. I got him because the defense didn't question the evidence about where the woman's stuff was found . . . You really should be proud of me . . . I ought to get some kind of award for repre-senting the people so well. Call it the 'kick-'em-when-they're-down-prize.' "

Startled by this outburst, Willoughby looked up sharply,

but he did not smile. Instead, he shot back, "Cut it out, Harold, for Christ's sake . . . Don't slobber all over me about it . . . The law's the law. If you always want it perfect, why don't you get a job on television?"

Rogers had lowered himself into a chair, but now he was on his feet staring menacingly at the older man. "Now, listen, you son-of-a-bitch," he shouted. "I feel bad. Don't get high and mighty with me. This is one of the really stinking cases in the history of the world. I'll slobber on you or anybody else if I feel like it and if you don't like it you can go straight to hell."

Willoughby bridled but exerted the effort to control himself. After several seconds had passed, he said, very quietly, "All right, Harold, I'm sorry. I can't say anything else about it. Now let's you and me not argue . . . I'm *sincerely* sorry. It's obviously been a very bad day, and I'm grateful to you for handling it for me. I don't want to quarrel with you."

Rogers turned and opened the door and walked into the hall. But in a minute he stuck his head into Willoughby's office and said, "Good night, Paul, I'm going home."

The older man said good night and turned his attention to the papers on his desk.

Rogers walked slowly down the hall.

Judge Pearce arrived at his home a little before six o'clock. Greeting his wife in a perfunctory way, he sat down heavily in the library and accepted a martini from her. For several minutes they sat in silence, the judge looking absently at the headlines in the newspaper on the table beside his chair.

As the judge finished the martini, his wife asked, "Bad day, dear?"

"A horrible day," the judge answered, shaking his head. "The most unpleasant day I've ever put in. If it didn't sound so phony, I'd say that 'duty is a stern guide' or some silly-ass thing like that."

Then Judge Pearce, usually reticent in discussing his duties, began to tell his wife of *State v. Adam Johnson*. Toward the end of the story, he said, "The thing that convinced me, the thing that really cut through everything else, was that the woman's possessions were scattered along Johnson's trail."

"Of course."

"But," the judge continued, speaking out loud, but as if arguing with himself, "the testimony there was so general. As soon as the officer testified, I expected the defense to nail this down. Where exactly were these things, were they in the alley itself, in the bushes or what? Were they strung out down the alley, or were they found in a pile or scattered over a small area so that they could have been thrown away by a man *crossing* the alley? . . . If I'd been the defense I'd have asked these questions, but this Sawyer boy didn't. Then I decided I'd ask the questions myself, if he didn't. But then at lunch, I got to thinking about it . . . The judge isn't supposed to try these cases for the lawyers. He's not supposed to be God. The whole idea of the adversary system is to leave it to the *parties* to try the case . . . When I was practicing it infuriated me for a judge to get into a case and take it away from the lawyers . . . So I decided that the system was more important than this one case. When I was in law school one of the professors used to say that 'hard cases make bad law,' and he was right. So I didn't ask anything about it, and this meant that the boy was guilty on the record. But, God, it was difficult."

"Well, you did do the right thing, Clifford. I'm not a lawyer, but I see what you mean about this. It was a case of legal principles or this poor boy, and you decided on the legal principles. That's what you're supposed to do. I'm sure you were right."

Gratefully, the judge smiled at her and shrugged. "I hope I was . . . but I'm not so sure."

8

Lying in the ambulance working its way through the rush hour traffic, Adam slipped slowly into an almost comatose state, a mixture of absolutely hopeless depression and overpowering nervous fatigue. He was not quite alone because of the two deputies in the front seat. They had the glass partition partly open and were talking about a baseball game. After an initial close look, to make sure that their inert charge was really alive, they only occasionally glanced back at him.

Rocked by the motion of the ambulance, Adam actually dozed off as the vehicle moved through the city. But his sleep was very brief. Underneath the tiredness and despair, a glimmer of will and spirit was there, and all of his nervous reflexes were not yet stilled. The ambulance had reached the highway and was beginning to pick up speed when he woke with a start. He was frightened as he opened his eyes and it took a few minutes to remember where he was. But he soon recognized the plush interior and caught the voices of the deputies and again sank back. Slowly and tentatively, he found himself beginning to think imperfectly about where he was going.

Until now, Adam had been able to avoid thinking about the prison. It had occasionally flashed through his mind, looking always like the prisons in the movies—cold, efficient and full of tense and desperate men, most of them with hideously scarred faces. Now that this was to be his destination, Adam momentarily permitted these pictures to flood his mind. At once he was driven again into hopelessness. He became wide-awake and apprehensive, but he could not think of any way to evade the prison.

The ambulance drove on, its other occupants oblivious to Adam's mood. Because of the lateness of the hour, there was no stop for supper. At last, at about eight-thirty, the vehicle approached the outskirts of the small city where the prison was. His attention called to this by conversation of the sheriff's men, Adam twisted around and raised his head enough to look through the windows into the growing darkness. At first he saw open fields and occasional houses. But then these gave way to a dark cement wall, so high that he was unable to see the top of it. Suddenly the vehicle slowed to a stop before huge metal gates.

As soon as the ambulance stopped, it was flooded by the beams of searchlights which came on from above as if by magic. The deputy who had been driving stepped out into the light. As he did, Adam saw that there was a small brick office building on each side of the gate. The sheriff's man walked to a window in the building on the left and pushed a button.

A voice from a loudspeaker said, "Aren't you guys a little late? What's up?"

Looking up, the deputy called out, "We're from Marion County. The sheriff called ahead and said we'd be here. We've got a convict here who's paralyzed and we had no place for custody. Open up."

There was a pause and the loudspeaker said, "O.K."

In a few minutes the gates swung open, disclosing a small, brightly lighted yard area. The deputy got back in the ambulance and drove through the gates into the yard. Two guards, with black uniforms and police caps, were waiting. The ambulance stopped and both of the sheriff's deputies got out. The gates closed behind them.

To one of the guards, a tall, red-faced man, the deputy who had driven said, "Hello, Ed, how you doing?"

"Why, hello, Sheriff, glad to see you again," the guard said. Turning toward his companion, he added, "This is Sergeant Rockhill."

"Glad to meet you," the deputy said, and he introduced the other deputy to the prison men.

One of the guards said, "Is this the Johnson guy, the back injury?"

"Yeah," the deputy answered.

Sergeant Rockhill said, "I checked up with the warden a minute ago and he approved the admission. The receiving room is closed, though, so we'll put him in the hospital for the night." Motioning toward a doorway to the left of the yard area, he added, "Come on into the office and I'll take the commitment."

All four men entered the doorway and disappeared, leaving Adam and the ambulance alone in the yard. In a few minutes they returned. One of the deputies and Sergeant

Rockhill got into the ambulance and started it up. The vehicle moved slowly forward until it came to two solid metal doors at the interior end of the yard. These opened and the ambulance moved again, turning to the right and following a road along the inside perimeter of the wall.

Adam strained to see the inside of the prison compound. There seemed to be a large open area and buildings of various sizes and shapes, but he could really see very little.

After a few minutes, the ambulance stopped at the dock of a three-story white building. The guard got out and entered, returning promptly with two orderlies, one white, the other a Negro, both in white coats and pants. As the guard watched, the orderlies opened the back of the ambulance and began to pull Adam's stretcher out. It was dark and Adam could not see their faces and no words were spoken.

The orderlies carried the stretcher up a stairway and, while the guard held the door, entered the hospital and stopped at a small out-patient room with white walls and a single bed. At the guard's direction, they lifted Adam to the bed. One of them immediately detached Adam's catheter and waste bottle, returning in a few minutes with these articles washed and cleaned. Then both orderlies left the room.

The guard remained with Adam. Looking at him in a kindly way, he said, "Adam, I'm Sergeant Rockhill . . . would you like to have a cigarette?"

"No, thank you," Adam said mechanically.

"All right." The sergeant hesitated and said, "Now, you'll only be in this room for tonight . . . until you can be properly checked in tomorrow. These orderlies will be instructed to get you washed and cleaned up and to get you some supper and breakfast in the morning . . ."

"Yes, sir."

"Incidentally," the sergeant continued, "these men are fellow inmates, not guards." Then he pointed to a goose-

neck light extended over Adam's bed. "I think you can
reach that lamp. After you've eaten, you can turn it out . . .
I'll see you in the morning."

"Yes, sir," Adam said.

The sergeant left. In a few minutes the orderlies returned. In the light, Adam saw that they were young men,
perhaps his age. Their names were Red and Eddie. In contrast to their previous austerity, both men now seemed
friendly and outspoken.

As soon as their names were exchanged, Red said, "What's
the rap?"

Adam hesitated. "I don't know what you mean."

"I mean what are you in for . . . what's the charge?"

"Well, some woman said I robbed her, but I didn't."

"You didn't . . . what do you mean, you didn't?"

Although tense and a little bewildered, Adam said, "I
mean I'm not guilty . . . I didn't steal it."

Smiling and glancing at his Negro companion, Red said,
"Well, what do you know, Eddie! By God, the bastards
framed him . . ." Then he looked again at Adam and lowered his voice. "O.K., kid, we're for you. Now let's us get
you washed up. The guard says this bullet screwed up your
bowels and kidneys. Is that right?"

"Yes." And then because Red had reassured him, Adam
also said, "I'm awfully sorry . . . It's the worst thing about
it."

Shrugging his shoulders elaborately, Red said, "Don't
apologize . . . For Christ's sake, we wouldn't be on this job
if we was known for weak stomachs . . ." To the Negro he
said, "Come on, Eddie, give me a hand."

With surprising finesse and gentleness, the prisoners un-
dressed and bathed Adam and put him in a clean gown.
Then they left. But Eddie returned later with a tray of food
which Adam, his head propped up with pillows, ate while
the Negro sat silently beside him.

After he had eaten, Adam forced himself to ask Eddie to turn him on his stomach for the night. The man quickly and competently accomplished this. Then, after a quiet "Good night," the orderly left the room.

Adam lay still at first, eyes open, wishing that he had had the courage to ask Red and Eddie what the prison was like. Finally, having tried unsuccessfully to reach the light switch from his stomach-down position, he closed his eyes and fell asleep.

At 6 A.M. someone touched Adam and he awakened at once. In the too bright morning light, he looked up into a new but broadly smiling face, surmounting the white uniform of an orderly. Adam started. The face was astonishingly ugly—scarred, pockmarked, almost toothless and poorly put together in the first place. But above the nose—it was large and had apparently at one time been sliced off and carelessly sewed back on—were large and wholly benign eyes. Before Adam could organize his thoughts about the face, it spoke to him in the hill-billy accents of Arkansas or southwestern Oklahoma.

"Name's Sam, son. Sam Masters, if you care for the whole thing . . . which around here don't have much importance . . . I'm s'posed to get you ready and fed so's they can take you to the receivin' room."

Almost transfixed by the face, Adam could say nothing. Finally, he looked down from the face to the body. Although Sam was obviously an old man, he was slender and hard-looking, with muscular arms protruding from the short sleeves of his uniform.

Having waited long enough for Adam to say something, Sam asked, "How you feelin'?"

Adam said, "I'm all right." And then, assisted by the fact that Sam was an old man with white hair, he asked, "What's the receiving room?"

"It's where they sign you in, mister . . . it don't take long." Sam was silent a few moments. "What's wrong with you anyway?"

"It's my legs. They're paralyzed . . . I can't move them."

"Why?"

"They . . . the police shot me . . . in the spine."

With apparently genuine shock and concern, Sam whistled loudly. "*Jesus,* you're in a bad way, boy." But he immediately brightened. "Well, maybe you'll get better. I bet you will."

"Thanks," Adam said.

But Sam was not yet satisfied. Pointing to the tube, and the glass container under the bed, he asked, "What's that?"

"It's a catheter." Seeing that Sam did not understand, he slowly added, "This bullet, it also wrecked my bowels and bladder. That's for peeing . . . because I can't do it myself, and I have to take enemas . . ."

Sam shuddered and curled his lip up over his few teeth. His mobile features then settled down again. "Christ, boy, don't worry about Ol' Sam and enemas. If I didn't give somebody an enema every day, I'd miss the day entirely." Looking very thoughtful, he said, "You know, if you ask me, it's a good deal better way to crap anyway . . . I mean it . . . I think it's probably better for you. Don't you?"

"I guess it is."

"Well, fine," Sam said, as if the issue was closed. "Now, boy, you wait here, and Sam'll fix you up . . . inside and out, you'll see."

The old man turned and disappeared, but he was back in a minute and expertly administered an enema. Having turned Adam over on his back, Sam brought in a basin of water, soap and a towel. "Here. You can't shave yet until they give permission. I'll go get some food." He put the toilet facilities down, and with one wiry arm propped

Adam's head up, setting pillows behind it. Then he put the basin on Adam's stomach, set down the towel and soap and left again.

Adam washed himself as well as he could. He was interrupted several times by men passing up and down the hallway. Each one looked in inquiringly and several said good morning.

Sam soon reappeared with a tray of food—orange juice, toast, fried eggs, bacon and coffee. "Here it is," he said, replacing the basin with the tray.

Adam thanked him and began to eat as Sam, leaning against a small table in the corner, watched.

After a few minutes of silence, Sam began to talk. "You ever been in prison before?"

"No."

Sam smiled. "Sam thought not . . . I can tell most of the time and I told myself already that this was your first time around."

Adam was tempted to try to explain how he had gotten where he was, but he kept on eating and said nothing.

Sam waited a minute or two before continuing. "It's not as bad as you think once you know the ropes . . . Sam's kind of an old-timer . . . been here thirty-four years off and on . . . and if you use your head, it's got lots of advantages . . . I've tried it both ways, inside and out, and I say that guys like Sam has a better break in than out . . . And that's a fact."

These were certainly new ideas to Adam, and he looked fixedly at the old man.

Interpreting Adam's attentiveness as skepticism, Sam pressed his point. "Now, look at it this way . . . On the outside there's always somebody ready to kick you in the ass . . ." He shook his head for emphasis. "I mean it. You try to do all right and wham! . . . you're out of a job . . .

or you owe somebody a hundred dollars and maybe you're broke so some big son-of-a-bitch calls you a dirty name or calls the cops on you." Sam shrugged elaborately. "Now in here, it's different. You take the guards, they're all right . . . I'm not saying you'd pick 'em out to be your special pals if you was pickin' special pals, but they're O.K. . . . They don't bother you if you don't bother them . . . And then there's the prisoners. Most of them, at least ninety percent, is absolutely O.K. The others is poison like a snake . . . So you just be choosy, that's all, and you're O.K., too."

Carried along by Sam's glowing description of his companions, Adam began to feel better. He had finished his food and said, "How do you tell who the snakes are?"

"Why, you ask Sam, son. Sam knows the snakes on sight . . . You ask Sam, ask me anything, 'cause I *know* and the guys that count are Sam's friends. See?"

"Yes, I see," Adam said tentatively. "Thanks."

Before the older man could resume, two guards entered the little room. Sam saluted with his left hand and they smiled at him. "Mornin', gentlemen," Sam said. "This here is Adam Johnson." Turning to Adam, he said, "Adam, this is Fred and Ken . . . they's all right."

The guards answered Sam's greeting and nodded to Adam.

"Is he ready, Sam?" asked the guard named Ken.

"He is. Ol' Sam's took care of him."

Sam removed the tray from Adam's stomach and took the pillows from behind his head. Then he opened a closet at the end of the room and produced a canvas stretcher which he unfolded and laid on the floor. He and the guards lifted Adam up and lowered him to the stretcher. After placing the waste jug between Adam's legs, Sam got on his hands and knees and put Adam's shoes and socks on. The old man then stood aside. The guards squatted at either end of the stretcher and raised it up.

"O.K., Fred, you go first," said Ken. As they moved out of the room, he said, "Thanks, Sam, see you later."

Sam followed them to the hospital doorway and held the door as they passed through.

The summer sun was up and shining very brightly as Adam was carried into the yard. Looking around, he saw a number of buildings and beyond them, on all sides, the high wall. There were not many people about, just a few guards and a few inmates wearing white coveralls. Adam's attention was particularly taken by the lawns and the numerous flower beds around the buildings. On either side of the walk which his stretcher followed was a border of marigolds.

After a walk of perhaps half a block, Adam came in sight of a limestone building with a sign over the door, SERVICE BUILDING NO. 1. Here the guards turned in and carried Adam up a flight of stairs into a hallway. They walked down the hall, past rooms marked COMMISSARY, BARBER SHOP and LI- BRARY, before entering one with RECEIVING ROOM above the doorway. There, beyond a lobby outfitted with metal chairs, were three open doors, each leading into a smaller room equipped with a desk and a chair. A guard sat at the door of one of the smaller rooms and he came forward as Adam was brought in.

Pointing to the nearest of the smaller rooms, the guard said, "Put him in there, Fred . . . Gibson will take him now. We want to get him through before the others arrive."

The stretcher carriers veered and entered the room.

Mr. Gibson, a receiving clerk in civilian clothes, sat at the desk, a file before him. He looked up and greeted the procession and introduced himself to Adam. To the guards he said, "Put him down, please. I already have the commitment and have it checked and numbered."

The guards lowered Adam's stretcher to the floor and sat down in chairs near the door.

The receiving clerk asked Adam a few questions. Then he said, "Johnson, it will be necessary for you to remove the hospital gown and wear this uniform." He held up a pair of white coveralls like those Adam had seen in the yard. "Then you'll be sent to the Administration and Orientation Unit." Turning to the guards, he said, "Help him here, men, to put the coveralls on."

Despite their obvious distaste, the guards got down beside Adam and, having clumsily manipulated the catheter, pulled the gown off over his head. After further trial and error, the coveralls were put on and buttoned up.

At another word from the clerk, the stretcher was again raised up. As it passed out into the lobby, Gibson called out, "Good luck, Johnson." Adam inaudibly said, "Thank you."

From Service Building No. 1, Adam and his bearers proceeded to the Administration Building, a new structure of several stories. The second floor housed the Administration and Orientation Unit. It contained fifty single cells and Adam was told that all new inmates were assigned there during their first thirty days at the prison. Adam and his guards were carried to the second floor on an elevator operated by another guard. Leaving the elevator, they went through two sets of metal, electrically operated doors.

Inside the highly polished and lighted Administration and Orientation Unit, Adam was presented to the officer-in-charge, Lieutenant Richman. Unlike the other officials, the lieutenant visibly reacted to his physical condition. He greeted Adam in a faintly friendly way, but his face set again at once. He questioned the guards sharply. "What's the matter with him?"

The man named Ken answered. "Well, his legs are paralyzed."

The lieutenant started. "*Paralyzed*—for good?"

Ken said, "That's what they say."

Richman spoke irritably. "Did they or the warden say

what I'm supposed to do with him? We're not set up here to handle an invalided man . . . I haven't got that kind of help, Jesus Christ."

Ignoring the latter part of the lieutenant's outburst, the guard said, "We were told to bring him here. That's all. Where do you want him?"

Richman looked at Adam, who lay quietly in the stretcher suspended between the guards. "Can't you sit up?"

Adam said, "I . . . I don't know . . . I don't think I can by myself. I haven't since I was hurt."

Richman pushed a straight back chair forward. To the guards he said, "All right, men, sit him up in this chair and hold on to his shoulders for a minute. I'll see what I can do about him."

The guards put the stretcher down and, grabbing hold of Adam, placed him upright on the chair.

Adam was stricken at once. He uttered a muffled cry. His arms shot out and his head fell forward and he vomited. Choking on the vomit, he lurched forward and would have struck the floor if the guards had not held on to his shoulders. Moaning, he continued to retch, his entire body jerking wildly. The guards let him down to the floor. Stomach down and breathing heavily, he settled into a shapeless mass and seemed to subside, although his body continued to twitch.

Richman and the guards were white. For a minute they simply stared stupidly at Adam and each other. All three seemed to be on the verge of getting sick themselves. With an eye on Adam, Richman finally picked up the telephone and got the warden on the line.

"This is Richman," the lieutenant said, speaking in a restrained voice. "I've got a new admission here who's paralyzed in the legs, and very sick. They just brought him in. I'd like to know how I'm supposed to process him?"

There was a pause as the warden spoke. Then Richman

said, "Yes, I can photograph and print him all right, but I can't very well give him the whole program. He's already puked all over the office. I can't keep a sick man . . . Who'll feed him?"

Another silence took place, followed by Richman's saying, "All right. I'll get him started, but we'd better decide on it right away. Thank you." He hung up and sat down heavily. "Fellows, let's put him back on the stretcher, carefully . . . and maybe one of you would get some paper towels and wipe up this place."

The guards knelt down and turned Adam over. He said nothing. He was terrified and his body was very rigid above the waist. Although his face was flecked with vomit, he made no effort to wipe it off. The guards lifted him onto the stretcher and one of them brought some paper towels. All three of the men began to wipe up and Richman even wiped Adam's face.

After the towels were disposed of, at Richman's direction Adam was carried down the hall to the identification room. With Richman and the two guards dourly standing by, a flustered clerk improvised a means of photographing Adam lying down with the identifying number resting on his chest. The clerk then took Adam's prints and he was carried back to Lieutenant Richman's room.

Warden Ross M. Bartlow and the deputy warden in charge of custody were waiting in the lieutenant's office. They were introduced to Adam by Lieutenant Richman.

The warden, a tall, slender man in his early forties, crouched beside Adam as he was lowered to the floor. "To tell the truth, Johnson, we're not entirely familiar with the kind of situation which your custody presents. I've gone over the records here and I realize now that you're a paraplegic. You've also got a bowel and kidney problem. Is that so?"

Adam nodded.

"You see, Johnson, you're supposed to be in this unit for thirty days . . . for educational testing, orientation and classification . . . but we don't really see how we can handle you here. So I'm sending you back over to the hospital until we've figured it out."

Adam did not understand that his opinion was being sought, but he said, "All right."

Bartlow turned to Lieutenant Richman. "I'll call the hospital and talk to Dr. Forbes about this . . . You have two of your men take him back over there. Maybe a social history will help us decide what to do, after we get more medical stuff, so send a counselor over as soon as he's settled in." To the deputy warden Bartlow said, "This is your baby. We've got to work out some arrangements here."

The deputy warden nodded, and he and Bartlow left.

Richman and the guards followed their superiors out of the room, leaving Adam alone. He waited for almost half an hour before the guards returned. Then he was picked up and carried again to the hospital.

9

WHILE Adam and his guards were on the way to the hospital on the return trip, the deputy warden in charge of custody telephoned ahead to arrange for a regular bed. At the entrance to the hospital, Sam was waiting to tell of Adam's assignment. He smiled a welcome to the group. "Back pretty soon, ain't you?"

"Yes," one of the guards said. "They can't really take care of him over at the unit . . . Where do we go now, Sam?"

"Follow Sam," Sam said. As they started up a flight of stairs, he added, "You know, Sam kind of expected you back. Fact is, I would of expected the big boys to already know that you couldn't keep a hurt man over there in a damn cell. It don't make sense."

The guards were silent with their burden, but Sam was not. "You see, Sam could of told you all along that we know how to take care of a sick man, but them guys there don't . . . Do you know what I mean?"

Accustomed to Sam's infallibility, the guards ordinarily did not resent it. But on this occasion one of them answered, "Yes, Sam, you're right . . . We get the point . . . You needn't explain it."

Sam looked back over his shoulder and smiled innocently. "Well, I'm glad you see it . . . *now*. This way you won't be luggin' him back and forth again, at least."

By the time Sam had finished, the group had entered a ward. It was bright and terribly sanitary looking and contained twenty beds. Four other prisoners were there, widely scattered over the room, but the rest of the beds were empty. Sam guided the guards to a bed near a window, removed from the other occupied beds. Adam was deposited, the catheter was arranged and the guards left.

As soon as they were out of the way, Sam removed the coveralls and again put Adam in a hospital gown. Noticing the smell of vomit, he bathed him and then, at Adam's request, helped him get over on his stomach.

"Now, Adam, the doc is going to talk to you," Sam said. "He told Sam to tell him when you got here."

"All right," Adam said.

"Sam will go get him now. You wait."

Sam left the room and returned shortly with Dr. Forbes. He introduced the physician and sat down on an empty bed next to Adam to participate in the interview.

Ignoring Sam's presence, Dr. Forbes drew up a chair and sat down. "Johnson," he said, "there's apparently been a mixup here. I assume that there are medical records on you, but they aren't here yet, so I must ask you a few questions."

"Yes, sir."

"Sam here tells me you were shot. Is that correct?"

"Yes, sir."

"Where?"

"In the back."

"Let me have a look at it . . ." the physician said.

Doctor Forbes threw back Adam's sheet and pushed up his gown. He examined the bullet scar and also looked at the scar on the buttocks left by the sore that Adam had had at City Hospital.

"Do you know whether they took the bullet out?" the doctor asked.

Adam said, "No, they didn't . . . They said they couldn't."

"I see. And they say the cord was damaged?"

"Yes, sir. They said it was cut in two."

As if to himself, Dr. Forbes said, "Well, that figures." Then he asked, "You were at City Hospital, weren't you?"

"Yes, sir, the big one."

The doctor rose. "All right. We must get the records here and we'll run them down right away. Thank you, son. You've been very helpful."

"Yes, sir," Adam said, as the doctor walked away.

Sam moved over to the end of Adam's bed. Craning his neck so that he could look at Adam's face, he said, "Can you read?"

"*Yes,* I can read."

Noticing the protest in his voice, Sam said, "Well, I'm askin' because I'm tryin' to think of how to help out. Lyin' on your face, or your ass, either, for that matter . . . you ain't going to be too easy to entertain . . . unless you read."

The necessity of answering Dr. Forbes' questions had aroused Adam briefly, but the painful and frightening episode in the Administration Building had deepened his depression and withdrawal. He simply could not cope with Sam. "I don't want to read," he said finally, and he closed his eyes.

Sam made a face and was silent. He seemed to be thinking about his next move. After perhaps three minutes, he said blandly, "What you plannin' on doin', son, if you ain't gonna read?"

Adam said, "What?"

"I said, what you gonna do? You gotta do somethin' and I'd like to help you out."

"I can't do anything. I don't want to do anything."

Although seriously perplexed, Sam proceeded instinctively. Assuming a slightly different tone he said, "Look here, Adam, ol' Sam is on your side . . . I don't want to hurt your feelin's, but I think you better make up your mind. Are you goin' to lie there and just sort of die or are you goin' to try a little? I'd like to help you."

"I don't *want* any help," Adam said with surprising vigor. "I'm not asking for help . . . and even if I was, you couldn't help. There isn't any help." Adam swallowed. "And . . . as for dying . . . I don't care about that."

Sam stared at the boy and seemed about to say something, but he checked himself and got off the bed. Hands in his pockets, he walked over to the window and looked out for a long time. Finally he turned around and moved back beside Adam. Slowly he let himself down to the floor and sat there, his face directly opposite Adam's.

Sam smiled before he spoke, and his voice was very even and soft. "What you said was kinda funny, Adam. I guess maybe you didn't ask for my help . . . I didn't say you did . . . but I reckon *I'll* decide who I'm gonna help, and who I ain't. That's *my* business, nobody else's, and I don't stand on too much ceremony about bein' asked."

Adam looked directly into Sam's face and his blank eyes seemed to flicker, but he said nothing.

"Now as for not wantin' help, and thinkin' about dyin', that's your privilege. I think somebody who's got two eyes and two ears and two hands, and who can talk and think . . . and eat and sleep . . . I think that a man like that who just don't care is crazy. I just don't figure him . . . Even if he's got a right to, I got a right to say he's wrong." Sam shook his head. "He ain't only wrong, I say he's a God damn fool . . . but, of course, that's his privilege, irregardless. You hear me, Adam?"

"Yes," Adam answered.

"So since a man like that is such a fool, I don't reckon I have to pay much heed when he says he don't want no help. You see, he don't really know what he's talkin' about, when that fella says that, because everybody's got to have somebody helpin' him . . . *everybody*. You think about that . . . Even some rich guy walkin' around on the outside with his pockets stickin' out full of money, even he's gotta have help, everybody knows that." Sam nodded his head for emphasis. "So, like I said, Sam don't bother much about your not wantin' help, since you ain't really a fool, or if you are, I know better. See?"

"Yes," Adam said.

"What I'm sayin' is that Sam's goin' to help you, no matter what, because as I was sayin', I'm on your side . . . and I'm goin' to help no matter how you act . . . But it'll be a lot more fun if you try a little. And at least you had ought to try a while. You just got here last night, boy, you hadn't ought to quit until you see what it's like. Now, should you?"

Adam blinked. After several moments, he said, "Maybe not."

"There ain't really no maybe about it, Adam. Don't you get what I'm sayin'?" Sam said firmly.

"Yes, sir, I do."

"Well, that's *fine*." Sam's comic face switched from its serious look to a smile. "Now you quit callin' me 'sir' and call me 'Sam,' like a proper friend, and I'll get you somethin' to read."

Sam stood up and left, but he was back almost at once and, using a chair, rigged up a platform to hold several dog-eared magazines he carried. A test showed that Adam could turn the pages. Having congratulated himself several times, Sam turned to leave again. Just before he was out of earshot, Adam spoke to him.

"Thanks, Sam," Adam said softly.

The old man looked back and smiled broadly. "Don't mention it, Adam."

The days that immediately followed Adam's admission to the prison were crowded with visitors. He was first interviewed at length by a staff social worker. Following an official form, this man carefully obtained the materials for a report. Adam saw that the form contained a space for data about *Family, Childhood, Adolescence, Adulthood, Neighborhood, Employment* and *Plans*. On the basis of his report the social worker was later to submit his recommendation to the Classification Committee:

> *Custody and Discipline:* Hospital
> *Transfer:* Not indicated
> *Social:* Community investigation, to determine
>   nature and circumstances of the crime
> *Special Treatment:* Medical aid
> *Program:*
>   *Work:* Not employable
>   *Educational:* To school if practical in view
>   of physical
>   *Religious:* No recommendation

> *Recreational:* No recommendation
> *Reclassification:* None indicated—except for clemency or parole some years hence.

On the heels of the social worker came a staff psychologist who also spent several hours with Adam. Having administered a number of tests, the psychologist's report identified his IQ and educational achievements.

The psychologist also filled out a printed form concerning the new prisoner's *Present Demeanor and Attitudes, Abilities and Aptitudes,* and *Personality and Special Problems.*

The psychologist's *Summary,* which Adam did not see, said that Adam was "friendly, cooperative and soft spoken; he appears to be intelligent and his grammar and diction are good." Following this the *Summary* said:

> Despite some withdrawal, he is not reticent although he seems to control his statements. He does not demonstrate hostility or resentment toward the unfortunate events of his life. He is, in short, *adjusted,* with some repression of the feelings which he must inevitably have.
>
> Adam Johnson will adjust well to institutional life. He will constitute no custody problem.

The report of the psychologist to the Classification Committee was much like the social worker's, except that it urged cell study courses in view of the prisoner's relatively superior intelligence and educational training.

Chaplain Adcock, an elderly Presbyterian, was the last to report to the Classification Committee. Although kind to Adam, the minister reported that "it is difficult to commucate with the prisoner regarding things of the spirit." Noting Adam's lack of religious training or experience, the chaplain concluded that "no specific religious needs exist;

the relationship of the office of chaplain and the prisoner must await an awakening of his religious interests."

Confronted with these reports, for custody the Classification Committee decided to leave Adam in the hospital where he was. "No recommendation" appeared opposite all other headings of its report except "Medical." There the committee urged that "appropriate medical treatment" be given.

Backed up by the Classification Committee's recommendation, Warden Bartlow authorized Dr. Forbes to employ a consulting physician for Adam. A week had passed since Adam's entrance to the prison and his medical records from City Hospital had finally reached the prison hospital. With these before him, Dr. Forbes contacted Dr. William Warfel, a Chicago paraplegia specialist, who agreed to see Adam the following week.

Arriving at the consulting room in the prison hospital, Dr. Warfel first studied the X-rays and records forwarded from City Hospital.

Dr. Forbes at first silently stood by. After several minutes, he said, "I know very little about paraplegia, Doctor, but I do understand that it is irremedial."

Dr. Warfel only grunted as he looked at an X-ray through a view box.

Forbes continued. "The point, of course, is that this man is sentenced here for a long term. Robbery. We don't know what in the devil to do with him. I think the warden's hope is to build a case for getting him out of here some way. In the meantime, and I am aware of the risks of infection . . . the renal disfunction is especially risky, I know . . . we're obligated to keep him healthy."

Without looking away from the X-ray, Dr. Warfel said, "The antibiotics are the saviors of these cases. Twenty years ago, they were terminated pretty quickly. Today, they can go on forever."

"Yes, I suppose that's true."

After several more minutes of study, the specialist said, "Let's have a look at him."

"All right," Forbes said. He walked to the door and spoke with Sam, who had somehow learned of Dr. Warfel's presence and the reason for his visit.

In a few minutes Sam wheeled Adam into the room on a surgical table. The specialist was still looking over a report and did not glance up. Dr. Forbes helped Sam place the table and position the powerful examination lights above it. Then Dr. Warfel moved over beside his patient and looked down into his face.

Turning toward the specialist, Dr. Forbes said, "This is Mr. Johnson, Dr. Warfel."

Dr. Warfel nodded, but said nothing to Adam. To Sam and Forbes he said, "Put him on his stomach, please."

They turned Adam over.

Dr. Warfel raised up the surgical gown and examined Adam's back. Noticing the scar on his buttocks, he looked up sharply. "When did he have this decubitis ulcer?"

"Before we got him, Doctor," Forbes answered. "I assume it happened while he was waiting for the trial."

"It was a nasty one," Dr. Warfel said. Bent down over Adam's back again, he asked, "What about muscle spasms . . . does he have them frequently?"

"I think not, Doctor," answered Forbes.

Having kneaded Adam's back a number of times, Dr. Warfel asked that he be turned over. This done, he began to maneuver Adam's legs and feet and question him directly about his reactions. After perhaps fifteen minutes, Dr. Warfel moved away and sat down. Lighting a cigarette, he drew deeply on it before speaking.

"Well, Dr. Forbes," Warfel began, "it's a fairly typical case. I might quarrel with the reports on the question of whether the cord is actually severed . . . It could be trauma. But the net effect is the same. Nothing can be done about the paralysis."

"That's what I had understood," Forbes said.

The specialist nodded. "The real fight is defensive, from here on. You're faced with a variety of risks, some of which can be minimized at least. A certain amount of circulatory deterioration is inevitable. Bone weakness . . . from porosity . . . is also largely unavoidable. Muscular atrophy is already pretty well advanced in the extremities immediately affected."

"Yes, I've noticed that, at least."

"Of course. Now certain specific things can be avoided." Warfel held up an index finger. "In the first place, the decubitis ulcers. He must not rest in any one position for more than three, or maybe four, hours at any time. Even if he were seated he'd have to shift around on his rump. This, plus keeping him absolutely clean, will avoid the ulcers . . ."

"Well, we can manage that, I think."

"Good." Holding up another finger, Warfel said, "Contractures are number two. He's lucky in this respect, so far, but his joints—hips, knees, ankles, even his toes—must be moved from time to time, or they'll lock. If he were trained to it, he could do it himself. If he can't do it, someone else will have to. Do you understand?"

"Yes, of course." Smiling ruefully, Forbes added, "All of this simply emphasizes how absurd it is for us to have him here."

"Yes, it is, I'm afraid. As to his bowels and kidneys . . . you mentioned the renal disfunction . . . this is a matter of hygiene, insofar as it is controllable. If there is infection, then you treat it in the ordinary way and hope for the best."

"We've been lucky there, thus far."

"Luck is a part of it, I suppose, and the general health and strength of the victim," Dr. Warfel said. He pointed at

Adam. "He was an exceptionally powerful man, I would judge, and he should have as good a chance as anybody . . . and this gets around to the really difficult questions."

Dr. Forbes had also moved to a chair and was seated by this time. Adam lay where he had been. He had hardly moved, except that he had raised his right hand to his eyes to shield them from the lights. Sam stood motionless in the corner of the room toward the door.

"The truth is, Dr. Forbes, that you must ultimately, and soon at that, get him off his back. All of these secondary physical problems are immeasurably lessened if the man is up, at least sitting and later walking . . ."

"I can see that," Forbes said.

Without acknowledging the interruption, the specialist continued. "And, of course, the whole psychological aspect of the matter is improved by physical improvement . . . I've made no specific psychological diagnosis here . . . it's really not my line, of course . . . but typically the psychological damage is extremely severe." Dr. Warfel paused to light another cigarette. Through the initial smoke, he said, "You know, the pain, the paralysis, the permanent harm to the urinal-genital system. It's emasculating, not technically, but effectively, to the patient. All of these things tend to break down the personality, and part of the therapy is to help the patient to *some* sort of life out of bed."

Dr. Forbes shook his head dolefully. "This man ought not be here. It's absurd to confront such a medical program with this kind of facility."

"Of course. In my written report I will express this view . . . the things that are essential in treatment, both physically and psychologically, are unavailable here. But suppose he nevertheless remains on your hands? What I'm suggesting is that it is critical for him to get into a sitting position, and from the level of paralysis I don't think it will be much of a trick in this case . . . if you go at it gradually so that he can adjust. Otherwise, of course, he'll be nauseated, and a severe lowering of the blood pressure will result."

"That's happened once," Dr. Forbes said.

"Well, that's too bad, because it unnerves the patient for later attempts. By the way, I assume that you have a wheelchair?

"Oh, yes, we've several."

"Well, that's the next move. Of course, he won't be able to move it himself. What he really needs is an aluminum chair, the lightweight kind that a paraplegic can move himself . . . Then, if he were a private patient and after the physical therapists said 'O.K.,' he'd go to leg braces and cuff type crutches. The braces would have locked knee joints and the ankle joint might have a 90 degree stop." The specialist looked over at Adam speculatively. "The precise character of the braces can't be predicted. Judging from the level here they would probably extend to a pelvic band, ischial weight bearing . . . probably. It would be a long hard pull but, depending a lot on the patient's *will*, the extent of the psychological damage, it could probably be done and he'd be on his feet. His chances, ultimately, unless he gets to walking, are not good. All of this could happen in the proper environment. Here . . ." The physician shook his head and looked at the floor. "I'm not so sure."

"Of course not," Dr. Forbes said. "Among other things, a full program for this man would cost a fortune."

"Yes, it would." The specialist rose from his chair. "But I'll put all of this in my report. I'll set forth the standard procedures and recommendations, even if they are impossible in the circumstances . . ." Warfel looked directly at Forbes. "There isn't any standard *makeshift* program for paraplegics. If there was, I'd tell you, Doctor."

"I know you would," Dr. Forbes said. He, too, had risen

and stood with his hands in his pockets. "Based on your report, we'll move heaven and earth to get him out of here. If we can't do it soon, we'll just have to care for him the best we can."

"Right," Dr. Warfel said, picking up his medical bag.

To Sam, Dr. Forbes said, "Get him back in bed, will you please."

Sam nodded and the physicians walked out of the room. As they went down the hall, Dr. Forbes said, "There's one thing I'm not clear on, Dr. Warfel."

"What's that?"

"Well, regarding these braces, I'm wondering what sort of time schedule would ordinarily be observed. If he were a regular patient of yours, when would the braces come into the picture, to get him on his feet?"

"I don't like to deal with that issue on a general rule basis, Doctor. I made no neurological findings, of course, and he has not been seen in this respect since the early days of the injury."

"I see," Forbes said.

"Yes. However, judging from the reports, and in view of my own examination, I'd say that he'll have to be in braces relatively soon . . . or not at all."

"You mean . . ." Forbes began.

"I mean simply that the indications are that he'll have to be in braces within six months . . . say by about March 1 of next year . . . or the bone weakness and muscular deterioration will be too far advanced for him to make it."

Forbes whistled under his breath. "That soon?"

"Yes, I think so, at least in terms of any existing orthopedic devices which would permit him to get around and be useful at all . . . I should say, incidentally, that despite his obvious physical vigor, the City Hospital reports establish that his bone structure was not of the strongest, apparently as a result of childhood malnutrition . . . not severe, but sufficient to have marked him. In the ordinary circumstance this might never have manifested itself symptomatically, but when you're talking about forcing other parts of the skeleton to bear the weight of his body and carry the braces, it becomes material. This is a factor which prompts my view of the six months."

The physicians had by this time reached the hospital exit. "Well," Forbes said, "that means that we'd better hurry in arranging placement for him out of this hospital."

"Yes, I suppose it does, Doctor." Warfel bade Forbes goodbye and left the building.

While the doctors were talking, Sam was maneuvering the surgical table down another corridor toward Adam's ward. After several minutes of silence, he slowed down. "I hope that don't make you feel too bad, Adam, all that big doctor talk. Maybe they're wrong about it anyway."

"No, it don't bother me much anymore, Sam. I've heard it all before."

"Of course," Sam said, enthusiasm returning to his voice, "even that doc admitted that you could learn to sit up and then walk. That don't sound so bad, does it?"

To Sam's infinite pleasure, Adam said, "No, not bad at all. I'd like that a lot."

By this time, they were beside the bed and Sam got Adam into it. Looking at the boy, he said earnestly, "We're going to start gettin' you used to sittin' up some in bed. It won't feel so good at first, but we've got to do it before you get into a wheelchair."

"All right."

Sam moved immediately to the end of the bed and began to operate the cranks and levers there. Slowly the bed rose under Adam's back, pushing him toward an upright position.

With his eyes unusually wide open and bright, he clutched the mattress and began to sweat. The bed stopped with Adam in a halfway sitting position. He breathed heavily and blinked a number of times, but finally seemed to settle down.

Watching closely and still at the foot of the bed, Sam said, "How about it, boy? You O.K.?"

"I think so."

"Good work." Sam moved around beside the boy. His comical face folded into its most grotesque grin and he put a heavy hand on Adam's shoulder. "You've just took the first step on the road to recovery. Tomorrow you'll take another . . . every day we'll take one. Won't we?"

Adam turned his head toward Sam. He was a little pale, but he said, "I think so, Sam."

"That's *fine,*" Sam said, and he walked briskly away.

Adam's "sittin' up exercises," as Sam called them, continued for the rest of the week, while Dr. Forbes awaited the formal report of Dr. Warfel. Relying on his own understanding of the proper regime, each day Sam insisted that Adam sit up in bed a little straighter and a little longer. It was an effort but Adam did not complain, despite the back pains and fatigue, and the dizziness which he always conquered just as it was about to conquer him.

Shortly after breakfast exactly one week after Dr. Warfel's visit, Sam approached Adam's bed pushing a venerable wooden wheelchair with a cane back and seat. Sam could barely restrain his enthusiasm. "Here's your chair, Adam, and *today* is *the* day . . . ol' Sam knows."

Although sitting almost upright in bed, Adam looked scared. Nervously opening and closing his fingers, he said, "Well, Sam, *you* know, but I don't . . . how am I going to get on it? What if I get sick?"

"I'll get you on it, and you won't get sick." Sam stood directly beside Adam and seized the sheet to throw it back.

But Adam's face was very flushed and his jaw was fixed. Holding the sheet down, he said through his teeth, "Sam, I don't feel like getting on that chair . . . *I don't want to . . .*"

Sam stiffened. He stood completely still for a minute, looking down at Adam, whose eyes were averted. "All right, Adam," he said finally. "Sam sure as hell can't make you do it . . ." Relaxing his grip on the sheet, he stepped back and sat down on the wheelchair. "I wish I could, by God, but nobody is gonna make you get off your big ass, but *yourself.* And if you don't get off your ass, you ain't gonna get them braces and walk. Sam just wanted you to get them braces so's you could walk."

Adam's natural color had returned. He sat now with his head bowed, his hands limp in front of him on the sheet. Sam saw the tears begin and saw his chest heave with silent sobs.

A few minutes passed before Adam said, "Sam, I do *want* to sit on that God damn chair . . . but . . ." Adam breathed heavily and spoke very slowly and carefully. "I *don't* want to get sick, and I *don't* want to fall on my face like . . . like a baby girl."

"You finished?" Sam asked.

Adam did not look up and said nothing.

"Well, if you are, I'll tell you Sam don't want you to get sick either, and if you start to get sick, I'll put you back in bed . . . and you can't fall 'cause Sam won't, by God, let you fall." Sam's voice had risen as he finished. Now he dropped his tone. "Do you hear me?"

"Yes," Adam said, "I hear you." He ground his teeth. "Now let's try the chair."

Sam got up slowly and pulled the sheet back. He placed the chair facing the bed and set a lock on the wheel so it would not roll. Then he wedged himself behind Adam and clasped his arms around his chest from behind. By a combination of lifting and dragging, he pulled the boy over the seat. Adam caught the arms of the chair with his hands and lowered himself. Sam grabbed his legs and placed his bare feet on the footboard.

Adam leaned his back against the chair, but he was pale and sweating. He gulped for air and murmured, "Catch me, I'm falling forward!"

Sam stepped quickly to the side of the chair and placed one arm tightly across Adam's chest and the other behind the chair. "You ain't goin' to fall, Adam, you ain't even leanin' . . . Take it easy."

"My head's beginning to spin," Adam said desperately.

"All right," Sam shouted. "I'll *hold* it." He grabbed Adam's head with both arms and pulled it roughly against his chest. Assuming a dictatorial tone, he said, "Use your arms, Adam, God damn it, hold to the chair and brace yourself. You ain't goin' to fall."

Perhaps two minutes passed. Both men were sweating profusely in their odd embrace, but neither spoke.

Finally, Adam said, "O.K., I won't fall. Let go of me kind of gradual."

Sam relaxed his head lock and slowly withdrew his arms. He stood back.

Adam was still pale and his face was very wet, but he turned his head tentatively from side to side and the terror slowly left his eyes. "I feel pretty good, Sam," he said, beginning to smile.

"Should I move the chair, or let 'er set? We don't want to overdo it, you know."

"Let it alone, Sam. I'll just sit a while today, all in the same place."

Adam spent most of the day in the chair, too much by the

standards of proper care. On the following day, although his arms and upper back muscles were terribly sore, he agreed when Sam suggested the chair. The nausea and fear were there again, but only briefly, and on the following days they gradually disappeared entirely. Soon Adam was pushed freely about by Sam and the first steps toward what Sam persisted in calling "recovery" had been completed.

Dr. Forbes was pleased by Adam's unexpected showing and he was genuinely surprised by Sam's ingenuity. "If they ever have a contest for the-most-unforgettable-habitual-criminal I've known, we could win it hands down with Sam," he told the warden when reporting the event. "The guy is astonishing."

"He is, indeed," Warden Bartlow said. "He's smart, determined, well organized. He has real integrity when he's here . . . but on the outside he's terrible. Armed robbery, assault and battery . . . with intent, as I recall it . . . auto banditry, burglary, bank robbery and every kind of petty stuff in the book. It's really incredible."

"Have you read the report from Warfel?" asked Forbes.

"Yes, I've read it, and forwarded it, but I already know the answer. Unless he can get a Governor's parole . . . and it's too early for that, he's only been here a month . . . we're stuck with him until normal parole procedures become timely. I've sent in the strongest possible request for a Governor's parole, but it simply won't happen fast." Warden Bartlow spread out his hands. "So there you are, Doctor."

"There we are is right. I assume you noticed in Warfel's report the problem of getting him into braces soon, or never. He says that we've got about six months."

"Yes, I saw that, and I also saw that braces are an ultimate step in a physical therapy program and a psychological program we're unable to give here. If we can't take the first steps, I don't see how we can anticipate the last ones, do you?"

"I suppose not," Forbes answered, "but I still hope we can move him in time."

"Well, I do, too, Doctor. I surely do," Bartlow said.

Despite Adam's pleasure at sitting up, Sam was unwilling to have him rest on his laurels. In early October, having loaded Adam into the chair, he announced, "You gotta learn to push this yourself. Then you could get around without me."

Adam twisted his shoulders and head around and looked inquiringly at Sam. "How can I, Sam?"

"It's easy, boy," Sam exclaimed, smiling broadly. "You just push and pull on the wheels. Your arms is very strong. You can push and pull." Sam raced on, arguing his point in anticipation of Adam's objections. "You gotta learn to do it, so's you can get them braces. It'll take practice, but other people not half as strong as you can do it. They've got special chairs, and we ain't, but we're stronger than they are, so we'll do it with this one."

"You really reckon I can?"

"*Sure.* Sam's got the chair ready. I went to the machine shop and got some graphite for the axle." He pushed the back of the chair and stopped it at arm's length. "See there. It's as loose as a goose. A baby could push it."

"All right," Adam said tentatively. "I'll try."

Sam pushed the chair into the aisle between the rows of beds. He stopped it and moved around in front. Except for the two of them, the ward was empty, but Sam spoke as if he were addressing a multitude. "Take hold and push forward."

Dutifully, Adam grasped the wheels and began to push. The chair did not budge. "God damn it," he said.

"*Try,* Adam," Sam said with considerable asperity. "Sam's an old man and I could do it easy. *Push!*"

Adam pushed hard and, pivoting on his seat, slipped gro-
tesquely in the chair. Sam darted forward and caught him,
returning him to a sitting position. Adam was sweating and
about to cry. Desperately, he said, "I can't do it. I can't get
any leverage on the footboard 'cause I can't push on my legs."
He sat back and closed his eyes.

Sam moved to the back of the chair. Putting a hand on each
of Adam's shoulders, he said in a low voice, "You *is* gonna
move the God damn chair, boy. Suppose Sam got a parole.
Who's gonna push you around then? You *gotta* learn to push
yourself . . . That's all there is to it."

Adam was silent.

Sam began slowly to push the chair. "I'll get you goin'
and then you keep goin'. Put your hands on them wheels."

Adam grasped the wheels and pushed as Sam did, forcing
his hands to follow the arc of the wheels as far as he could
reach, then bringing them back and repeating the maneuver.

"Now, I'm gonna turn loose, Adam, and you *keep pushin'*."

Sam let go and Adam pushed, straining as hard as he
could. The chair moved about five feet, slowing down as it
went. When it stopped, Adam was bent forward from the
waist almost at a right angle from the back of the chair. The
muscles of his neck were distended fearfully. Red faced and
exhausted, he pulled himself erect.

Sam shouted enthusiastically. "See, you *can* do it. Ol' Sam
knew you could."

Adam answered sharply. "Don't crap me. I didn't do a
thing . . . not a thing. It stopped."

"Now look, Adam, Sam ain't gonna argue with his friends,"
Sam said haughtily. "You done it *some*. From now on it's
practice we need. This is enough for today, but you'll be
pushin' it all by yourself soon. *Sam knows.*"

As the dreadful days passed, it became perfectly obvious
to Adam that it was impossible, but despite the severe sore-

ness of his hands and arms and the terrible broken blisters on his hands, he had stopped challenging Sam. Each morning he resignedly and doggedly tried, but it had become only a matter of routine, until the morning that the chair teetered magically and moved agonizingly forward. The next morning was a failure and the expletives of Sam and Adam, and their despair, were unavailing. But three separate starts were made on the following day, and finally Adam could start the chair at one end of the ward and move all the way to a toilet at the other end.

It did not get easier as such things are romantically believed to do. It was done each time with grinding effort and pain, but it was done and became a matter of course.

IO

For many prisoners, sleep is the principal resource in the penitentiary. Every hour not required for some other activity —employment, outdoor recreation or school attendance—is passed, and passed more quickly, in sleep.

For Adam Johnson, cruel physical effort had become the order of the day. Driven, at times unwillingly, by the persistent Sam, Adam's regime had continued.

On the morning of November 20, three months to the day from his entry into the prison, he rolled violently back and forth on his bed and finally drew a pair of white duck trousers over his limp and unfeeling legs and buttocks.

Having caught his breath and wiped the sweat from his chest and arms, he put on a blue cotton shirt.

Then he reached up and seized the rings of a trapezelike structure which had been erected over his bed by inmates of the machine shop working under Sam's direction. He pulled himself up from the bed, dragging his legs and feet. With an occasional assist from Sam, he caught two other rings dangling above the space beside his bed and let himself down heavily into the wheelchair. Having manually pulled his legs and feet off the bed and manipulated them onto the footboard, he blinked, grunted, coughed and again caught his breath. With Sam trailing beside him he then pushed the chair to Dr. Forbes' office.

Adam and the physician were by this time old friends. At Sam's suggestion, Forbes had recently employed Adam to do clerical work for him in the office. But these tasks were performed in the afternoon. This morning the two men had a different errand.

They stopped at Forbes' doorway. He was there, as was a surgeon summoned to perform an appendectomy on an inmate. The surgeon was in the act of leaving, so Sam and Adam waited until he had gone.

Sam opened the interview. "Doc, me and Adam has been havin' a little talk about his legs, and the braces and canes that other doctor said he had ought to have . . . We figure if he don't get them he'll get sicker. We was wonderin' how to go about gettin' them."

Dr. Forbes did not answer at once. Instead, he sat down at his desk and, lighting a cigarette, motioned to Sam to be seated in a chair beside Adam's wheelchair.

At last the physician said, "I won't pretend I don't know what you're talking about, Sam." He shifted about in the chair. "It's true that Dr. Warfel recommended leg braces for Adam and discussed the importance of his walking. But the truth is that such things are horribly expensive. They have to be carefully fitted and then refitted from time to time, and expert therapy must go along with them."

The doctor hesitated, but his listeners said nothing. They continued to look directly at him.

"Well," Forbes continued, "because of the cost, there was nothing we could do about it . . . at first, that is. Of course, I did discuss it with Warden Bartlow, but we decided to wait and see . . . how Adam seemed to get along. I really don't know quite what to do about it now."

There was a moment of silence during which Sam looked at Adam.

"How much do they cost, sir?" Adam asked.

"About $400 apparently, depending on exactly what kind of braces you'd have to have, and that's quite a lot of money, of course. That's just for the devices themselves, not counting surgical fees for the fitting."

"But if I don't get them, will all these other things happen to me?"

"That risk is present, I'd say, yes, but, of course, there are always risks and we're never certain about these things." The doctor looked away from Adam and waited.

"Sir," Adam began, "I don't want to get any worse . . . I'm getting better now . . . and I *sure* don't want to get worse." He leaned forward and put his hands on his bony knees. "Will you please see about the braces?"

Dr. Forbes smiled expansively. *"Of course,* I will, Adam. I'll see about it right away. It may take time, of course, and you understand I'm not promising anything. But I'll see what I can do at once."

"Thank you," Adam said.

Sam added, "Yeah, doc, thanks a lot. Me and Adam knowed you'd be all right about it. We'll count on you."

Sam turned Adam's chair and they left the office. But in a minute Sam returned alone. Making himself comfortable on the edge of Forbes' desk, he said, "Doc, I didn't want to nail you down when the boy was here, but when do you figure you'll get them braces?"

Dr. Forbes was flustered and spoke thoughtlessly. "Well, if we get them at all we'll have to by about March 1."

Sam said, "Why?"

Aware that he had made a tactical mistake, the physician tried to dissemble. "Well, that would be the best time, that's all, Sam . . . Now look, I'm busy, Sam. I . . ."

Sam looked shrewdly at him. "Doc," he said, "I don't guess a man like you would lie to me, now would he . . . I mean, with me helpin' out here in charge of Adam, it'd be a God damn shame if you was to hold out on me. That's why I'm askin' why you said that about March."

Forbes was annoyed by Sam's tone, but there seemed something compelling about the odd old man. He heard himself saying, "No, Sam, I would not lie to you. It is important for the braces to be available by March 1. Otherwise . . . well, otherwise it will be very difficult for them to serve any practical purpose."

"You mean it'll be too late, don't you?"

Meaningfully, the physician said, "It might be."

The prisoner slid off the desk and looked down at Dr. Forbes. "Well, doc, as I and Adam said before, we're countin' on you, real hard, we are."

"Yes, Sam, I understand," the doctor said.

"Good," Sam said and he strode from the room.

Returning to Adam's ward, Sam caught up with the boy, parked in his wheelchair beside his bed. He greeted Adam in an especially breezy way, but Adam was in a different mood.

"Have you been talking with Dr. Forbes?" Adam asked.

Sam stopped short and looked beyond Adam. "Well . . . I . . ." he began lamely.

"I know you have, and I'd like to know what about . . . It was about the braces, but what about them?"

Smiling too casually, Sam unwisely said, "Well, we was

talkin', me and the doc, about how fast we'd get them braces for you, so's you could get to walkin' . . . that's all."

Adam waited for a minute and then, very slowly and carefully, he said, "Sam, you and I . . . are what you'd call friends . . . pretty *good* friends . . . aren't we?"

Sam was solemn. "Yes, we're real good friends. About as good friends as there ever was, I reckon . . . I really mean it. We are."

Adam looked down at his hands and bowed his head. Then he quickly raised his hands to his eyes and cleared his throat. "Well, since we are real good friends, I think you ought to tell me what Forbes said. You ought to tell me straight."

Affected by Adam's inarticulate affection, Sam gave in, in spite of himself. "All right, Adam. What the doc said was that we had ought to have our braces by early next year . . . maybe March . . . if they was goin' to do any good."

"I see." Adam counted off three months on the fingers of one hand. "We've got about three months, maybe four. Do you think they'll get here by then?"

Relieved at the chance to be reassuring, Sam said, "Why, *of course* they will. Ol' Doc Forbes said they would . . . you heard him. They ain't criminals. They knows how important they are."

Infected again by Sam's spirit, Adam smiled. "I guess you're right. I won't worry about it. I won't even think about it."

Dr. Forbes was as good as his word. Carrying Adam's file, he went to Warden Bartlow's office before lunch. "You remember my talk with you, Ross, in September, about braces so that this boy could get up?" he asked.

"Yes, I do."

"Well, it looks like we're going to have him indefinitely, doesn't it?"

"I guess so." The warden smiled sardonically. "It's the old 'hot potato' situation. We got it . . . taken unawares, of course . . . but nobody in his right mind will take it off our hands now that the impossibility of the problem is apparent . . . Yes, we got him, *indefinitely*, I'd say."

Dr. Forbes said, "Well, if that's the case, we can't very well avoid this braces problem . . . He's in our custody and we're stuck if anything happens."

"Of course we're stuck, or rather *I* am," Bartlow said. "The professional fees, for fitting and therapy, could probably be absorbed in the general fund, but this figure of $400 for the braces and the canes alone, regardless of fitting and therapy, is bound to be an issue with the Department." The warden lapsed only briefly. "Jesus! I've got a per diem budget, per prisoner, plus certain specified general appropriations . . . you know that. And it's like getting on the rack to get anything else from the capital."

Forbes held up his hands sympathetically. "I know the problem. No kidding, I do. And I also know that any warden hesitates to requisition to the Department over the budget . . . No news is good news to those guys and they think highest of the man in the field who squawks the least."

"Exactly!"

"But," Forbes said, "this can be sold in a way that won't hurt you. As a matter of fact, if the PR men at the Department used it, they could get a good press treatment for everybody. I'm sure of it."

The warden's attention was arrested. "What's the angle?"

"Well, it's really simple. The point is that this man is already a public charge, and he's likely to be one for the rest of his life. If he *does* develop the secondary symptoms at stake here, the public will pay for them anyway, and they'll be a damn sight more expensive than these braces. In other words, hit the rehabilitation idea. I *honestly* feel that the public'll be saving money by preventing his being a messy invalid for the rest of his life."

Bartlow was convinced. "It's unavoidable. I can't disregard it, even if I were built that way. Your approach is good. I'll forward the request and get the thing in the works at least. In the meantime, we'll have to keep our shirts on."

Less than a week later, the warden's request was dispatched to the Department of Correctional Institutions at the state capital. A powerful letter from Dr. Forbes went along, referring to "the necessity of avoiding painful, crippling and expensive hospitalization and treatment, at public expense, either *during* or subsequent to the inmate's custody by the Department."

As a matter of course, the chairman of the Department of Correctional Institutions referred the warden's letter to the Comptroller of the Department. He, in turn, dispatched it to the office of the Attorney General, so that no issue could later arise when the Auditor of State or the State Bureau of Accounts reviewed the expenditure.

The Attorney General's office was deluged daily with similar inquiries from the many departments of the state. But in a very few weeks a deputy presented the draft of a memorandum to the Attorney General. This draft was the basis for the Attorney General's opinion, written before the next week was out.

Addressed to the Chairman of the Department of Correctional Institutions, the opinion, prefaced by the appropriate references and identification, stated:

The question of proper public liability for this extraordinary expenditure is not free from doubt. It is our understanding that at the time of injury—the direct cause of the requirement of the expenditure—the prisoner was not in the custody of the Department of Correctional Institutions. As a matter of fact, we are advised that at that time he was not the charge of any public department.

Following the injury on May 19, 1960, and until his conviction and immediate sentencing, the prisoner was not in the custody of the Department of Correctional Institutions. During the interval between the injury and the beginning of said custody, the prisoner was in the custody of the Marion County Sheriff. As an indigent, his medical and hospital expenses during this period, due and owing to the City-County Health and Hospital Corporation, were paid by the County Welfare Department. (This payment was presumably made pursuant to Chapter 300, Section 401, of the Welfare Act of 1947, Cairns Annotated Statutes, 48-107.)

Without passing on the propriety of that payment, but taking it into account, it is our view that the Department of Correctional Institutions is without statutory authority to expend the money here in question.

Warden Bartlow soon learned of the fate of his request. Endorsed by the chairman of the Department of Correctional Institutions, a copy of the Attorney General's opinion was forwarded from the capital. Dr. Forbes was asked to come to the warden's office to read it.

"Legal mumbo-jumbo always irks me," Forbes said. He was sitting opposite the warden at the latter's desk and had threaded his way through the letter. "What now, Ross? How about the regular poor relief funds, through Johnson's township trustee?"

"Well, I'd thought of that, too, but that's apparently the one source that's clearly out of the question."

"How come?"

"For about a half a dozen reasons, apparently. In the first place, the trustees are an unruly lot and do pretty much what they damn please. It's also pretty clear that this kind of medical expense, as distinguished from hospital room and board, isn't covered by the poor relief laws. Finally, there's a township residency requirement, and Johnson wasn't in his township long enough before he was shot. And he's sure not living in it now."

The doctor said, "Well, what are you going to do, no kidding?"

The warden placed his hands before him on the desk. "I've decided to take the bull by the horns, although I may lose my own in the process."

"What's the plan?"

"Well, I just can't afford to ask my department to contact Welfare. I can't let my board think I'm a crybaby and unwilling to swallow my medicine. On the other hand, I can't let Johnson down either." The warden turned his face away and momentarily concentrated on a photograph of the Governor on the wall. Then he turned back. "So . . . I'm going to write the welfare people directly and instruct them to respond directly." He smiled. "We'll keep the Department out of it, and see what we can do on our own."

"*Very* good," Forbes said with feeling. "At least we know we're doing our best."

"That's the point, exactly," the warden said.

By a disturbing coincidence, Sam was waiting for Forbes when he returned to the hospital from his conference with the warden. Without waiting for the doctor's greeting, Sam said, "How you doin' on them braces for the boy . . . any news?"

"Yes, Sam, there's been some news, news today as a matter of fact, and it's a little bit discouraging, to tell the truth." Seating himself, Forbes added, "There's some legal question about whether the department of prisons or the welfare people should buy them."

Sam looked blankly at the doctor. "What's the difference . . . it's all one, ain't it, the government?"

"Yes, it's all one . . . but it has different departments and everything is set up on the basis of laws." The doctor had begun with a condescending tone, but he dropped this now, feeling that he was already getting beyond his depth.

Sam waited in silence but soon realized that Forbes believed that the subject was exhausted. The prisoner smiled and said, "Doc, Sam knows about laws, but I still don't see what's wrong about the braces." He stammered and finally asked, "It ain't against the law for Adam to get 'em, is it?"

Forbes answered in a tolerating voice. "No, it's not *against* the law, but it is *subject* to certain laws. You must understand . . ." The doctor hesitated. Then he said briskly, "Look, Sam, old friend, it's much too complicated to explain right now . . . I'm busy and . . . you're busy. The important thing is that Warden Bartlow is following it up. He's going after the welfare department now. You may be sure that we're doing all we can."

Sam shrugged and turned to go but said, "I hope he keeps after them. It's been almost a month since I and Adam talked to you about it. I was hopin' they'd be here for Christmas . . . kind of like a Christmas present . . . but that's next week already."

"They won't be here by then, Sam, that's for sure, but we're trying and you and Adam must be patient." Forbes turned to his desk to end the interview.

"O.K., Doc, but I hope everybody gets the lead out," Sam said. He walked away slowly, in his mind converting the bad news to good news for Adam.

The next day, Sam stopped off at Adam's bed after breakfast. He had been with the boy on the day before, but he had been upset and nervous and had cut their time together short. He arrived now, as usual, to supervise Adam's dressing and see that he made the precarious morning journey from the bed to the wheelchair.

To Sam's practiced eye, Adam looked as if he had not slept well. He was considering this when Adam suddenly said, "I saw you talking to Dr. Forbes yesterday and you've been acting funny ever since. What's eating you?"

"Me?" Sam answered. "Why nothin's eatin' me, Adam. I'm just fine."

Adam completed his dressing and lay quietly to get his breath. Then he said, "Sam, you're not kidding me . . . there's some kind of trouble. And I know what it is."

Sam was angry. "There ain't no trouble," he said sharply.

"Oh, yes, there is, and you might as well admit it. I know what you and Forbes talk about. It's the braces, and they're having trouble. Isn't that right?"

Sam felt trapped. Perhaps, he thought, Dr. Forbes had already told Adam, or perhaps he would tell him, and tell him the wrong way. "All right, Adam," he began guardedly, "since you're so damn nosy, I'll tell you. There was a little trouble, but it's all over now."

"What was it?" Adam said tensely.

"Well, it didn't amount to much . . . It was about who was going to buy the braces, which one, like the prison people or the people in the welfare."

"What did they decide?"

"Well, it ain't exactly decided yet."

"So they haven't got them yet. Is that right?"

"That's about the size of it, Adam, but they will. I ain't gonna worry about a little thing like that."

Adam suddenly turned his face away. In a bitter voice Sam had never heard, he said, "Hell no, you aren't going to worry. Why should you worry. It's nothing to you."

Utterly taken aback, Sam bit his lip. "Now look, Adam, that's a real ignorant thing to say. I mean I ain't worried 'cause I know we'll get them braces."

Adam turned to him again. His face was flushed and he

began to talk loudly in a high voice. "Sam, you're wrong. I'm not going to get any braces, ever, and you know it . . . and I don't care. I don't . . ."

Desperately, Sam interrupted. "For Christ's sake, what's got into you. We're gonna get the braces, I'm tellin' you . . ."

"I don't want them!" Adam shouted, raising up on his elbows. "I never did want any braces. They were your idea, and you lied about it . . . You knew damn well there weren't going to be any braces, but you said . . ."

"Adam, you're crazy," Sam said harshly. "I . . ."

But Adam was out of control. "No," he screamed. "There aren't any braces, but you and Forbes decided to play a trick so it would be easier to take care of poor old paralyzed Adam. You're the doc's pal . . . you get all your privileges from him . . . so you do what he says, and you screw me. Well, I don't give a damn, and I'm not going to bust my guts for your phony braces." Adam stopped short. He twisted his head around, his face contorted with anger. Lowering his voice, he said, "You're a dirty, lying son-of-a-bitch . . . I hate your guts . . . I really do!"

Sam had had enough. "Shut up!" he shouted, shaking with rage. "If you was on your feet, as old as I am, I'd knock you down and break your head, you bastard . . . accusin' me of double-crossin' you after I've been helpin' you, and worryin' about you like you was a baby, and you . . ." Sam was almost snarling. He raised a big fist as if he was actually going to bring it down on Adam's face. But seeing his hand ready to strike seemed to check his outpouring. He dropped his hand to his side. "God damn you, boy," he said hoarsely. "God *damn* you."

Adam, too, seemed spent. He did not shout back but, as if to himself, said, "I'm glad I found out now, instead of in March." He added coldly, "Well, so what . . . So I'm going to be in bed the rest of my life . . . I don't give a God damn." He turned toward Sam. "Leave me alone, Sam, just keep plumb away from me."

Adam's tone withered Sam. For a moment, he stood there, and then he turned and walked away.

Sam could only take Adam's injunction—to keep away from him—literally. Sadly the old man saw to it that the assignments of the orderlies were rearranged so that other prisoners covered Adam's ward. It was a physical impossibility for him to avoid passing through Adam's room, but the reassignments would keep him from getting close, and this was what Adam had said he wanted.

Adam spent the day of the argument in bed and, at his own insistence, the head of the bed was not elevated. Sam passed through the ward once during the late afternoon. Although he tried not to see anything, he saw the empty wheelchair beside the bed and Adam's listless body, eyes closed.

The next day, at Sam's secret suggestion, Adam's orderly tried to coax him to get dressed and earnestly offered to help him into the wheelchair.

"I can't," Adam said blankly. He again would not let the bed be elevated. He did not read and quietly rejected the orderly's clumsy efforts to talk with him.

That night, as on the previous night, the new orderly was cross-examined by Sam when their rounds were finished.

"Is he any better?" Sam asked.

"No, he ain't. He don't seem like the same guy. I mean it's just like he's all shriveled up, kinda, all of a sudden."

Sam cursed and struck the palm of one hand with his fist. "God damn it, that settles it."

"What you gonna do, Sam?"

"We gotta switch back for tomorrow. Let me take your trick and you take mine."

"Sure. It don't make no difference to me."

"It *does* to me, son," Sam said. "It does to me."

On the following morning, Sam entered the ward and walked slowly toward Adam's bed. He was armed with the usual morning accouterments, the enema kit, a clean catheter and waste jug, soap, water and towels and a shirt and pants, all neatly arranged on a service cart. He also had a sheaf of letters in the pocket of his shirt. These, borrowed from the warden, were to be his proof that the braces, though not yet acquired, were not a figment of his imagination.

The old man drew up slowly beside Adam's bed. He had expected he might be rebuffed, but Adam simply looked up at him in silence.

"Mornin', Adam," Sam said with as much dignity as he could muster.

"Good morning," Adam said.

Neither spoke further, but the boy did not object to Sam's initial ministrations. Sam placed the pants and shirt in the usual place on the bed where Adam could reach them. Then he left, to return shortly with breakfast. Without asking permission, he raised the head of the bed so Adam could feed himself. During the meal, he sat by as he often had in the past, but this time he was silent.

When Adam was done eating, Sam took away the remains and came back. He seated himself on Adam's wheelchair and looked directly at the boy, who remained in his sitting position because Sam had not lowered the bed.

Sam had carefully planned what he wanted to say. Having rehearsed it again in his mind, he said, "Adam, I'm gonna have to talk to you for a minute . . . it won't take long."

Adam made no objection. He looked straight ahead, so that his gaze missed Sam's intense eyes.

"I ain't gonna argue with you. I really ain't. You say you

hate my guts . . . well, you go right ahead and hate 'em. Other people has, and maybe they got a right to, so that's your privilege."

Adam seemed to slump down a bit in the bed as Sam said this and Sam, who was already digressing from his prepared remarks, was prompted to digress some more.

"You see, it really ain't too important . . . I mean your hatin' my guts." Sam smiled ruefully and shook his head. "I'm sure sorry about it. I don't mean that. *Jesus,* I'd give anythin' if you wouldn't do that, even I'd beg you not to . . . I really would, but askin' people not to hate you don't help any, and anyway, what I'm sayin' is that that ain't the point. Whether you hate my guts is *your* business and I'm not discussin' that. Do you hear?"

Adam nodded.

"All right, now, leavin' that aside, Adam, the point is about you and them braces." Sam pulled the letters out of his pocket and held them up. "Now . . . here is the letters from the *warden* about that. You said I was a liar and that I was kissin' Doc Forbes' ass and makin' it all up about them braces and not tryin' to help you. Well...I ain't concerned about what you think of me. If you want to think I'm the kind of dirty son-of-a-bitch like that, just mean as hell, why, you go right ahead and think it."

Adam looked up. He looked at the letters and it seemed that interest, in what Sam was saying and in himself, was beginning to struggle through the despair.

Sam again strayed from his point. He couldn't seem to say what he had wanted to say so directly and simply. "You can believe what you please about ol' Sam. I really ain't mean. I ain't never done anythin' dirty, like trickin' people who was my friends, and you bein' sick like this. I just ain't the sort to do what you said about me . . . and you can ask anybody around here and they'll tell you the same. Sam ain't much, they'll say, but, by God, he don't abuse his friends, or anybody else, just so's he can get ahead . . . That's what they'll tell you."

Sam stopped talking. He was getting excited, and was angry with himself for saying all of the things he hadn't wanted to say. Suddenly he said loudly, "But, God damn it, Adam, like I was sayin', *that* ain't the point. Sam ain't the point . . . you is the whole point! Do you get what I'm sayin'?"

Adam looked hard at Sam. He barely shook his head from side to side.

"What I'm tellin' you," Sam said excitedly, "is that there *is* such a thing as braces. I ain't askin' you to believe me or even give me the time of day. Let's say ol' Sam is a rat . . . you hate him, O.K., and everything you say about Sam is true. He's a low-down skunk. But you can still get the braces." Sam threw the letters into Adam's lap. "Bein' as much of a rat as I am, it don't change the fact that you can maybe get them braces and really get up and walk around . . . and Sam can drop dead and ol' Adam . . . Adam is walkin'." Sam swung his right arm in front of him. "Yes, sir, God damn it, Adam's walkin' around!"

Sam sat back in the chair. Tears had come to his eyes and he didn't bother to brush them away. "That's what I wanted to say, Adam," he said more quietly, "so's you would please, for the love of God, not lie there on your ass like that. Don't you see? If you know that maybe you can get the braces you'll try like you been tryin', and you'll be all right, and that's what I want. That's all ol' Sam wants, more than anythin'. God damn it, I really do."

Sam finally put his hands to his face, covering it almost entirely. Adam tentatively touched the letters. He didn't try to read them, but he glanced at them and saw his name and the warden's. He looked back at Sam, but said nothing.

Sam got off the wheelchair. He was again composed. He stood beside Adam's bed and said, "One more thing. If you decide you're gonna keep goin', that's enough for Sam. But you still gotta have somebody around sometimes. I told you that before. The day you came here, I said you did, 'cause everybody has got to, and you're no different from anybody else. So . . . whether you lie down or get up, irregardless, you gotta have somebody . . . Well, I'm the one, 'cause *I* say so, not you. Even with your thinkin' I'm a rat, which is your business, like I said, it's *my* business who I help out, and I decided last night that you ain't man enough to throw me out. So I'm stayin', do you hear?"

Adam nodded his head.

"All right. Now that's that. Now I got to go, and you think about one thing—whether you is gonna get up or stay down. Either way, I'm for you, but I'm sure hopin' you'll get up."

Sam turned abruptly and walked purposefully away. "I'll be back later, Adam," he called, without looking over his shoulder.

For almost an hour, Adam was alone in bed. He looked around the room a dozen times and, still without reading them, folded and unfolded the letters Sam had thrown on the bed.

Sam busied himself elsewhere in the hospital. As if dreading to return to Adam's ward, he insisted on cleaning one of the latrines, a chore he had steadfastly refused for years on the ground that his seniority entitled him to better things. But as an hour drew to a close, he washed up and headed for Adam's bed.

Entering the ward, Sam's glance traveled ahead of him. He almost shouted as he saw that Adam was in the shirt and pants. And when Sam reached the bedside, Adam spoke first.

"Sam," he said softly, "if you'll move that wheelchair up

here under the trapeze, I'll get in and take a little ride."

Sam smiled his most grotesque smile. "My pleasure, Adam," he said grandly.

Seated in his office in the City-County Building, the Director of the County Welfare Department received Warden Bartlow's request with something less than enthusiasm. He put it aside until after the holidays, always a hectic period in the agency, but it was on top of his desk on the first Monday in January. He called for his assistant, who soon entered the office.

"What is it, Stan?" the assistant asked.

"It's this inquiry from the prison," the Director answered, passing it over. "I'm showing it to you so you can commiserate with me."

Without waiting for his colleague to read it carefully, the Director said, "Now here we are, struggling with the new budget and the hearings before the Council and the Commissioners set for next month . . . here we are and the warden wants a mere $400, and wants it real fast, at that. And he wants it for orthopedic devices, for an inmate, an inmate in the first year of a minimum ten-year sentence for robbery."

Still glancing at the letter, the assistant said, "Well, he needs the damn things, apparently . . . pretty badly."

Pounding his desk the Director said, "*Of course* he needs them, the poor devil, but you know the heat we're getting. The Taxpayer's League and the newspapers will grab onto a little thing like this like a tall dog. My God, the papers never quite say it but they imply that this agency really exists in order to encourage illegitimate children. You remember that series last year that said that after three illegitimate children A.D.C. should be cut off? . . . And I was called an apologist for promiscuity when I asked if the fourth child should simply starve?"

The Director was by this time quite heated. The assistant said, "Come on, Stan, relax. It's always tough around here at budget time, but we'll get through it. We always do, finally."

The Director shook his head. "Yes, I know we will, but the question is what compromises we'll have made with the program . . . I'm like everybody else in the world, I guess. I like to go to bed at night thinking I've done what I'm paid to do. But in this business, we're always put on the defensive and we get . . . or I get . . . more and more dishonest about the thing." He put his hands to his eyes. "The trouble with me is I remember the brave new world. That's when I began in welfare work and then I have to remember things like the graduation dress we bought last year for that Wills girl . . . so she wouldn't be the only kid in the God damn high school on the stage in rags . . . and I actually apologized to our Board and the newspapers for an oversight. *Ugh!*" He actually looked sick.

"All right. You can punish yourself if you want to." The younger man spoke almost harshly. "But we got the budget through, didn't we? We let them cut out the air we'd left in it, but the agency's still here. If that's dishonest, and it isn't, it was for a good cause. Why don't we just say we're realists. We're *pragmatic,* because we have to be."

The Director had subsided. "O.K. Histrionics now over . . . Will you do something with that damned inquiry?"

"Yes, I will. I'll dispose of it." The assistant turned and moved toward the door. "Don't let them get you, Stan."

In his own office, the assistant picked up an IBM Form 70 and attached it to the correspondence from the prison. He wrote, "check legal" across the top of the form. Then he assigned the claim to a staff caseworker. In a few minutes, the file was picked up from his desk and delivered to the desk of the caseworker.

On the following day, the caseworker forwarded the file to

the agency's lawyer. By the end of the week, this man had turned to the case, and he immediately saw that Adam Johnson had been a resident of the state for only a few weeks at the time of the shooting. Several months more would have to elapse before he would have been in the state a full year.

The lawyer always had too much to do. Exhilarated by the simplicity of this issue, he was prompt in dictating an opinion to the caseworker. It began with the facts concerning time, and proceeded:

Chapter 209 of the Acts of 1931, Sec. 8, disqualifies "non-residents" for welfare payments. The term "non-resident" is defined so as to include any person not born in this state who has continuously resided here for less than one (1) year. Subject does not, therefore, meet the residency requirement. He is a "non-resident" within the plain meaning of the statute.

It may be noted that payments were made May to August, both inclusive, 1960, in subject's behalf, to the City-County Health and Hospital Corporation, pursuant to warrants issued by the Marion County Sheriff's Department. Said payments reimbursed the Health and Hospital Corporation for expenses borne by it during the period of subject's custody by the sheriff. These payments were proper according to the Welfare Act of 1947, which statute contains no residency requirement and, indeed, mandates the Welfare Department ultimately to bear indigency charges during such custody. Thus, the fact of said payments does not constitute any waiver of residency requirement in relation to the instant claim. The 1947 legislation, *supra,* and the residency statute must be read *in pari materia.* (It is in any case doubtful if any doctrine of waiver can be applied against a public agency with reference to the discharge of its statutory authority. *State ex rel. Pearson v. Department of Public Works of the City of Peru,* 1907, 48 App. 214.)

In order to anticipate a later issue, it will be seen that subject will have completed twelve consecutive months of "residence" in this state as of April of this year. At that time, this claim may be renewed. If it is renewed, the question will be whether he has fulfilled the residency requirements in view of the following considerations:

A. The injury requiring the claimed expenditure long pre-dated the acquisition of "residency." (It is believed that this fact would not disqualify subject for the claim in view of the continuing character of the disability.)

B. Subject, a convicted felon, has by statute been deprived of his civil rights for twelve (12) years. It is doubtful that a felon, in prison and without civil status, can acquire *residency* in a legal sense for purposes of the welfare statutes. Further inquiry on this question may be made if and when the claim is renewed after the one (1) year period of time.

When the lawyer's opinion became available, the worker assigned to the case prepared a draft of a letter for the Director of the County Welfare Department, advising Warden Bartlow of denial of the claim. The caseworker's draft was used by the Director, who also added two final paragraphs to the letter:

The theory of the residency requirement (with which I personally do not agree) is that the state of origin should bear the public welfare expenses of its own indigents and that this state should not have that obligation until the indigent acquires an identification with this state. The requirement is not, of course, unusual. Many states have adopted it.

In the instant case, I should like to be able to recommend forwarding the request to Tennessee. But experience of this Department would indicate that that state would be wholly unresponsive.

Warden Bartlow called Dr. Forbes to his office when he received the Welfare Department's letter. Having read it, the physician said, "What do you make of it, Ross? Is this the end of it?"

"Yes, I guess it is, though it doesn't seem right to me. *Someone* ought to have this appropriation. This guy can't be caught between third and home like this . . . It just doesn't make sense!" The warden was silent for a minute. Then he looked directly at the physician. "But, frankly, whether it makes sense or not, this is the situation. So there we are."

Dr. Forbes shook his head. "O.K. It's not the end of the world, of course, but the question now is who'll tell him. I'll have to, I guess . . . He'll be all right about it . . . although the better he feels the less docile he seems to be . . . but that damned Sam will make me feel like Judas for a year or so." The physician got up and extended his arms at his sides. "Oh, well, that's the way it goes."

"Thanks, Doctor," Warden Bartlow called after him. "For taking the responsibility for me, I mean."

"Don't mention it," Forbes said.

Neither Sam nor Adam quarreled with Dr. Forbes. Adam received the news with his customary quiet. Instead of complaining, the older man tensely thanked the doctor for his efforts. For the rest of the day, however, Sam did not leave Adam's bed except to get food for him. The physician saw them and knew instinctively that Sam, seated on the bed, was trying to cope with Adam's desperation at the news. He did not complain that Sam neglected his other orderly's rounds. It would be a small price to pay, he thought, if Sam could handle the boy.

There was really no question of Sam's handling Adam. They were no longer on this footing. Adam now understood how recklessly he had risked Sam's friendship by doubting and falsely accusing him. He also understood vaguely that he had not destroyed their friendship, in spite of himself, simply because Sam had not permitted him to. He was still terribly anxious about the braces, but some saving instinct had told him that his relationship with Sam was probably even better than walking. And Sam had sensed some of this, and it meant that he was candid about the difficulties over the braces.

After the initial disappointment at Forbes' report, Sam and Adam turned again to efforts to obtain the braces. "Have you got anybody down at the capital . . . any friends we could ask for help?" Sam asked suddenly.

"I . . . I don't think so."

Sam looked at him closely. "You act like maybe you have, but don't want to tell ol' Sam . . . This ain't no time for secrets."

"Well, it isn't a secret, Sam, it's just that I'm not sure."

"That don't make no difference, bein' sure. We got to take chances." Suddenly Sam looked very knowing. "Now look, Adam, you can trust me. If it's some guy that's hot, we can protect him. There's ways of gettin' word to him, you know, outside the ordinary mails. They're friends of mine in here who can get ahold of anybody anyplace, and nobody's the wiser."

Adam shook his head and almost smiled. "That's not it, at all . . . It's a girl."

"Your girl?" Sam said sharply.

"Sort of . . ." Adam looked embarrassed. "She wrote me a letter."

Sam had begun to cheer up. "Is that who sends you them letters? Well, I'll be . . . I always wondered about that."

"No, not those letters. That's different. They're from my folks, the Abernathys in Tennessee."

"Oh," Sam said uncertainly. "Well, what does this girl say?"

Adam seemed to be trying to decide what to do or say next.

Finally he moved his wheelchair to the head of the bed and reached into the pillowcase. He drew out a small, soiled envelope and hesitantly handed it to Sam.

Sam opened it up and took out a letter. He read it quickly, and then looked back at it and looked up at Adam. "I don't understand this, son. This was wrote clear last year."

"But I didn't answer it."

Sam seemed really puzzled. "Look, ol' Sam ain't too bright. Is this the only time this . . . this Anne wrote you?"

"Yes . . . But she said if I needed anything I should write her. Well . . ." Adam shrugged self-conciously. "I didn't ever write her, because I didn't know what to say. But if I had, maybe she'd have written more. She says to write if I need her . . . So maybe we could write her now."

Sam put the letter into the envelope and gave it back. He lay back on the bed for a minute, holding his head between his arms and looking hard at the ceiling. Finally, choosing his words carefully, he said, "I'm sure this girl is a nice girl and I'm sure all for her, and for you and her . . . But we ain't got time to go off on any wild-goose chases, Adam. She's a fine girl, like I'm sayin', and I wouldn't want you to think that ol' Sam is knockin' your girl, but people who are gonna help out like we need now don't write letters and tell *you* to let *them* know. People who are gonna help, well . . . they just start helpin'."

Adam carefully put the letter in his pants' pocket. "Maybe you're right."

"I think I am, at least talkin' about friends. Now . . ." Sam suddenly seemed alert. "If you're talking about some charity, that's different. They only know about you if you ask, and we ain't even asked. We gotta ask, by God."

"What charity?"

"All of them, Adam. We're actin' pretty dumb, you and me. All of them big charity companies sittin' around with a pile of money, and we ain't even asked 'em! By God, we'll just ask, and we'll get the money." Sam jumped off the bed. He was genuinely cheerful. "You go to bed. Ol' Sam has got it all figured out. We'll get the chaplain over here and we'll start in all over again. This time, we'll get 'em. Ol' Sam *guarantees* it!"

"All right, whatever you say," Adam said hopefully.

Adam did go to bed, as usual, and Sam did, too. Neither slept very well, but Sam, at least, seemed fresh and frisky the next morning.

After Adam had gotten into his chair, the old man went again to the hospital office to see Dr. Forbes. Following salutations, Sam said, "Doc, I and Adam ain't give up on this thing yet. We figure there may be some charity that could be hit, so we'd like to see the chaplain today. Can you get him over for us?"

"Of course, the reverend will come. But surely you don't expect him to have the money?"

"No, but he *ought* to know about charities, and we need a charity right now. So we want to see him. O.K.?"

"Sure, Sam, I'll call him for you. How about just after lunch? Do you think that would be a good time?"

"That's fine," Sam said, and he left the office to begin his rounds.

At one o'clock, the Reverend Mr. Adcock arrived. After stopping briefly beside the beds of other inmates, he moved on to Adam's. There he first greeted Sam, whom he knew well, and then he turned to Adam and shook hands before drawing a chair up beside the bed.

Adam and Sam found it as hard as most laymen to start a conversation with a clergyman, so a more or less clinical discussion of the winter weather proceeded at first, for perhaps five minutes.

Suddenly, so explosively that the minister started, Sam

said, "Look, Reverend, we want you to do us a favor. How about it?"

Mr. Adcock recovered himself and eyed the two men warily. To himself he thought: Never sign a blank check for these fellows. Aloud he said, "Well, Sam, I'd like to help you, of course. What is it that you want?"

"Well," Sam began, "it's for Adam here, about his braces and sticks, so's he can walk. There's some kind of red tape that's shut our water off, and that's where you come in."

"I see. But can you be a little more specific about what you want me to do . . . where I 'come in,' as you put it?"

"Sure." Sam very inaccurately sketched the impasse in government that had victimized his friend. Then he added, "Now, Reverend, what we think is some of them charities ought to help out, like the March of Dimes or the one that puts out them stamps with those sick kids on 'em." Sam was suddenly affected by the contrast between Adam and the crippled children. His voice rose. "Jesus, Reverend, every one of them is standin' up in them pictures, smilin' like and lookin' sweet, and this poor bastard"—he pointed at Adam—"he's been on his ass since last May and he'd have been on his ass *forever* if he didn't have more God damn guts in him than a fat horse."

Even before the minister spoke, Sam knew he had transgressed. Adcock drew himself up. "Sam, you should watch your language. Blasphemy, oath-taking and vulgarity have never solved any man's problems."

Sam began to answer quietly. "I apologize, Reverend, honest to God, but we've been kind of on a strain, Adam and me, about them braces . . . It's really me more'n Adam . . ." Sam's voice began to get louder. "You see, Reverend, if you was me and you watched this . . . guy . . . draggin' them legs and skinnin' around like a monkey every day on them rings so's he can get out of bed and then rollin' that chair by hisself with the sweat runnin' off him like a nigger on election day and his eyes bugged out and his blood veins stickin' out like cordwood, because it hurts so bad and because it practically busts his gut tryin' every time . . . but he don't never holler and he don't hardly ever complain, if you was me . . ." Sam mopped his brow with one of his long arms. "If you was me, Reverend . . ." Sam stopped. His eyes narrowed. He clenched his teeth and lowered his voice sharply and suddenly looked surprisingly dangerous. "If you was me, you'd have a hard time understandin' why in the name of the Lord God Almighty, amen, no one was able to get them braces here for him . . . Would you please write them charities for us, Reverend, that's all we wants to know?"

Sam strolled to the window and looked out. Adam lay very quiet. The clergyman folded his hands and was silent. Finally he said, "I think perhaps you're on the right track. I'm not entirely satisfied that there aren't public funds available. I think that should be pursued at first. But if there aren't, I'll be glad to do whatever I can in an approach to private funds." The clergyman thought for a moment. Then he turned to Adam. "Johnson, you had a lawyer, didn't you, someone appointed by the court?"

"Yes, sir, I did. I don't remember his name, but I had a lawyer in the court."

"Perhaps he's the key man here," Adcock said. "The trouble with this kind of thing is that you're at a disadvantage proceeding by mail. You need someone right on the ground . . . to *talk* to the Department of Correctional Institutions, the welfare people and, if necessary, some of the private agencies. Suppose I write the lawyer and enlist him in the cause? If he worked for nothing before he probably would again, and this shouldn't take too much time. How about it? Is that agreeable with you two?"

Adam looked at Sam.

Sam said, "Sure, Reverend. If you think that's the way to do it, you do it that way."

"All right, I'll write him today. I can get his name from the information in the warden's office . . ." The minister hesitated before going on. "Johnson, I'd like to make the letter as strong as possible. And I should like to refer to the doctors' reports. Is it all right with you if I talk with Dr. Forbes, and maybe even with Warden Bartlow, before I write? They will cooperate, I'm sure."

"Sure," Adam said. "That's all right with me."

"Well, then, it's all settled. By tomorrow morning the lawyer will have my letter . . ." The clergyman got up, shook hands with both men and walked away.

"A nice guy, the reverend," Adam said.

"He's all right as a chaplain," Sam said. "I just hope to God he can write a good letter."

II

In the office of the Legal Aid Society, Bill Sawyer winced as he read the opening paragraphs of the Reverend Mr. Adcock's letter. To himself he exclaimed, "Adam Johnson, the poor devil," and he briefly recalled the miserable day in Judge Pearce's court.

The letter was plain enough. Believing that Adam was entitled to the orthopedic devices from public sources, Adcock asked that this avenue be checked again before a private agency was approached. In a roundabout way, the chaplain also conveyed the urgency of the situation. He suggested that the braces should have been at the prison already, even before his letter was written. If they were not obtained by at least the beginning of March, the prisoner would probably be unable to use them.

At the reference to March, Sawyer glanced up at a large calendar on the wall. Most of February was left, but a number of the remaining days were already circled, set aside for appointments, hearings and appearances. The lawyer felt a twinge of anger. The people at the prison should have written him sooner.

Having finished the letter, Sawyer put it down and sat back in his swivel chair. It seemed to him that Adcock made sense about the public responsibility. Surely, he thought, public sources were available, and it also occurred to him that they might have been readily available if his intervention, on the scene at the capital, had been solicited at the outset, before the warden had plunged into the bureaucracy by mail. Although inexperienced, Sawyer had been around long enough to know that the routine channels of government were inert, if not actually stopped up entirely, by gratuitous complications. The fact that Adam's problem was already tangled up there meant to Sawyer that it would be doubly difficult to accomplish anything.

Shaking off his regrets about the way the matter had thus far been handled, Sawyer accepted the charge and docketed it, although "the gratitude of Mr. Johnson and the blessings of God" were the only rewards promised by Mr. Adcock. To his secretary, the lawyer dictated a brief answer, requesting copies of the correspondence between the warden and the Department of Correctional Institutions and the County Welfare Department.

Despite the deadline for Adam Johnson's problem, Sawyer was unable to do anything about it immediately. But late in the week, with prior matters with their own deadlines disposed of, he decided to start with the Department of Correctional Institutions. Having checked the statutes cited in the letters and made a few notes, he left his office and walked to the State Office Building.

The lawyer located the offices of the Department of Correctional Institutions and was referred by a receptionist to the deputy director. He was courteous and professional, but Sawyer was wholly unsuccessful in his objective. The obstacle was the Attorney General's opinion.

"Look, Mr. Sawyer," the deputy director explained, "all state departments are under constant scrutiny by the newspapers and everybody else for spending too much money. Last year *The Chronicle* had a three-week series on this department alone. They said we were 'coddling' prisoners. Now on top of that the Attorney General says we haven't got the legal power to spend this money. I admit it seems strange . . . not to be able to take care of a prisoner like this . . . but your quarrel ought to be with the Attorney General. He's *our* lawyer, and we have to act on his advice."

"Suppose the Attorney General does reverse his position?" Sawyer asked. "Will you people buy these braces then?"

The deputy director smiled. "I'm not saying that, quite. I will say that we'll reconsider if the Attorney General says that it's within our authority."

"O.K.," said Sawyer, "that's good enough for me. I'll see the Attorney General."

"All right, sir. Good luck and thank you for your cooperation."

Sawyer walked from the deputy director's office into the large lobby through which he had entered the department. A few minutes earlier, the lobby had been almost empty. Now a large crowd of men was assembled, some carrying television and photographic equipment. The lawyer moved through the lobby and had reached the corridor when he heard his name called. Turning, he saw a disreputable-looking and vaguely familiar little man coming toward him from the crowd.

Extending his hand, the man said, "Sawyer, I'm Medlicott of *The World*. We met at the time of the Johnson trial. Do you remember?"

Sawyer smiled agreeably. "Yes, I do, Mr. Medlicott, and it's a coincidence that I'm over here right now working on that same case. What are you here for?"

"The Governor's office has just announced the firing of a purchasing agent at the Girls' Reformatory, for some kind of kickback deal. The press people are here for the kill." Medlicott switched the conversation back to Adam Johnson. "What's new about the case? Are you working on a pardon already?"

"No, nothing like that. I'm trying to help him get some metal braces and canes so he can walk."

The newspaperman's manner, up to now friendly, became antagonistic. "Did he have to hire a lawyer for *that?*"

"Well, apparently . . ." Sawyer answered. "It's kind of a long story. If you want to hear it, I'll buy you a cup of coffee."

Medlicott hesitated, torn between a real interest in Adam Johnson and a professional one in the goings on in the lobby. "All right," he said, "I'll come with you. To hell with the Girls' Reformatory."

Falling into step, Medlicott accompanied Sawyer to a canteen at the end of the corridor. There they sat down and Sawyer told of the problem about the braces.

As Sawyer finished, Medlicott erupted. "It stinks, it absolutely stinks."

Sawyer was taken aback by the newspaperman's bitterness. "Well, it is too bad," he said, "but there apparently is a genuine legal problem. The statutes don't quite dovetail and this case falls sort of between them."

Unassuaged, Medlicott said, "Of course there's a genuine legal problem. There's always a God damned genuine legal problem . . . It makes me want to puke."

Sawyer bridled but lapsed into silence before he spoke again. This time he sought to end what had unaccountably become a trying conversation. "Well, I'm going now to the County Welfare Department, Mr. Medlicott. I haven't given up yet. I'll also talk to the Attorney General as soon as I get the chance, but I think Welfare is the next place to go."

"And suppose they rely on the genuine legal problem?" Medlicott snarled. "What happens then? Couldn't you file some kind of a lawsuit?"

"No, I don't think litigation has any promise. I thought, or rather I agree with the chaplain up there at the prison, that we ought to hit one of the private agencies."

Medlicott said, "Well, do me a favor, will you? If you're brushed off by the Welfare people, let me go with you to the private agencies. My newspaper isn't what you'd call influential, God knows, and this man's white anyway. But there are a few men on the big papers I know, and maybe they'd be interested in a sob story on this thing. As a last resort, it might work." He pointed a finger at Sawyer. "One way or another, we've *got* to get the money."

Reluctantly, Sawyer agreed to let the newspaperman go with him if a private agency was to be contacted. They parted and Sawyer walked the several blocks to the County Welfare Department in the City-County Building. The attitude there almost exactly duplicated that of the Department of Correctional Institutions. Harassment by the newspapers, and a strong and parsimonious citizens' Board of Directors were said to be responsible for the agency's technical position. Again Sawyer was told that he should talk with the agency's lawyer, but he was temporarily unavailable. Returning to his office at Legal Aid, Sawyer became involved with several other pressing matters. The Johnson case was temporarily put aside.

During the next week, Sawyer separately interviewed the Deputy Attorney General and the attorney for the County Welfare Department. Both were competent men and both were enthusiastic about the nice legal question presented by the case. Neither, however, would change his position. On the part of the Attorney General's representative, Sawyer suspected that this was motivated in part by a reluctance to acknowledge that an issue could exist where the Attorney General had spoken so positively. The attorney for the County Welfare Department contended that the Department of Correctional Institutions had a clear liability. Each lawyer insisted on assuming that the other's agency would step in, if his own agency was categorical enough in saying that it would not.

After the second set of interviews, Sawyer decided that the impasse with respect to public funds would take too long to break if, indeed, it could be broken at all. With some distaste, he called Jack Medlicott and told him of his plan to turn to the private agencies. The men agreed to meet at Sawyer's office in the United Fund Building at 9 A.M. the following day.

Medlicott was late for the appointment, a failing which the lawyer found practically unpardonable. But he arrived at nine-fifteen, looking himself a little like an applicant for some sort of public relief.

Accepting the reporter's sullen greeting, Sawyer said, "Please let me do the talking, Mr. Medlicott. I know a little about these agencies . . . damn little, really, because my own is unique and operates largely on its own . . . but we must be politic, if you know what I mean."

Medlicott smiled not unpleasantly. "O.K., Sawyer, I get it. I'm very subtle. And I know that I'm not cut out to wheedle money out of these people. I'll be quiet, at least as long as what you say seems to make sense."

Sawyer was not amused, but he did not quarrel. "The question is where to go," he said. "I've looked over this *Guide to Your Community Services* which the United Fund puts out"—he held up a printed booklet with a torch on the cover —"but I'm still not clear where our request fits. I think we ought to start out at the offices of the Fund."

"Good enough," Medlicott said. "Let's go."

They left Sawyer's office and walked across a terrazzo floor to the general offices of the United Fund. Sawyer explained their errand to a pretty receptionist at a switchboard bedecked with very realistic artificial flowers. She directed them to the nicely appointed office of Mr. Antoni, an Agency Coordinator.

After another brief description of the nature of the request, Mr. Antoni said, "Gentlemen, your problem cannot be readily classified, and actually the Fund itself does not attempt the classification process. We have, as you may know, a member agency, the Community Council, which was created for this very purpose. The Fund reviews all budgets, raises the money and allocates it to its members. The Community Council exists in order to coordinate all other agencies, to watch for duplication and the like. I think you should see the Council."

"That's fine," Sawyer said. "Perhaps you would tell us who to see there."

"Of course. Ask for Mrs. Ellis. She's in charge of intake. Room 404."

Although not understanding the reference to "intake," the men left and found the elevator. At Room 404, Sawyer asked for Mrs. Ellis.

Mrs. Ellis, a middle-aged but youthful woman, arrived promptly and Sawyer and Medlicott followed her into her office, noticing the plain but fine furnishings. For the third time, Sawyer sketched the problem and told Mrs. Ellis that Mr. Antoni had told them to see her for reference to the proper agency.

Mrs. Ellis spoke with assurance. "I think that's clearly a case for the Metropolitan Aid Bureau. You see, we've classified the agencies into four basic categories. The first is health, like the Red Cross, Muscular Dystrophy, the TB people, Mental Health . . . you know, all of those that specialize in diseases and things. Our second category is what we call casework agencies, like the Marital Adjustment Foundation, the adoptive agencies, and things like that. Then there are the religious agencies . . . Catholic Youth and the Jewish Welfare and the others. Then we have your type of agency, Mr. Sawyer, Legal Aid and the direct service agencies. There aren't any direct *relief* agencies as such, of course, because the concept of pure direct relief is not consistent with the principles of modern social work." Mrs. Ellis smiled disarmingly. "At least as those principles are interpreted by the United Fund in this community."

"I see," Sawyer said, although he did not see at all. He waited for a moment and said, "Well, Mrs. Ellis, this Metropolitan Aid Bureau . . . I assume that you classify our request as direct relief . . . if there aren't any such agencies, I don't quite get where we are."

Mrs. Ellis giggled. "I forgot to say that some of the casework agencies . . . that was my second category, you will recall . . . do have direct relief funds, *but*"—she held up a finger for emphasis—"they may only engage in direct relief if it is not *pure direct relief,* at least that's the general rule."

"Yes, of course," Sawyer said. "And does the Metropolitan Aid Bureau have some of this money?"

"Yes, they do. That's the point."

"Well, is our case what's known as pure direct relief, the kind that's out?"

Mrs. Ellis became very reticent. "You will understand, Mr. Sawyer, that this is surely not my decision to make. It could be treated as pure direct relief . . . or it could be regarded as *supplemental* to another service of the agency, and therefore permissible. The decision is entirely up to the agency, and I might say that MAB does a good deal of depth casework, experimenting with the sources of their clients . . . You might call it preventive casework, but it *does* have direct relief money. That's the point."

"Yes . . . MAB," Sawyer repeated slowly and helplessly.

"Metropolitan Aid Bureau," Mrs. Ellis said. "You know, Metropolitan Aid Bureau . . . MAB."

"Of course," Sawyer smiled. "Will you tell us who we ought to see at . . . MAB?"

"Oh, I can't do *that,* Mr. Sawyer. It's not permitted. You should simply go to the office . . . it's just down the hall, 409 . . . and report to the receptionist there. She'll advance you to an interviewer and you'll be all set."

Mrs. Ellis rose as if to end the interview. Sawyer and Medlicott thanked her and left the office.

Out in the hall, Medlicott said, "Boy, that was an experience, but if she'd gotten you clear into the teapot, I'd've pulled you out."

Sawyer turned and was about to try to understand his companion when they found themselves at Room 409 and the frosted glass doors of the Metropolitan Aid Bureau. They pushed open the doors and entered the reception area.

A young woman peered from behind a telephone switchboard and anticipated them. "May I help you, gentlemen?"

"Well," Sawyer said, "we have a request involving some expensive orthopedic equipment for an inmate at the state prison. We were sent here by Mrs. Ellis down the hall."

"All right, please be seated." She turned again to the switchboard and took several calls before looking up again. When she looked up, she had a printed form in her hand.

Nodding to Sawyer, she said, "Your name, please?"

"My name?" asked Sawyer.

"Yes, please."

"My name is William Sawyer."

"Your occupation?"

"I am a lawyer."

"Your name, please?" she asked, looking at Medlicott.

"Jack Medlicott."

"And your occupation?"

Suddenly annoyed, Medlicott said, "Well, I'm unemployed right now but I push dope—cocaine—when the heat's off."

The woman colored, as did Sawyer, although he was not wholly unsympathetic with Medlicott's reaction. The woman recovered herself and persevered.

"Who referred you to this agency?" she asked, looking hard at Sawyer.

"Mrs. Ellis, the woman down the hall."

"Well, I mean before that . . . Who indicated to you that you should seek the assistance of a United Fund agency?"

Although by now quite irritated, Sawyer spoke carefully. "Miss, I am a lawyer, as I've told you. I work for a United Fund agency, the Legal Aid Society. The inmate at the prison, the man on whose behalf we are here, is a client of mine. Knowing of the United Fund, it has occurred to me that one of its many agencies might appropriately be approached in behalf of this man's needs. The United Fund office sent us to the Community Council. The Community Council sent us here. Now that's about the only way I know to explain our being here."

The woman was obviously not entirely satisfied, but she subsided and placed a call through the switchboard. In a few minutes, a smiling young man appeared. He was introduced as Mr. Edwards, the agency's Classification Officer.

Before Sawyer and Medlicott could accept Mr. Edwards' invitation to go with him, the switchboard operator interrupted. Waving the printed form, she said, "Mr. Edwards, I need your help on the Form 801."

Edwards paused. "Yes?"

"Well," the woman said, "these men aren't here for themselves. They're trying to help somebody else. So I *can't* check 'Self-Motivated Inquiry.' And they weren't referred here by any of the usual reference sources, like 'clergy,' 'legal,' or anything. Mrs. Ellis sent them just now, but they aren't really 'interagency,' because they just came to the building on their own. What do I do?"

Edwards puzzled only a moment. "Mark them 'miscellaneous.'"

The woman nodded and Sawyer and Medlicott followed Edwards into his office. They were seated opposite his desk before he spoke.

"First of all," Edwards said, "I should welcome you to the agency. MAB was founded here in 1897. We are the oldest private social agency in the city in terms of continuous operation."

Since there seemed to be no ready response to this opening, Sawyer and Medlicott said nothing. Edwards said, "I am the Classification Officer. My job is to see that you are assigned properly to a caseworker specializing in your area of need. I am an administrative social worker. We can save time if you will outline your situation, leaving the details for the caseworker. Please tell me why you are here."

After a brief exchange of glances with Medlicott, Sawyer retained the spokesman's role and outlined Adam Johnson's plight. Edwards took notes as the account proceeded.

When Sawyer finished, Edwards said, "A most unusual and tragic situation. And it illustrates one of the reasons for the continued life of private agencies. As this case shows, there is an inflexibility about the publics. They're hemmed in by statutes and rules all the time."

"Yes, that's true," Sawyer said. Reassured, he asked, "Do you feel that your people can supply the funds? The need is very real and there's also some urgency about it."

"Perhaps we can, but I'm fairly sure that it will require Board action rather than Staff. You see, the case doesn't fit into any of the traditional departments here, and it poses the pure or supplemental question. I have to treat it as 'unclassified.' There's also the problem of the amount. These would be direct relief funds, either pure or supplemental, and we're prohibited from disbursing more than fifty dollars in relief funds in any one case without board approval."

"What board are you talking about?" asked Medlicott.

"Our own board. The Board of Directors of the agency. I can submit the request at the next meeting or, as a matter of fact, you can submit it yourself. We've recently been encouraging direct submittals, so that we can better interpret the agency to the community."

"When's the meeting?" Medlicott said.

"Well, the next meeting is Tuesday, a week from tomorrow, but the agenda on that meeting is already printed and distributed. The board meets every other Tuesday. You could come to the meeting after the next one."

"I don't see what the printed agenda has to do with it, Mr. Edwards," Medlicott said. "We don't have to be on the printed agenda. There's nothing formal about our appearance."

Mr. Edwards was unruffled. "I understand that, but it is generally understood by the board that the agenda will not be changed once it is distributed to them. The board people are all very busy in the community, and we are hardly in a position to impose on them."

Medlicott seemed not to understand. He had begun to sound unpleasant. "Look, Edwards, we've jacked around here for almost two hours about these braces, walking from place to place with our hat in our hand. It seems as phony as hell to me to postpone the question for an extra two weeks because of some procedural deal you have."

Edwards flushed and looked coldly at the reporter. "I'm sorry that our rules are disagreeable to you. They really make sense, you know, in the total administrative picture. But because of the peculiar hardship here, I'll see if the Director will waive this rule." Edwards rose from his chair and moved toward the door. "Excuse me for a moment, please," he said.

Sawyer and Medlicott sat silently. The lawyer was embarrassed by his companion's hostile manner, but secretly thankful that he had pushed the question of attending the meeting. The reporter was apprehensive because he felt that his anger might have jeopardized the chance to get the money. An uneasy quiet existed, as the two men seemed to study the room. They started when Edwards suddenly reappeared.

"Mr. Medlicott," he said, "am I correct that you are with the colored newspaper here?"

"Yes, that's right."

"And what is your connection with this case . . . I mean . . . are you interested in it as a newspaperman . . . or just . . . ?"

Medlicott interrupted. "Yes, my newspaper's very much interested. I can't tell you exactly the nature of our interest, but we are interested in this case and we're always interested in the conduct of the affairs of the United Fund agencies."

"All right, thank you, that's what I suspected," Edwards said. "Just a moment, please." He withdrew again, but reappeared almost at once. "Well, I've good news. Mr. Beemer feels that the Board should be concerned with your matter, regardless of the agenda, so you may raise it at the next meeting. You should realize that it will be a rather full meeting, but Mr. Beemer will give you an introduction at the close of the agenda. The meeting is Tuesday of next week, at one o'clock in Conference Room D on the ground level of this building. We'll see you then."

Edwards had not resumed his seat, and he continued to stand. Sawyer and Medlicott stood up and thanked him. They shook hands and left his office. But just as they were opening the frosted glass doors, Edwards came running out.

"Mr. Medlicott," he called, "I've something for you here."

The two men stopped and Edwards caught up with them. He handed the reporter a piece of paper, embossed at the top with the name and address of the Metropolitan Aid Bureau and captioned, "Practicing is Preaching," in bold type. "This is our Brotherhood Week release, Mr. Medlicott, it's not been distributed yet, but I thought you'd like an advance copy."

"Thanks," the newspaperman said. He glanced down at the body of the paper:

We would remind our friends that MAB has the following *Americans*—Negroes—employed on its staff:

1 Case Work Supervisor
2 Case Workers A
1 Case Aide I
7 Professional Assistants
11 Office Clerical

Charles Beemer
Director

A few minutes later, walking down the steps of the building, Sawyer and Medlicott agreed that they would appear together at the Board meeting.

"You're all right as a talker," Medlicott said, "but I represent the lords of the press, by God, so I'll sit and glower."

"Fair enough. And, incidentally, you'd better glare good and hard. I'm pretty sure we'll get the money from these people in spite of all this folderol, but we're just about down to the deadline. So I hope they act quickly."

Medlicott stopped on the bottom step. "What deadline?"

"Well, it's about now. If Johnson doesn't get the braces now, apparently his physical deterioration may be so far advanced . . . I don't understand all this medical stuff . . . but, anyway, he won't be able to stand up or walk around even with the braces."

"Who said that?" Medlicott asked fiercely. "I didn't know that. For Christ's sake, Sawyer, why didn't you tell me that . . . my God, that's appalling. Why in the name of God didn't you say so?"

"Of course it's appalling. I know that. You aren't the only guy who's upset by this, *and* you're not the only one who's trying to help, either. I thought I had told you. I thought you knew. I'm sorry."

Medlicott shook his head distractedly. "Well, I didn't know, but it doesn't make any difference now. God Almighty, the MAB had better come through . . ."

"That's what I say, too. And I think they will. Let's not get all excited about it. That won't help any. We'll go to the meeting and do the best we can . . . I'll see you in my office just before the meeting."

"O.K.," Medlicott said helplessly.

Leaving Medlicott standing on the sidewalk, Sawyer turned back and headed for his office.

12

Oɴ ᴛʜᴇ appointed Tuesday—it was now March—Bill Sawyer returned to his office in the United Fund Building at five
minutes to one. He took off his overcoat and gloves, removed
his hat and sat down impatiently to wait for Jack Medlicott.

In addition to impatience, the lawyer had also begun to
feel nervous about a letter he had posted the previous day to
the chaplain at the prison. The letter had reported on the
progress of his efforts and now he was insecure because it
had probably implied an unwarranted optimism about the
Metropolitan Aid Bureau. After all, he thought, he was permitted to present the request, but he had no assurance that
favorable action would be taken. He was momentarily angry,

with himself and with the chaplain. That was the trouble with being a lawyer, he said to himself, people tended to interpret your *efforts* as a *guarantee* of the result they wanted, regardless of the merits of the issue.

Sawyer's office door suddenly was thrust open and Medlicott, looking disheveled, actually jumped in. He looked at his watch. "One minute to go! How about that, Counselor?"

Sawyer had risen. "Well," he said dryly, "I'm glad you're not late. Let's go."

Medlicott put his wraps on a chair and followed Sawyer out of the office. They hurried to an elevator and soon located Conference Room D on the ground floor.

The door was closed, but Mr. Edwards was there waiting. Holding his finger to his lips, he whispered, "The meeting is just getting underway. Find yourselves seats and wait for Mr. Beemer to call on you. Good luck."

Edwards opened the door enough to allow them to enter. Sawyer and Medlicott tiptoed in and, disregarding the stares of the directors, took two empty seats in the corner.

The conference room was imposing. Three walls were paneled in walnut and a blackboard covered the other. In the center of the room was a large, highly polished conference table, surrounded by leather chairs with arms. These were occupied by the directors, before each of whom was a pad of paper, a sharpened pencil and a small stack of mimeographed documents.

Sawyer was at once reassured when he recognized the chairman of the board, the genial public relations vice-president of a bank. Always identified in the newspapers as "Howard ('Howdy') Stewart," he was middle-aged, quietly handsome and widely known among lawyers and business men as a "regular guy."

Although he did not know Howard Stewart, Medlicott also had reason to feel more at ease because of the presence of

Thomas Kern, an International Representative of the United Steelworkers. Once a legislator and still a minor power in Democratic politics, Kern had been interviewed by Medlicott on a number of occasions and had impressed the reporter with his direct and sensible manner.

Sitting incongruously beside the unpolished Kern was Mrs. Charles Berkeley, the beautiful and fashionable wife of a broker. Both Sawyer and Medlicott recognized her as a founder of the Christian Liberty Union, recently established to rid the public schools of left-wingers and radicals. Sawyer had just received a dramatic brochure from the organization, announcing that "WELFARISM and COMMUNISM ARE YOUR ENEMIES."

Next to Mrs. Berkeley was Monsignor Grover, the Archbishop's frequent representative in community affairs. The priest was enormously fat and unappealing looking, but had an habitual cheerfulness that offset his condescension about all nonchurch matters.

These were the only board members Sawyer and Medlicott recognized, but the others, including an affluent-looking Negro, did not seem formidable and the two men sat back to await their chance.

The chairman opened the meeting by referring to the mimeographed minutes of the prior meeting in the stack of papers at each place at the table. Since available in this form, they were not read and were quickly approved by consent. Then Stewart referred the group to the mimeographed agenda, and Charles Beemer, the Director of the agency, rose to make his regular report.

A dark man in his early forties, Beemer looked not at all like a social worker. Pipe in hand and wearing a nubby tweed coat, he reminded Sawyer of a Chaucer professor with whom he had taken a course in college. Alternately puffing on his pipe and using it as a baton, he spoke easily and only occasionally looked down at his notes.

"I should first say a word for the Joint Board-Staff Committee on Public Relations," Beemer said after having first welcomed the group. "This committee pursues its appointed tasks with very little fanfare, but it nevertheless does an exceptional and selfless job in putting MAB before this community." Beemer looked pointedly down the table toward a pretty and obviously Semitic matron, but did not otherwise identify the committee chairman. "I have here the report of the committee for 1960, and it is really rather startling." He looked up and waved his pipe for emphasis. "Especially having in mind that the United Fund knocked our public relations appropriation out at the budget hearings last year, while leaving in a similar appropriation for Cancer, the Heart Fund, the Bertha Biloe Orphanage, and a lot of others."

Beemer paused and looked around the table. Stirred up by his reference to the treatment the agency had received at the hands of the United Fund, a number of the Board members were nodding and exchanging dark glances.

Beemer resumed. "Bearing that in mind, folks, you will surely be gratified at this public relations progress for 1960 —seven TV shows, three of them during prime time and devoted to the multi-problem family project; eleven radio spots, *not* counting those allocated to us by the United Fund during the fund drive; forty-eight . . ."—Beemer paused and repeated himself—"*forty-eight* newspaper references in daily editions of the three major papers; four features in the Sunday *Chronicle*, including the one about Howdy Stewart in the 'Man in Motion' series in the financial section; and twelve stories in the Steelworkers' District 9 *Bulletin*. Now, this doesn't count many other breaks for the agency. For example, when Mrs. Berkeley was featured in 'The Turning Point' series in *The Chronicle*, she very generously referred to MAB a number of times in describing her own awakening to the Communist challenge."

Beemer stopped momentarily, long enough for Mrs. Berke-

ley to shrug off the admiring and grateful glances of her colleagues. She did not see Jack Medlicott's look, which was
admiring but seemed concerned entirely with her remark-
ably voluptuous legs.

"So much for mere reporting of the magnificent efforts of
our Board," Beemer said. "Now to issues which you must
decide. First, the annual convention of the Metropolitan Aid
Bureaus of America will meet this year in June, in New York
City at the Commodore. It will be a tremendously stimulat-
ing program, with many of the really significant people there,
from government, industry and the community. Last year,
we sent three delegates, two staff and one board, to San Fran-
cisco. We would like to send three this year."

Howard Stewart interrupted. "Why don't you give them
an idea of the program, Charley."

"Of course, Howdy." Picking up a printed announcement,
Beemer said, "The first seminar is 'What's Wrong with Our
Public Image.' It should be very good . . . they've really
got top people assigned to that one. In the afternoon on the
same day, there's a discussion on 'Priority for the Community Dollar,' another very timely issue . . ." Glancing up,
Beemer added, "I won't read the entire week's plan, folks,
but other seminars are called 'The Community Power Structure,' 'Social Work in the Affluent Society' and 'New Developments in Family Centered Case Work.' "

Stewart interposed again. "What's the budget for the trip?"

"Well, the round trip plane fare is $104.62 per person.
The fee for the convention, this includes room, breakfast
and lunch, too, is $70 per person for the week. That's
$523.86 for the agency. The evening meal is on the delegates
themselves."

Stewart tapped the table with his finger. "Perhaps it
would be expeditious to take care of this question now, ladies
and gentlemen, before Charley goes on with his report. Is
there a motion?"

Someone moved that the arrangements from the previous year be approved again. This was seconded and promptly carried and Beemer proceeded.

"Mrs. Cravens is leaving us," he said. "Her husband has completed his schoolwork and has taken a job in Denver. She has been a valuable staff member and the Board may wish to express its appreciation to her."

Mr. Kern promptly moved that the chairman address a letter to Mrs. Cravens, in behalf of the Board, thanking her for a job well done. This was seconded by another director, before Mrs. Berkeley was recognized.

"I really feel that we should be a little more concrete in these expressions of appreciation," Mrs. Berkeley said, in an oddly seductive voice. "Wouldn't it be possible to give them something they could display . . . not expensive, you understand, but something more permanent than a letter? When I was on the Courtesy Committee, we suggested this to the Board, but it was never acted on."

The Negro now said, "I agree with Mrs. Berkeley. I'd suggest that a small decorous plaque be adopted—a symbol less ephemeral, less transitory, something that will last."

With an enthusiasm hardly warranted by the circumstances, Howard Stewart said, "An excellent suggestion, Mr. Wood . . . we'll do that unless, of course, someone objects." Stewart looked up and down the group. "How about you, Mr. Kern, will you accept Mr. Wood's point as an amendment to your motion?"

"Yes, of course."

"Any further discussion?" asked the chairman. There was silence and the motion, as amended, was carried.

Beemer withdrew his pipe from his mouth. "By way of report, I should tell you that we're having a little difficulty with the United Fund about the transfer of funds in the budget. At last year's budget hearing . . . at least four of you board persons battled along with me at the hearing . . . the Fund was very sticky about our personnel account. Well, at the last meeting of this Board, you'll recall that you approved the transfer of funds made available as a result of some staff economies that had freed $1600 from salaries. You voted $1250 of that for office furniture and an electromatic typewriter and $350 for the direct relief account. The United Fund has to approve such transfers, and Mr. Stewart and I have not as yet secured approval."

"What's the trouble?" asked Monsignor Grover.

"I'll answer that," Stewart said, and he got to his feet. "The truth is . . . and we've noticed this before . . . we've certain enemies in the councils of the United Fund, I mean among the directors, or rather the professional people they rely on. The United Fund is fairly new, of course, and its directorships have been turned over to the big givers and their representatives. The agencies are ultimately dependent on these financial interests, and I don't quarrel with their right to run the Fund. But the trouble is these people don't know anything about social work, and they tend to be suckers for the agencies that have a superficial appeal. The Boy Scouts, for example, have increased their budget by forty-nine percent since the United Fund was set up, as compared to its situation under the old Community Chest."

There was a quiet chorus of clucking around the polished table.

Stewart continued when the clucking had subsided. "With unsophisticated board people, and I hate to have to say that these tremendous people are unsophisticated, the important thing is the advice the board gets. And this is where our problem with the Fund comes from. The professional fund raisers that the Fund brings in here for the drive are, of course, wholly insensitive to an agency like ours. They saturate the drives with the hearts and flowers agencies—the

Scouts, Crippled Children, Heart—or the scary ones, like Cancer. This stuff spills over on the Fund board people, inevitably, and they start out with an unfortunate orientation toward the solid agencies like this one. Do you see?"

Charles Beemer had taken a seat during Stewart's remarks. He now looked up deferentially to the chairman. "Howdy, there's something else that might be said here, if you feel that it's appropriate."

"Sure. You take it from here," Stewart said agreeably and he resumed his seat as Beemer stood again.

"Well, folks," Beemer said, "what Howdy says is true about the Fund board and some of our problems with it. But there's another reason for the attitude of the Fund, and I think that we're all big enough and old enough to realize it."

The people at the table looked expectantly at him.

"As you know," Beemer said, "the Community Council is the agency which has the constitutional function of relating the other agencies to each other and avoiding overlap and things like that." Striking a pose which especially reminded Sawyer of his Middle English class, Beemer continued. "Now, remember, the Council is *not* a superagency. It has *no* jurisdiction over MAB or anybody else, despite some of the empire-building that those guys dream about. But, inevitably the Fund consults with the Council in reviewing our budget and those of the other agencies, and"—Beemer stopped and looked slowly around the room—"the Council is *unfriendly* to MAB and it downgrades us, and the Fund board gives us the axe."

Kern of the Steelworkers asked a question. "Why are these guys against our agency . . . why would they try to damage this agency?"

"There are several reasons," said Beemer, who was now in complete control of the conversation. "In the first place, we're the biggest agency. We always have been. Our budget,

percentagewise, is the largest single budget in the Fund . . .
Incidentally, it is declining as a percentage all the time. Five
years ago, it was fifteen percent, today it is only twelve percent . . . But we're still the biggest and the big dog is always the one the others attack. And there's another reason.
We pay our people a little more than the other agencies. Our
Case Aide I classification, for example, gets about as much
as their Caseworker A. You and I know we have to because
we've got to get the best and most experienced people, because of the nature of our work. But much of our staff has
been hired away from the others, and they can't take it. The
Kessler Scholarship is another sore point. We send a social
worker to graduate school every year and the student is morally obligated to work for us for three years after he gets his
Master of Social Work degree. This rankles the others, too."

Another board member, an anonymous man toward the
foot of the table, said, "Back to Mr. Stewart's statement
about the directors of the United Fund, I sort of have the impression that those men really aren't committed to the idea
of social welfare . . . public or private. I mean, from what
I've seen, they accept the idea of welfare as kind of a necessary evil, but they really don't understand the premises of
welfare and approach the whole thing as if it was an effort to
keep the poor people from cheating the rich people . . . I
wonder about whether we haven't put the management of
the United Fund into the hands of the very people who really
have very little use for the whole idea."

As this man had begun his curious statement, his identity
had dawned on Sawyer. Until recently he had been the
pastor of a Methodist congregation that had just moved to
a large, new Gothic church in the suburbs. In the mysteri-
ous way that Protestant denominations accomplish such
things, he had been removed from his pastorate and lingered
awaiting a new call. Although a comparative newcomer in

the city, the reason for his dismissal was also widely known. Sawyer had been told that he was one of those obtuse and presumptuous clergymen that unaccountably use the pulpit to talk about "problems." In this man's case, race relations was the fault, and his congregation simply would not put up with it. Sawyer noted that Mrs. Berkeley was looking at the minister with evident distaste and, as Sawyer recalled who the man was, Howard Stewart began to answer him.

"I'm afraid none of us agrees with *that,* Reverend. I *know* these United Fund directors and they're fine people . . . the finest really. They *do* believe in social welfare, especially private funds, with the whole community putting its shoulder to the wheel to help the unfortunate." Pressing on with his answer, Stewart spread out his hands before him. "Why, just think, folks, some of these United Fund directors make $75,000 a year in their regular jobs. They're highly trained specialists in business management and financial control. Social work needs these skills . . . It must be run on a businesslike basis . . . And these men spend hours, for nothing, going over the program, budgeting and then raising the money. I say that we're fortunate to have them."

Although Stewart's remarks were plainly very pleasing to the board as a whole, the minister seemed undaunted. "What you say may be true, Mr. Stewart, although maybe social work *isn't* a business. Maybe it *oughtn't* to be on a business-like basis. But, anyway, I'd separate the two functions of the Fund. Let the money men raise the money, but let others allocate it, people who *feel* something about poverty and need and social issues and who might know a little more about them than the financial community does." He looked cheerfully about for a moment, as if expecting to find some-one to second his views. But there was silence, and it occurred to Sawyer that unlike most people who had failed in life, this man seemed to be without rancor or bitterness.

Chairman Stewart smiled manfully. "Well, those are interesting opinions," he said, "and everybody has a right to his opinions, that's for sure. But the United Fund is here and we must cut our cloth to fit it. Charley Beemer and I will stay after this transfer of funds question, and we'll see it through." He hesitated, glancing at the agenda. "Now, Charley, we're down to your report on the multi-problem family project. Where do we stand on that?"

Beemer rose again. "Well, we've a few problems there ourselves. As you know, we've picked the Brookfield area and we're going over County Welfare Department and police records to select five multi-problem families. We've gotten down to ten and we'll eventually reduce this to five for the pilot. We've passed up certain hopeless ones . . . One of the families we'd looked at . . . the township trustee has them . . . has a mother and father and seven children, living in a shack, literally a shack, with two rooms. The father is unemployed and has been for years . . . he's an alcoholic. The mother is terribly withdrawn and wholly inadequate. The small children are truant and get into trouble at school . . . very hostile. The fifteen-year-old daughter seemed to be the star of the family, but it now seems that she's a sexual delinquent of some kind, and the oldest boy was recently arrested in a gang fight . . ." Beemer shrugged. "Well, that's just too hot to handle, for anybody, and we're trying for the cases with some daylight in them, to make it worth the chalk . . . Now the question is, *who's going to run the show?* It was our idea, of course, and we sold the United Fund people, but the appropriation for the project wasn't what we asked for. So we've contacted the Settlement House Association and the Buchanan Neighborhood Group to see if they'd chip in . . . They say they will, *but* now it appears that they may try to muscle in on the management of the thing. Our position is, of course, that we're the agency that knows some-

thing about family-centered casework. We've got the personnel, and it was our idea, so we've got to run it in the final
analysis."

Beemer had paused for a breath and Stewart put in.
"It really is in the interest of all concerned that MAB keep
this project."

"*Of course,*" Beemer said. "Frankly, we've more negoti-
ating to do before the question of control is ironed out. If
the project can show some real gains, it will attract a lot of
attention. The gains will be in simple human values, salvag-
ing *people*, but this, of course, can be translated into dollars
saved in taxes and private giving. The United Fund understands this kind of thing, so we're going to hang on to the
project for dear life. We'll keep this board informed, of
course."

As Beemer concluded and sat down, Stewart, his attention
attracted by similar antics of several others, looked at his
watch. "It's a little after two folks," he said. "We're running
late." He turned to Mrs. Berkeley. "Jane, the last agenda
item is your report for the Agency Auto-Analysis Committee.
It's really terribly important, but would you be offended if
we carried it over until the next meeting?"

"No, Howdy, it's perfectly all right," Mrs. Berkeley answered, "although we do have a very thrilling report."

"I know you do, and we must hear it, but if you don't
mind, we'll pass it," Stewart said. Leaning over, he whispered to Beemer and the Director got to his feet once more.

"Ladies and Gentlemen," Beemer said, "we have another
matter to consider today. It's not on the agenda, but it concerns our Special Relief Fund and I've taken the liberty of
going beyond the rules just this one time." Nodding toward
Sawyer and Medlicott, he continued. "The spokesman for
this matter is Mr. William Sawyer. Some of you may know
him as the attorney for the Legal Aid Society, a United Fund

agency. With him is Mr. Medlicott, a reporter from the colored newspaper, *The World,* which has always given Fund campaigns generous coverage. Mr. Sawyer would like to address you briefly . . . Mr. Sawyer."

Sawyer stood and bowed slightly. Before he could begin, two members of the board rose and with exaggerated apologetic signals to Stewart withdrew on tiptoe from the room. After the door had closed, Sawyer began, telling plainly and chronologically the story of Adam Johnson.

Even the skeptical Medlicott was impressed with the performance by the lawyer. Without getting hopelessly technical, he described the unlikely impasse between the Department of Correctional Institutions and the County Welfare Department. The whole presentation took but a few minutes and concluded with the request for the $400.

Monsignor Grover was the first to speak when Sawyer had finished. "Mr. Sawyer, although the court found this unfortunate man guilty, your statement seems to imply that he is innocent. Are you telling us that he didn't commit this crime?"

"No, Monsignor," Sawyer answered quickly, "that is not my point. I frankly don't know whether he did or didn't. I would express the opinion, respectfully, that whether he's guilty or not is irrelevant."

Unaccustomed to this kind of demurrer, the monsignor colored and Sawyer at once suspected that he had erred in characterizing the clergyman's question.

Mrs. Berkeley took up the monsignor's line. "Mr. Sawyer, in one sense you are quite right that the man's guilt or innocence isn't involved here. But in another sense you're quite wrong." She smiled and it occurred to Sawyer that she was, indeed, "the beautiful Mrs. Charles Berkeley" that the society pages frequently mentioned. "You see," she said, "our direct relief funds are limited and most of us feel that they should be for that matter because of the tendency of these people to become dependent, to lose their incentive, if there's a known source of financial help available. But be that as it may, whether we should have more or less for direct relief, your request would account for a large portion of our Special Relief Fund. I think it's only reasonable for us to consider whether this man is *really* deserving, because there are other deserving people, you know, who'll be deprived of direct relief if we spend so much now."

Another woman, who had not participated in the meeting thus far, now came to Sawyer's defense, at least on the issue of guilt or innocence. She spoke with feeling. "I don't think that whether this man is guilty or innocent has *anything* to do with it. I frankly don't even like the implication of our considering that part at all. But I do admit that the question of available funds is significant. We must consider whether it's worth the price, whoever the applicant and no matter how sympathetic we may feel."

After this initial barrage, there was a lull in the comments. Howdy Stewart said, "Well, folks, does anybody else want to say anything?"

The union man, Kern, suddenly spoke up. "Sawyer," he began, "what I don't like is the way the Welfare Department is acting about this thing. Those guys are always ducking out . . . I know from my own experience about that because of something that happened during the Washburn strike. The people was out there for nineteen weeks . . . nineteen weeks is a lot of weeks . . . and some of them applied for aid to dependent children and the damn welfare people wouldn't grant it. I went over myself and talked to the head guy there and he got real snotty, and we never got no help. Somebody had ought to teach those guys a lesson, and if we pick up the tab here, they'll have gotten away with it again."

To his horror, Sawyer sensed that this unlikely point had scored heavily with the board. The lawyer was wholly unprepared for it and had to fight for control of himself. Turning to Stewart and Beemer, he asked, "I wonder if it's appropriate for me to answer these comments?"

Both men assured him that it was.

In a strangely even voice, the lawyer began. "I should like to say that I'm perfectly understanding of your problem about limited funds. I wouldn't try to substitute my judgment for yours about what the agency can or can't afford. But . . . I implore you *not* to feel that the public authorities can be disciplined by your not helping out here. The question is a clear one—is this man's cause worthy of your concern? I assure you that that's all there is to it."

But to those who spoke out, the question seemed not clear at all. Monsignor Grover had a new thought. "Sawyer, let me ask you this question: Do you believe as an attorney that either of these two public departments is required by law to pay for these things . . . after all the man *is* a ward of the state, isn't he?"

"Yes, Monsignor, I think I do feel that one or the other is really supposed to do it. But . . ."

The priest interrupted. "Well, if that's so, it means that this agency is being asked to subsidize the government, doesn't it? In addition to the taxes we pay, we're now supposed to pay privately donated money to do what the taxes were supposed to do." He was plainly pleased by the irrefutable logic of his analysis. With an unexpectedly unfriendly smile, he said, "What have you to say about that?"

Sawyer's answer, framed only in his mind, was "irrelevant," loudly and clearly. But he was alert enough not to make this mistake again, and he tried to rally with the timeworn "Well, sir . . ." But the priest had finally articulated a point of deep interest to Mrs. Berkeley.

"Monsignor Grover is quite right," she said, looking toward the chairman of the board. "I don't wish to provoke a partisan political quarrel, but there's one thing all real Americans agree on, I think, and that is that the government is about to consume us all in this spiral of taxing and spending. Now here we've a case of taxing *without* spending, and it's . . . which is much worse . . . the plainest road to Socialism and Communism, if you ask me." Mrs. Berkeley suddenly seemed transported. Her voice rose. "We all know that you can lose your liberties in more ways than one. The destruction of the people's money is one way . . . and isn't this an example of it? As a matter of fact—" Mrs. Berkeley lowered her voice and looked down at her beautiful hands—"in my *other* work I have learned a great many startling and *frightening* things." Her voice quavered. "I propose to find out more about this matter, too. I should like to assure you all that I'll get to the bottom of this."

Honestly perplexed, Sawyer waited for someone, or everyone, to ask Mrs. Berkeley what in the world she was talking about. But the group acted as if she had made perfect sense, until the erstwhile pastor of the Gothic church spoke up.

"Mr. Sawyer," the minister said, "for my own sake . . . I can assure you that it will serve no other purpose . . . I should like to disassociate myself from the remarks just made by my colleagues. I for one think that they are pursuing irrelevancies. I think that we should long ago have approved your request."

"Thank you, sir," Sawyer said, but he also sensed unmistakably that the clergyman was alone in his view. His heart sank and a feeling of inadequacy overcame him. Medlicott pulled at his coat and he leaned down.

"You're through the looking glass now, boy," Medlicott whispered. "Tell the son-of-a-bitches to forget it and let's go."

As Sawyer strove to quiet the reporter, the still genial Howdy Stewart came to his rescue. "Well, Mr. Sawyer," he began, "you've presented your case very well . . . very well, indeed, and all of us are grateful to you and Mr. . . . ah, Mr. Medlicott for bringing our attention to this matter." Stewart coughed nervously. "Despite what has been stated here . . . and we have, as usual, let the discussion run its own course, enriched by the divergent views of the representatives of all segments of the community, the rich and the poor, regardless of color or creed . . . we will give the matter careful thought and vote, in secret, of course, as is really only right. I can assure you, as chairman here, that the decision will turn entirely on only the most proper considerations."

Pleased to have it over with, Sawyer thanked them all and he and Medlicott bolted from the room, closing the door behind them.

Medlicott was shaking with rage and was sincerely sorry for Sawyer. He took hold of the lawyer's arm. "It wasn't your fault, Bill, you did as well as anybody could . . . you were very fine. But . . . they stink!" He threw his head back and almost shouted. "They *absolutely* stink! I've never been so revolted in my life . . . Jesus, what a bunch of pure blooded phonies!"

"It was pretty bad, all right," Sawyer said, "I admit it. Honest to God, I felt as if I was in quicksand or something. Those people really put you through the paces. We'll really have earned that money, every cent of it."

Medlicott said, "You're right. You would have earned it, except, of course, they're going to turn us down."

Turning abruptly toward the reporter, the lawyer said, Oh, no they won't. We'll get the money."

"What makes you think so?" Medlicott said, surprised. "Almost every damn one of them went on record against it. They're not crazy. They've practically turned us down already."

"That's just the procedure," Sawyer said earnestly. "It

makes these agency boards feel important to deliberate like that, but they can't really say no to a case like this. People like that wouldn't let this boy down . . . Why, I'm counting on it."

The two men had reached the street floor and had stopped walking. They faced each other. With an unbelieving look, Medlicott spoke bitterly. "The trouble with you is, Sawyer, that you're ignorant, or at least naïve! That people like that wouldn't let you down is one hundred percent wrong! When you've been around as long as I have you'll learn that the people who you'd most expect to help out in this town are the ones who *always* let you down, unless there's an angle in it for them . . . And the opposite is true, too. The people who are the least secure . . . the people who can least afford it . . . are the ones who always go to bat."

Offended both by Medlicott's adjectives applied to him, and also not accepting his querulous generalizations, Sawyer said, "Look, I don't go for this 'down-with-everything' line of yours, and I don't believe you for a minute . . . But I also don't want to quarrel with you. Let's forget it. I still say we'll get the money. They're good, substantial people, obviously. They've got the money, plenty of it, and our case is a good one."

Medlicott had subsided. "O.K.," he said. "I agree with you that we shouldn't be arguing, and disagree with all your other youthful appraisals of the world and its creatures. We'll have to see what they say. How will you get the verdict? Will they call you?"

"I guess so."

"Will you let me know?"

"Sure, I'll call you . . . and then we can celebrate," Sawyer said.

"O.K., and for the record, I hope to God you're right about what they'll do."

"I'm right, Medlicott, you'll see. I think Howdy Stewart

really tipped us off at the very end when he practically apologized for all that nonsense and talked about proper considerations."

Medlicott smiled ambiguously but said nothing.

Drawn together now by their odyssey, the two shook hands as they said goodbye.

13

Sawyer's telephone rang in the late afternoon on the day of his appearance at the Metropolitan Aid Bureau. He picked up the receiver and heard the voice of Charles Beemer.

"Mr. Sawyer, this is Charley Beemer, at MAB."

"Yes, hello," Sawyer said expectantly.

"Well, I'm afraid the news isn't too good."

Sawyer said, "Oh, no—surely they didn't vote against this."

"Yes, I'm sorry to say they did, and in spite of my personal recommendation in your behalf."

The lawyer was speechless, trying to believe the news. At

last he said, "Is it final? Is there a chance they'd reconsider?"

"I'm afraid not," Beemer answered. "But I'd like you to know the reason. It wasn't anything along the lines of the discussion at the meeting. Most of that was garbage. It was really a question . . . well, it boiled down to whether a man like this, in the penitentiary, you know, was really deserving in view of our limited funds. That's all there was to it."

"Yes, I see," Sawyer said absently. "Well, thank you for calling."

The lawyer hung up and sat quietly for a few minutes, twisting a pencil in his hands. Then he reached for the phone again and dialed *The World*. He passed along the news to Jack Medlicott.

"God, I'm sorry," Medlicott said. "I won't say 'I told you so' . . . it's just so damned sad."

"Yes, it is sad," Sawyer said helplessly.

"What are we going to do now?" Medlicott asked. "It's almost too late, but we've got to do something."

"Well, I'm going to write the chaplain and tell him I've been unsuccessful thus far . . . I really think we're licked in view of the time problems. I still have a vague hope that the log jam may break at the Welfare Department or with the prison people, but I don't really know what to do about that and I'd better write to the chaplain now, to let him know."

To Sawyer's surprise, Medlicott said, "Look, Sawyer, we can't write that letter. What about Adam? Can't you picture him getting that news . . . it's enough to break my heart, let alone his."

"I know that, but facts are facts. We can't simply be silent. That doesn't make sense either."

"No," Medlicott said harshly. "Don't write that letter, at least yet. Let's think about it for one more day . . . We can't just stop . . . Let's at least talk about it. Will you be in your office tomorrow? Could I come over?"

"Well . . . I could see you in the morning, maybe about ten o'clock. I don't guess one more day will hurt."

"Good. I'll be over there in the morning, and in the meantime, for God's sake, rack your brain for ideas and I'll do the same."

"O.K.," Sawyer said. "See you tomorrow."

Arriving at Sawyer's office at midmorning the next day, Medlicott was unusually morose. He also seemed embarrassed and oddly apologetic, new characteristics in Sawyer's experience with him.

With hardly any preliminary, Medlicott said, "I tried last night to get the money, but I can't do it."

"What do you mean?"

"Well, I tried to borrow it first, from my boss at the paper, and from the few other people I know who might have it. But"—the reporter stopped and stammered—"the truth is that because of a wholly misspent life I'm broke and I haven't any credit or collateral. I've never given a God damn before."

"I'm sorry, Mr. Medlicott," Sawyer said.

"*Don't* be sorry for me, for Christ's sake," Medlicott said angrily. "I don't want anybody to feel sorry for me . . . ever, and here the guy to feel sorry for is Adam."

"Of course," Sawyer said quietly.

"I also tried to sell my car . . . and I can get $85 for it . . . it's a lousy car, a '52 Plymouth, and I guess that's all it's worth. If that much will help, I can go ahead and sell it and we can use the money."

The reporter had slumped down into one of Sawyer's chairs. His confession at an end, he seemed to have nothing more to say.

Sawyer said, "I tried last night, too, and I didn't get as far as you did."

"What happened?"

"Well, I don't have any money, either, and I disapprove of asking other people for a thing like this . . . After all, people give their time and money to community and public services, and it isn't right for them to be hit privately."

Medlicott seemed to revive and almost said something, but he slumped down again.

"Well," Sawyer continued, "I made some phone calls last night . . . I'm not very good at that kind of thing. I just can't bring myself to call a stranger, and I really don't know any of the substantial people. But I tried the people that I could possibly approach, and it didn't work."

"Who'd you try?" Medlicott asked with interest.

"I don't think I should identify them, Medlicott, especially since they couldn't help. One guy wanted to know if it was deductible . . . I'm no tax expert but, of course, it isn't. Gifts like this to individuals don't help out the giver taxwise. Another one said he might consider making a contribution but he wanted a written statement of the facts and circumstances . . . and we haven't time for that. Another man had just given a good deal of money to this fund to send the Jenny McKean High School Band to the Chicago relays . . . Every one of them had a good excuse, and I don't mean that sarcastically."

Medlicott said, "I'd never really thought about a campaign for small gifts . . . Could we do it?" Answering his own question, he said, "Time! The God damned time is so short. And who'd do the soliciting?"

"You and I aren't adequate, I'm afraid."

"That's right, we aren't. We'd get a dollar here and a dollar there. If you've noticed, there's kind of a cult about money raising. The idea seems to be to get rich people as the solicitors, and then they solicit the other rich people. That's the way it's done."

"That's true," Sawyer said. "I've noticed that about these so-called finance committees . . . Since that's out, I'm afraid we've got to face up to the fact that we couldn't get the money quickly enough, if we just picked it up a little bit at a time." Facetiously, he added, "We might try a raffle. A good many organizations do that. Some of the churches do it."

Medlicott got up from his chair and turned to the window. The room was quiet except for the occasional squeaks of Sawyer's swivel chair.

Suddenly Medlicott turned around and faced the lawyer. Speaking to no one in particular, he said, "By God, I wonder."

"Wonder what?"

Medlicott snapped his fingers. "It's a chance, Sawyer. It's a little tiny chance."

Annoyed by his companion's mysteriousness, Sawyer said, "*What's* a chance? What are you talking about?"

Medlicott sat down again. He seemed to be consciously restraining himself. "Did you ever hear of Father Gleason . . . Patrick Gleason . . . out at Holy Rosary, the Catholic church?"

Sawyer answered with a disdainful smile. "Sure, you mean the Bingo Priest."

"That's the guy."

"What about him? You don't think he'd give the money do you?"

"Why not? Maybe he would. At least he's got a slush fund without a big board of directors. If he was approached right, maybe we could get some of it. Maybe we couldn't, but . . . anyway, it's a chance." Medlicott continued earnestly. "Look, Sawyer, Gleason has it. What do you say?"

The lawyer seemed to be considering the matter. "Well,

I'm not impressed with Gleason. From all I hear he's at least a nut, and an illegal nut at that. That bingo game he runs isn't just a nickel-and-dime affair. It's a big game."

"Sure it is. But to hell with the bingo. I wouldn't care if he stuck up a bank. I also don't care if he's a nut. I'm not talking about marrying him or joining his church. I just want to get a little of his money for our boy Adam."

Sawyer shook his head. "There's no sense in kidding ourselves. Gleason is working for his church. People say he's in hock right up to his ears trying to finance that little village of his out there. He wouldn't throw away this kind of money on some person he'd never heard of, who wasn't even in his flock. I hate to discourage you, but there simply isn't any reason to believe it would work."

Medlicott's enthusiasm had left him. "I guess you're right. Gleason would really have no reason for chipping in here. We've got no cards to play with him." He paused. "But it is a source—*a* source—of funds. Why shouldn't we try it? Aren't we really in the no-stone-unturned situation? Suppose, for Christ's sake, he would have given the money and we ended up not asking?"

Sawyer smiled. "We'd never know that anyway, so what difference does it make?"

"I'm not thinking about being able to say to ourselves that we did the best we could," Medlicott said. "I'm thinking about, by God, getting the money. As silly as it may seem . . . I admit it's farfetched . . . I say we've got to try Gleason."

Sawyer still was not convinced, but he did not reject the whole idea. "Who would go to see him?"

"You, of course, you're Adam's lawyer."

Sawyer sat up abruptly. "Oh, no you don't. Count me out. That's absolutely out of the question. This isn't a *legal* problem. It's *your* idea, and since you think it's such a good idea, you're the one to see him."

Medlicott shook his head. "Now, listen, Sawyer. I *can't* do it. I've been involved in a ruckus with him because of an article I wrote for the paper. He doesn't like me. He's snotty to me every time I see him. It would be absolutely foolish to send me out there. I don't like him . . . he gives me the creeps. I'm the last guy who ought to go. No kidding."

"Well, that's too bad," Sawyer said firmly. "I'm not going to do it. I'm willing to go after the Welfare Department and the prison people again, but otherwise I'm finished. If anybody is to see Gleason it will have to be you."

Overcoming an urge to swear at Sawyer, Medlicott sat back in the chair. Despite the most severe misgivings, he realized that he was doomed to see the priest himself if anyone was. He sat quietly for a moment and then stood up. "All right, God damn it, I'll go see Gleason, but it's a mistake. I can't think of anybody else if you won't go, but my going doesn't even give the long shot a fair chance." Without another word, he turned and left the office.

Medlicott walked directly to his decrepit car, parked in the lot of the United Fund Building. He got in and started driving purposefully toward Holy Rosary. As he moved through the downtown traffic, he tried to think of a likely way to approach the priest. But there seemed no likely way and he felt more and more foolish as he proceeded on his way.

In ten minutes, Medlicott had cleared the late morning downtown traffic and moved into the slums which ringed the downtown area. Soon he drove into one of the Negro neighborhoods, where shacks and filthy weathered houses crowded along the littered street, separated occasionally by a new warehouse or light manufacturing plant.

Suddenly, several blocks ahead, the tower of Holy Rosary was visible. As Medlicott drew nearer, a series of vacant lots appeared, recently cleared of shacks and tumbled down houses, and carefully posted, "Property of Holy Rosary Church." Beyond these and closer to the church itself, Medlicott passed new houses, mostly one-story brick veneers with an occasional two-story clapboard house, each with its own fenced yard. Reaching the intersection where the church was located, he saw that the new houses extended in all directions and that there were other newly vacant lots and other lots where men were working tearing down the shacks so that new houses could be built in their places.

The reporter parked his car in front of the church and, despite his unease at the forthcoming interview, he stood on the sidewalk and looked up at it.

In any setting, the church would have been arresting. Here in the midst of blight it was startling—glass and white stone put together in a contemporary design wholly unlike the usual rootless church architecture. In partial relief over the wide doorway was a series of large red stone beads from which a stunning crucifix hung. The sun was almost directly overhead and the shadow of the cross fell at Medlicott's feet. Beside the church was the tower Medlicott had seen from a distance. It stood free of the church itself and was inscribed:

WHERE THERE IS NO LOVE,

PUT LOVE

AND YOU WILL FIND LOVE

St. John of the Cross

Medlicott looked down from the church and the tower and walked up the steps. Looking through the glass, he saw that the church was free of the clutter that marked the other Roman churches he had seen. Except for the Stations of the Cross, the only ornament was a large wooden cross above the altar, extending almost to the vaulted ceiling. The reporter started when he saw the feet of a man sticking out into the aisle from a pew located toward the front. He realized that someone was sleeping there.

The newspaperman turned slowly from the church and

looked to his left toward a large school building, also obviously a part of Holy Rosary. Between the church and the school was a small white frame house which fronted on a lawn. The walk Medlicott stood on ran from the church to the frame house.

Medlicott started to follow the walk, noticing as he advanced that two men, one white and one a Negro, were more or less aimlessly spading the ground around a hedge in the yard. Recognizing their rancid pasty look as he got closer, he realized that they were derelicts. They stopped their work and peered furtively at him from sickly eyes as he walked opposite them.

"Good morning," Medlicott said.

The men grunted and one of them coughed heavily. "You got a smoke?" he asked.

"Yes," Medlicott answered, and he handed over what was left of a package of cigarettes.

The man nodded and, accepting this as thanks, Medlicott walked on toward the house. Another man sat on the steps of the porch smoking a pipe and eying Medlicott as he came on. The man did not look up even when Medlicott stood beside him.

"Is this where Father Gleason lives?" Medlicott asked.

"Yeah," the man said.

"Is he here, do you know?"

The man kept his eyes straight ahead. "He might be . . . are you a cop?"

Medlicott almost laughed. "I am *not* a cop," he said emphatically. Then, overcoming his final reluctance for his unlikely errand, he rang the door bell.

In a few minutes an aged Negro woman opened the door. To Medlicott she looked just like a picture he had seen of Sojourner Truth, even down to the curious shabby costume. "Yes?" she said.

"I'd like to see Father Gleason."

The woman said, "Come on in." She turned from the door and disappeared.

Medlicott pushed the door aside and entered a tiny hall. On the walls were two of Eichenberg's typically stark prints, one of St. Francis, the other of the guardian angel. The reporter closed the door behind him and stepped tentatively into the living room to his right. It was a long, narrow room, plainly furnished, with white walls and pale blue curtains. A wildly colorful exhibition of children's art was Scotch-taped to the wall above the fireplace at the far end, surrounding a large reproduction of Roulat's Head of Christ. On the wall to Medlicott's right was a framed scroll, containing not an illuminated picture of the Pope but these words, in black letters:

> *For the millions who go without two meals a day,*
> *the only form in which God dare appear is food.*
> GANDHI

Otherwise the walls were plain, except for one which was partially lined with bookshelves. From where he stood Medlicott could barely make out the names of several books on the nearest shelf, among them *The Idiot* and *The Brothers Karamazov*.

Next to the fireplace was the entryway to an adjoining room and Father Gleason's voice emanated from there. The priest was talking on the telephone and Medlicott was to be an unwilling eavesdropper.

"What time was it supposed to have been?" the priest said. "I see . . . yes, it's possible . . . Of the seven names, I recognize four . . . Sure, I'll take all seven if the judge will let me. The big trouble will be on Dunham. This is his second time around and he was paroled to my custody the last time . . . You might remind the police of the luck we had last year on that Garcia boy—the narcotics business—and this isn't nearly as dark as that."

The priest was now silent for several minutes, only occasionally saying yes or no to his caller. Then he said, "Of course, I'll come down whenever you say, Max. I was there most of the night on this other business. It's been a bad week. And I will call the psychiatrist. You tell the judge he can rely on that." The priest's voice suddenly sounded anxious, "Max, for God's sake, do the best you can—I know you will—we can't give up on them. Thanks."

Medlicott heard the receiver click and in a minute the priest, shielding his eyes against the bright light reflected into the room, walked in. His coat was off. He wore a black rabat on top of a T shirt and his collar was open and askew. His dark face looked deeply distraught and inexpressibly tired out. To Medlicott's surprise the man also seemed strangely vulnerable. At the instant that these things occurred to him, the reporter also realized that the priest was unaware that anyone was in the room with him. The light momentarily prevented his seeing Medlicott and Sojourner Truth had apparently not bothered to announce him.

Medlicott coughed and said gently, "Father Gleason, it's Jack Medlicott."

The clergyman actually jumped and looked sharply toward the end of the room where Medlicott was. Then he smiled self-consciously and said, "Oh, hello, Mr. Medlicott, how are you?" He strode to the reporter and extended his hand and Medlicott took it.

"I'm all right, Father, thanks, how are you?" Medlicott said mechanically.

"Well, I'm fair right this moment, I think, with a few parish problems . . ." He smiled. "Sit down, please, so I can, will you?"

Medlicott sat down in a chair and the tall priest sank heavily into a couch that occupied most of one of the longer walls of the room.

The priest said, "I haven't seen you since that United Fund party . . . the night that I was so unpleasant. I hope you've come to see the church."

At last confronted, Medlicott said, "To tell you the truth, Father, I haven't come to see the church . . . I've come to ask a favor." The reporter stopped short and clapped his hands together. "I'm not much of a politician, I guess, so I'll just come clean and tell you what it is."

The priest smiled. "Good . . . and don't worry about not being a politician. I have the same problem . . . No finesse, that's always been my trouble, so you needn't worry about the small talk. What's the favor?"

Medlicott twisted uncomfortably in his chair. In spite of his declaration, he simply could not be as direct as he wanted to be. "Well, it concerns money . . . quite a lot of money—$400—which I need . . . not for myself, but for somebody, a man you don't even know who needs the money . . ." By this time so tangled up that he felt foolish, Medlicott held up both hands and said, "Look, Father, for God's sake, it's a long story, and I'll begin at the beginning."

The priest leaned forward from the couch and put both hands to his head. Medlicott caught the signal and stopped talking, believing that his request was about to be denied.

Father Gleason said, "I'll give you the money. I happen to have it available, and you can have it . . . I'll get my coat and write you a check."

The priest got up and disappeared into the room in which he had been telephoning earlier. Medlicott sat dumbly in his chair until he returned and sat down again.

"Father," Medlicott began, "surely you want to know what it's for?"

"Not necessarily, no, I don't." The priest laughed and said, "You haven't come out here to swindle me have you, Mr. Medlicott?"

It was Medlicott's turn to smile. "No, I haven't, but suppose I had?"

"Well, that's a chance I'm always willing to take." Balancing his checkbook on his knee, the priest was now writing the check. Quietly, as if to himself, he added, "When somebody reaches out for help, who can say he doesn't need it? . . . I've never wanted to make that kind of judgment."

Medlicott said nothing, but his newspaper article about the "Bingo Priest" and his conversation with Gleason at the United Fund dinner somehow passed through his mind. Suddenly he felt that he disliked being a supplicant a good deal more than the priest pretended to dislike the role of benefactor.

Gleason tore the check from the book and waved it before him to dry the ink.

In a nasty tone that surprised even him, Medlicott abruptly said, "Well, Father, don't leave me dangling. What strings are attached to the money?"

The priest looked up sharply. His blue eyes flashed and his dark face colored perceptibly. Rising from the couch he took Medlicott's right hand, twisted it open and put the check into it. *"My friend,"* he began, a note of anger distinct in his voice, "my system here is my business, but you choose to question my motive. Stated quite simply, my system is 'first come—first served.' Your friend meets this test . . . I happen to have the money at the moment. *There are no strings* . . . Now please take the gift to your friend with God's blessing."

The priest did not resume his seat and Medlicott stood up uncertainly, feeling deeply embarrassed and uncomfortable. He had somehow managed to get the money and also to offend the good man that had given it to him. "Father," he stammered, "I . . . don't know how to thank you."

"Good," the priest exclaimed. "Don't thank me."

"But, my God, Father, if you could imagine this man's situation and the efforts we've made . . ."

The priest shook his head and put a large hand on the reporter's shoulder. "Mr. Medlicott . . . I know how you feel, I do understand that, but I *want* you to take this for granted, for my sake." He looked directly at Medlicott and smiled. "Don't you see, I'm being selfish when I ask you not to thank me. There's a sin of pride, you know . . . To me it's most ugly and unfortunate . . . And you must not help *it* against me . . . We are all under the same commandment and I've chosen the easy way to obey it, the obvious way which affords me the security of knowing that I *am* obeying it . . . *I* should not be thanked or praised, God knows . . . Think of all the people who are trying to fulfill the same obligation and also do all the other things they think . . . they honestly think . . . they're supposed to do . . . *Don't* thank me, please."

Medlicott felt that he understood at least part of what his companion had said. "O.K.," he said, "but let's not kid each other about obeying your commandment. The rest of us, who don't do it your easy, direct way, end up not doing it at all."

"I don't believe that," the priest said flatly.

"Well, I know it's true," Medlicott said, but he added, "I suppose it wouldn't have to be . . ."

Neither man spoke now and Medlicott longed to extricate himself from the interview. To break the spell, he said, "Look, Father . . . I *won't* thank you . . . if you want it that way that's the way it'll be, at least for now."

The priest smiled and stepped back. "Good."

"But," Medlicott began again, "if I can't thank you, you've

left me without anything more to say. That's a pretty dirty trick."

Gleason laughed aloud. "It's not a dirty trick at all. It's good public policy. We all talk too much, anyway. At least I do. Today I surely have . . ."

Medlicott turned slowly toward the door. "Can I come again and visit you?"

"Sure, I wish you would. I'm kind of off the beaten track out here and I'd love to see you . . . I mean it. Come back."

"I will, and the next time I'd like you to show me around."

At the door the men shook hands. "Goodbye, Father."

"Goodbye, Mr. Medlicott, and God bless you."

"Thank you for that," the reporter said and he stepped out on the porch as the door closed behind him.

Medlicott hurried down the walk toward his parking place. The men who had been in the yard were now gone. When he reached the street, the reporter looked back toward the rectory. Still looking unkempt, Father Gleason had come out on the porch and he waved his hand. Medlicott answered this salute before moving around to the street side of his car. There, shielded from the priest's view, he glanced thoughtfully down at the check in his hand. He shrugged his shoulders and smiled wryly. Then he got into the car and drove quickly away from the curb.